his
father's
son

'It's perfect. Absolutely perfect. One of the best books I have read in
2013. Fantastic.' – The Book Boy blog

'A breathtakingly beautiful read.' – Random Things Through My
Letterbox blog

tony black

his father's son

BLACK & WHITE PUBLISHING

First published 2013
This edition first published 2014
by Black & White Publishing Ltd
29 Ocean Drive, Edinburgh EH6 6JL

1 3 5 7 9 10 8 6 4 2   14 15 16 17

ISBN: 978 1 84502 736 0

A CIP catalogue record for this book
is available from the British Library.

ALBA | CHRUTHACHAIL

Typeset by RefineCatch Limited, Bungay, Suffolk
Printed and bound by Grafica Veneta S. p. A. Italy

For my son,
Conner

Prologue

Marti didn't get it. He knew when Dad said it was "just one of those things" it was because he couldn't be bothered explaining.

"But why, Dad?" said Marti. It was burning hot outside and Dad was stretched out in the yard under the coolibah tree. Marti had seen him put the newspaper over his face when the sun broke out from the shade. He was still under the paper when Marti asked the question again. "Dad, why Blue?"

"Like I say, son, it's just one of those things."

Dad must know, thought Marti. He had never heard him say he didn't know about something. He must know, really. "Just one of those things" was something grown-ups said when they couldn't be bothered. It was like, "Go away and play with the cat's eyes on the road."

"But Dad, why Blue?" Why did they call Dad 'Blue'? Pete, their neighbour with the swimming pool with the leaves in and the car with no wheels, had called Dad 'Blue' every time he passed by. And Pete wasn't even a very good friend of Dad's, thought Marti. Pete didn't even support Liverpool, so Dad couldn't really be good friends with him.

"Marti, it's an Australian thing, all right. That's what they call you in Australia when you have red hair like me, *Blue*."

Marti really was confused now. "Well, why don't they call you Red?"

"Because Marti, it's Australia and they do things differently here. It's the other side of the world."

Marti knew Australia was on the other side of the world from Ireland. Dad had shown him on the map, and on the globe in the library he had shown him where the boat had come across all the ocean and how it was the best money he'd ever spent. He told him the story about how they needed men like him because the country was so big they had to fill it up and he paid all his money for him and Mam to come on a boat from Ireland.

"But why because it's the other side of the world?" Marti knew he was pressing his luck. Dad put down the paper and tipped back his cap. It was bright sunshine outside and he had been trying to sit in the shade of the coolibah tree and read the news, but he was there so long the sun had followed him and the shadow was on the other side of the tree now.

"Right, Marti," he said, and picked up the rug he was lying on and moved it into the shade again. "If I explain this thing for you, will you give me some peace?" Marti nodded. "Right, now first things first, get out of the sun – *eleven to three, under a tree*, remember." Marti moved over into the shade of the coolibah tree with Dad.

"Now, in Australia everyone – well, mostly everyone in Australia – comes from Ireland or Scotland or the Other Place." The Other Place was England; Marti knew Dad didn't like England, except for Liverpool but that was as Irish as Molly Malone, he said, whoever Molly Malone was. "So, Australia is on the other side of the world. Australians think this is a funny thing, it's like everything is the opposite. It's summer in Australia when it's winter in Ireland and the water goes down the plughole the other way." Marti's eyes widened. "Ah now, forget that about the water, son, that's a whole other story, but so you see what I'm saying? That's why red becomes blue in Australia. Do you get me? Do you see it now, Marti?"

He kind of got it. He didn't know why the Australians wanted to call red blue, but he got the bit about doing things the other way around. It made him wonder because he had black hair like Mam, maybe they would call him white.

He was still a bit confused, then Dad leaned forward and lifted him up on his knee. "Don't worry your head about this nonsense, son. Sure won't you get it all for yourself when you go to Ireland."

"Are we going to Ireland?" said Marti.

2

"No, son, we've no plans to go to Ireland. Australia's our home now, but sure, won't you want to go and see the place one day, to see where your mam and dad were born and where the giants come from, and sure won't you have to try the Guinness on home soil. There's nothing like a pint of Guinness poured on Irish soil, son – when you're a man, of course."

"Will you come with me, Dad?"

"No, Marti, I won't be going back to Ireland."

"Never, not even when I'm a man and I get the Guinness?" He knew Dad would never go back to Ireland. Mam had said it was because he was too fond of foostering his days away in the sun, and didn't Ireland only remind him of himself.

"No, Marti, I never will. Sure why would I want to – would you look at this place? Isn't it God's country entirely; you can't grow oranges in your yard in Ireland."

"Then I won't go, Dad. I'll stay here with you." Marti hugged him and Dad laughed.

"Son, you're choking me – that's some grip you have there. Do you fancy yourself a wrestler?" Dad pretended to bite Marti's arm, and the pair rolled around on the grass. "That's enough now. There could be trapdoors around here," said Dad.

Trapdoor spiders were sneaky bleeders, Mam had said. They bury themselves in the yard and then jump out of their little grass trapdoors to bite you if you're not careful, she had told Marti.

"Do they have trapdoors in Ireland, Dad?"

"No, son."

"Then could we wrestle in the yard if we lived in Ireland, Dad?"

"You'd be soaked through in a millisecond, Marti. Sure, there's no sunny days over there. It's all rain, rain and more rain. No, this is the place, Marti, God's country, like I say. Now away and play."

"Dad."

"What?"

"Will you show me the flower dancing?"

"No, son."

"But, Dad, please."

3

"No, son. Come on now. I think I hear your mam calling you. Is that a cake she's been baking?" Marti knew there was no cake. He had never known Mam to bake a cake. Dad was having him on.

"Dad, can I see the flower dancing, in the wind like you say it, Dad?"

"Aren't you getting a bit big for that, Marti?"

"No, Dad. Please, please, Dad." Marti felt sad when Dad said this. He really was getting too big at eight to see the flower dancing, but he liked the way Dad did the trick. It was his favourite trick in the world.

Dad looked at Marti. "And if I show you the – what is it?"

"I know it's not a flower, but I forget. Is it a sha . . . sham-m—"

"A *shamrock*. What is it?"

"A shamrock." Marti spluttered out the word and knew it as soon as he said it. He knew he'd forget it again, too. It was the green flower thing on Dad's arm that he could make dance in the wind.

Dad rolled up his sleeve over the shoulder and showed Marti the shamrock. "Here it comes then, son." The shamrock stood there, square in the middle of Dad's arm.

"Once there was a lucky little shamrock that stood in a field," said Dad. Marti laughed. He loved to see the shamrock. It was something he could never grow tired of. "A lucky little shamrock in a lucky little field," said Dad, "and all through the day he'd stand in his field, thinking, What a lucky little shamrock am I, am I, what a lucky little shamrock am I, to stand in a field and grow strong, said he, to stand in a field and grow strong." Dad turned his arm and the shamrock's stem straightened.

"He's starting," said Marti.

"And when the night turns to day, I go wild, he said, when the night turns to day I go wild. Wild for song and the dance of a song, and I dance in a field all night long!" Dad turned his arm back and forth, making the shamrock dance. It rolled and reeled on his shoulder like a proper cartoon, thought Marti. Then Dad tugged his sleeve down again. "Right, son, that's enough. Now off and play like a good boy."

Marti grabbed Dad round the shoulders. "I love the shamrock, Dad," he said.

4

"And the shamrock loves you too, son. Now off and play, before your mam really is calling you in."

Marti loved playing in the yard.

He could remember when there was just a yard and Dad took them to buy the house to put in the yard. It was a big field full of houses all up on big tree stumps and Mam said she liked the one with the white rails that went all the way around. "I like that one too," said Marti, "because you could walk under it and I could climb out through a secret passage." But Mam said you couldn't because the big tree stumps would go away and you wouldn't be able to walk under the house anymore.

A man in a hat and a vest, with a big belly and freckles on his arms, said Mam had an eye for a bargain and she could look around the house if she wanted, but Dad said he wasn't made of money.

"You wouldn't need to be, mister. This is a repo'," said the man with the freckles on his arms, and Dad went over to talk to him. When he came back everyone went to look around the house. Dad had to lift Marti up over the big gap and the wood made a noise like a twig snapping, but Dad said it was all right, and the man with the freckles on his arms shouted out, "No worries, sonny. You're as safe as houses." And Mam smiled.

Inside Marti ran around the empty house. There were some things left behind, like a big wooden chest, which was nailed shut. He thought it might have treasure inside and told Dad, but Dad said they nailed everything down when they moved the houses. "How do you mean?" said Marti.

"They move them on the road, like a big lorry comes for the house and you take it to where you want to live."

"Isn't it the strangest thing, son?" said Mam.

Marti didn't answer but Dad said, "Sure, how's he going to know any different. Isn't the lad an Aussie? You only think it's strange because your imagination's running wild with the big old house driving up the Connemara Road!" Mam laughed, and Marti went off to explore the rest of the house.

In one of the bedrooms there was a picture of Superman and Marti decided this would be his room. "Can I have this room, Dad? Please, *please*?"

"Calm down, son. Haven't we hardly had a chance to check the place now."

"But Dad, someone else might buy it – look, there's Superman!"

"Where, where?" said Dad, and he looked out the window, putting his hands over his eye like a telescope. "I don't see him. Have I missed the man of steel again?" he said, and everyone laughed.

"It's just a picture," said Marti.

"A picture of Superman, here? Well why didn't you say sooner? That seals it for me. Mam, what do you say?"

"Well, the boy's right. If there's a Superman picture up we better move fast. Where's the man?" said Mam, and they went to find the man with the freckles on his arms. The man wrote something in a big blue book and gave Dad a piece of paper. Dad said that it was a chit, and they couldn't lose it because it meant the house was theirs, then he put the chit in his back pocket and there were smiles from everyone.

Marti liked to think of the day at the big field full of houses all up on big tree stumps. He liked to think of the day when the house with the white rails that went all the way around became theirs and there were smiles from everyone. He liked to think of these things because when the house came to the yard and everyone moved in to live, there were no more smiles.

1

Joey sometimes wondered, had Australia been a good move? God yes, had it ever. Sure wasn't it all blue skies and sunny days, he thought, and weren't the people just the best of craic, even the bosses. There were no bosses in Ireland would give you the steam off their piss, but sure Macca there was all right. Hadn't Macca been the greatest lately, even after all the bother with Shauna? Wasn't Macca the first to say, "Take some time, Joey. Get her right." No, Australia was the Lucky Country all right, and wasn't it the best of places to be raising young Marti. It was a million miles from Ireland and talk of Banshees and little old women with shawls and wispy beards who would only be scaring the b'Jaysus out the boy.

Joey took the trailer to be washed before the afternoon smoko with Macca and the men from the transport section. The cab was hot inside and the wheel felt like it would scorch his palms if he didn't spin it quickly enough. Driving a trailer filled up with iron ore day after day mightn't be the best job in the world, he thought, but it was a regular wage and there was a lot to be said for a regular wage in this day and age, was there not?

Driving the trailer mightn't be the highlight of his thirty-four years, but it had bought them a grand enough house and it had kept Shauna from sitting at a checkout or behind some counter or other. The family was looked after, Marti especially wanted for nothing, money was being set aside for his education and Joey was proud enough. The boy had a brain on him and if he were raised right and there was money enough for an education then there would be a fine job waiting for him when he was ready. Who could want more than that?

When the water from the hose hit the trailer there was hissing and steam raised off as the splashes evaporated. It was a blinder of a day – even the corellas that flew in from the bush were too hot to scratch about for a feed and sat hidden under branches and leaves in the gum trees for a bit of shade. The air seemed to hum when it was this hot. It was as thick as soup to walk through and the light played tricks on your eyes, making the road and the paddocks and the trees quiver like they were about to disappear in a shimmering mist.

On days like this Joey sometimes thought how different his life had become since he left Ireland on that wet May morning in 1968. He remembered his first job at Gleesons Bakery in Kilmora and the days spent carrying the flour in and the bread out. The faces and the air as white as a maggot, the men opening the windows and hacking out floury spit to the street, the pigeons below pecking away at it. He'd felt grand the day Gleeson had shown him the door – wasn't the job only a favour to his father, the mighty hurling player Emmet Driscol. He felt glad to be turning his back on the pair of them.

Bitterness was all he felt for his own father. Bitterness and hatred was what he'd been made to feel. It could never be that way for Marti, he'd make sure of it. Joey had nothing but a pile of desperate memories left over from his own childhood, which in darker moments would come back to haunt him. It was always the way of it. The darker things looked, the more he remembered. It was at the core of him. He could still see his father now, the whole family living in fear and awe of him, mealtimes held in silence in case a noise tipped him into rage.

Joey could only have been about the age of Marti himself when he brought the whole family close to despair. His sister, Megan, younger still, had appeared at the dinner table in tears. She was covered head to toe in muck and carried a stench that made the room seem suddenly emptied of air. Emmet stamped his fist on the table, swearing before God he had been pushed beyond the beyonds this time.

"What is this ye are bringing to my house?" he said. His voice was trembling so much that it seemed his next word might hurl the plates and dishes to the floor. No one would look at him. All six children kept their heads down, even the babe Clancy buried himself deeper into his mother's arms and scarcely dared breathe.

"I was looking for the fairies," said Megan. She was crying and blurting out her words. "'Tis a fairy rath we have in the yard. Joey showed me."

When Megan pointed at Joey all the eyes shifted on him. He was the eldest and used to being looked on, but he could only see his father's gaze racing towards him as he was lifted from his chair by one great hand. He knew he was in for trouble as his father dragged him by the hair into the yard. The fairy rath was the midden, he understood that now, but then he had been told about it by grown-ups and thought he was doing no wrong. His own mother had laughed about the midden being a fairy rath when he told Megan, but he knew this would have to be their secret now. He was glad it was him and not his mother or Megan being dragged out.

"Do ye see them?" said Emmet. He grabbed Joey's head – his whole hand fitted round it – and he pushed him face down in the midden. There was the sound of his brothers and sisters shuffling into place to see what happened next, and then there was his father's roaring. "Do ye see them yet? I'll put ye through it, I will," he said as Joey's mouth filled with muck and potato skins. "I'll put ye through it," said Emmet again and again. Joey tasted the muck and the rotting waste. His nostrils and his eyes filled with thick black soil that stuck to him and then the earth was frozen and hard where the midden ended.

He cowered from his father where he lay. Grown men had flinched from Emmet Driscol on the hurling field, but to a mere boy he was a terrifying sight when the rage was on him. His father looked lost in his fury, then a mouse scurried out from the midden and he shouted, "Vermin." Even with his eyes full of muck, Joey could see his mother and his brothers and sisters watching as Emmet's great boot was stamped, catching the creature's head. The children screamed at the sight and his mother gathered the little ones around her and led them back to the house. They had seen too much already.

Joey was left alone with the sight of his father bringing down his boot again. He could still remember the way the mouse's little legs kept going, it wasn't dead yet. Then his father brought down his boot again and again, until the mouse was no more than a bloodied tangle of flesh and tiny white bones.

The whistle shook Joey out of his memory and he saw Macca come out, smiling and waving for the men from the transport section to follow. "G'day, Bluey," he shouted.

Joey flicked the hose in a salute and Macca tapped twice on the packet of cigarettes in his shirt pocket to show it was time for smoko. "Come on, Bluey," shouted Macca. "What's the story today, mate?"

Joey knew he had become a bit of a legend for his stories. The men who took the ore out and the men who moved it about never tired of hearing his stories. Joey thought the stories were nothing special, just the way people talked all the time in Ireland. He knew nobody back there would think they were anything special.

When the men had their afternoon smoko they were forever saying what a rare treat it was to see Bluey Driscol jumping down from the rig, a grin on his face, saying the words, "Fellas, ye'll never believe this one . . ." He felt more at home with Macca and the men from the transport section than anywhere else in the world, and when they looked at him for a story at afternoon smoko he always felt it was his duty to think of something.

"So there I was, five minutes off the boat from Ireland," he said, "and I swear to you fellas, I'd never had the shits like it before."

There was laughter and back slapping. Some men sat back to savour Joey's story like it was a fine wine he was serving them, and others sat forward with big expectant grins on their faces, waiting for the next line to follow.

"So, I'm running and taking off my belt at the same time, and my dukes are dropping," he said.

"Your what?" said Pando the Greek, scrunching up his eyes.

"My dukes, trousers . . . *pants*, man. Anyway, I find the dunny in the terminal and I dive in there – I swear before the Holy Mother I was about to explode, so I was – and I plank myself down on the lavatory."

"*And?*" said the men together.

"And nothing . . . well, not quite nothing. No sooner had my arse touched the rim of the porcelain but this bright green, slithering mass of thorns and teeth and horns and a forkey little tongue runs right under the door . . . and then the bugger spits at me."

"Ha-ha-ha," broke the men.

"What a welcome, mate," said Macca.

"I swear, I thought it was some mickey biting bog lizard and it was gonna have my old fella away in those teeth of his. I froze. I swear, I bloody froze, and do you know what the little bleeder did? From nowhere it opens up this bright red umbrella thing around its neck and starts the spitting again and snarling too. By God, I thought I was a goner."

Pando the Greek had tears in his eyes with the laughing and Macca and the other men were grabbing each other for support. It was a good story, the Lizard Story, thought Joey. Didn't it always get a laugh? Sure, they liked a laugh, the fellas, and wasn't there no harm in that. It would be a long day, the working day, without a bit of a laugh and a joke. Wasn't laughter the greatest medicine on earth?

Joey laughed with the men but he knew his heart wasn't in it. Truth be told, he hadn't felt like laughing for a long time. Wouldn't you know it, bloody Shauna's tricks were creeping up on him. He thought the sun would do her the power of good, and it did sure, for a while there. For ten years they had been in Australia, but a fresh start cannot last forever, that was the fact of it. You could leave the old troubles behind and start again but sooner or later they'd catch up and scare the b'Jaysus out of you.

"Bluey, you're not yourself, mate," said Macca.

Joey Driscol hated hearing the obvious. Of course he wasn't himself, who would be? If he wasn't himself it was because he didn't particularly want to be himself right now.

"Is it the television you're in training for, Macca?" he said.

"What?"

"The television . . . some game show or other. It's mental gymnastics you're at, giving the old brain a workout, no?"

Macca closed his mouth and gave a little shake of his head, and Joey felt a sudden pang of guilt. It wasn't Macca's fault. It wasn't *his* fault either, he knew that well enough, but it was the way of things, so it was. People bark when they feel like dogs.

"Macca, mate . . . I'm sorry," he said. "I have my fair share of problems at the minute."

"Mate, we've all got them," said Macca. He was staring to the front. Joey felt he didn't even want to look at him.

"Macca, I know it, but sure mine are bad, real bad. Look, can you spare an hour for a few beers tonight?"

"Bluey, you're supposed to be keeping off the grog."

Joey knew he had sworn himself off the grog again. Couldn't he spend weeks off it, months even. It wasn't a problem, wasn't it only a little vice he had. He leaned into Macca's shoulder and directed his words carefully. "It's my wife."

Macca looked Joey squarely in the eye and Joey at once knew there was an understanding passed between them. He didn't like talking to Macca about his problems – they should stay his own, surely – but if Macca took a drink with him tonight then maybe he could forget about the problems for a little while. It was getting all messy again, he thought. Shauna had been the grandest catch of them all, with the face in a million, the black hair and half of Kilmora chasing after her. She was a beauty; they all said it. But weren't her lot known for the wildness, far and wide, as well. None of it mattered now though. Ireland was past, Marti was the future and Joey knew he had better start pulling himself together, for the sake of the boy. He checked himself suddenly. There was pity in him and that would never do.

"Fellas, ye'll never believe this one . . ." he said, and there were eyes dried around the table.

"You know the first day I got the trailer was the first day I ever sat behind the wheel of any vehicle."

"Nah, it is not possible," said Pando the Greek.

"I swear to you, I had never so much as honked a horn in my life. I had my driving test in the morning and my interview at the top office in the afternoon, and if I hadn't passed my test, I wouldn't be standing here beside this trailer today. Sure wasn't it a stroke of luck entirely. You see, the fella doing the test was from County Kerry and recognised my brogue. He came over with a wife and five chisellers and landed the job the day he got off the boat. Isn't this a marvellous country?"

12

"Oh yeah, it's the best country in the world, mate," said Macca. "We know."

"I won't fault you there. I won't. I won't." Joey leaned forward and the men followed. "Sure the Kerry man told me the test consisted of five questions on general road safety and if I got the majority of them right I could drive a car that day with a new licence in my back pocket. Now, I tell you not a word of a lie here, I got three of them wrong . . . but didn't he pass me anyway!"

The men laughed at Joey's story, and Macca said, "You Irish, bloody mongrels."

Joey laughed too. "Sure, we are, we are, but I think the Kerry men are the worst. But now, maybe I'm lying there because couldn't I still never drive a car in my life, and when I got the job with the trailer that afternoon I had to ask the Kerry man to drive it home for me. I didn't know another soul in the whole country. He did as well, and do you know what he told me?"

"I wouldn't like to guess, mate," said Macca, his face was the colour red with all the laughing he'd done.

"He said, 'Set out in the early hours when there's no traffic about, to get a bit of practice.' So I did. For the first couple of weeks I drove into work at five in the morning and arrived for the job two hours early. Christ, they must've thought I was keen, or retarded, I don't know which."

Macca laughed so hard his face was wet with tears and sweat and he had to take off his hat and scratch his head. The whistle blew again for the end of the afternoon smoko and Joey found himself with a wide smile sitting on his face as he watched the men from the transport section head back to work. They were a grand bunch of fellas to have around, he thought. They were mostly gone when Macca put on his hat and turned to Joey. "Bluey Driscol, you are a bloody rogue, but a man after my own heart," he said. "You have no need to be going on the grog when you can laugh like that."

"Don't I know it," said Joey, his smile fading.

His work was done for the day and he went back to the trailer and parked it in the shade of the depot to save the paintwork and keep the fuel tank out of the sun, then he punched his time card and headed for home.

The house looked deserted when he approached it from the road. The curtains were drawn and the front door and the mozzie screen were both closed tight. He looked up and down the street. All the other houses had windows open and doors jammed with gumboots and shovels and crates to let the rare and blessed breeze pass through whenever it could. Joey put his key in the door and turned the handle, but there was no sound.

"Marti, are ye here, son?" he called out.

There was no answer and then Shauna showed herself in the hallway. "Oh, you're home," she said.

"I am. Where's the boy?"

"I don't . . . I don't know."

"You don't know? What do you mean you don't know? It's gone five o'clock." Joey slammed down his keys and felt his teeth clench tightly. "He should have been home hours ago."

"Well, I heard him come in. I told him to feed himself. He must be playing."

"Jaysus, Shauna, you should be feeding him. You're his mother." Joey shook his head. He could barely bring himself to look at his wife, standing there in her nightclothes. "Has this been you for the day, ye haven't even dressed?"

"Oh feck off, will ye?"

"The boy needs looking after. He needs his mother."

"He can mind himself."

"Isn't he only eight years old . . . Christ Almighty, will ye ever take a look at yeerself, woman." He grabbed Shauna by the arm and forced her to stare into the mirror hanging in the hallway. "Look . . . look, would ye?"

"I won't, I won't look," she said and struggled to free her arm from Joey's grip.

"Look, look at what you're doing to yourself."

"No. I won't. Leave me. *Leave me.*"

Joey watched Shauna in the mirror, her face contorted, and then he threw her arm aside. "Gladly," he said and snatched up his keys, showing her his back as he walked for the door he had just come through.

2

When Mam and Dad had a fight Marti always missed what the fight was about. It was like someone had said, "Ready, steady, go," and they did. He knew he could listen forever, but there would be no clue to explain the fight. It was just what Mam and Dad did. Sometimes after a fight one of them walked off and slammed a door. If it was Dad who slammed the door, Mam would curl up on the sofa, start the bubbling with the tears and call for Marti to come and give her a hug. But if it was Mam to slam the door, Dad would sit at the kitchen table and smoke the cigarettes called Majors until she came home and say, "So, is that your tail between your legs now?"

This time it was Dad who slammed the door. Marti had come home to find Mam curled up on the sofa crying. He tried not to make a noise and creep past but Mam heard him and said, "Come here, come and give Mam a hug."

He didn't want to give Mam a hug. He felt too big to be giving her hugs all the time. He didn't want to feel too big to have Dad show him the trick with the green flower thing dancing but he wanted to be too big to give Mam a hug. Some boys at school were always getting hugs from their mam at the gate and they were called Mummy's Boys by the others, and he didn't want to be one of the Mummy's Boys.

"Marti, will you come over to me," said Mam. She was all puffy in the face and had black stuff round her eyes. There was some snot too, some snot and a lot of wet tears on her big red puffy cheeks. She would probably give him a kiss with the hug and he might have to get some snot on him then, which wouldn't be nice, he thought.

"Marti," said Mam.

"I'm coming," he said, and when he walked over and put his arms around her she grabbed him and started the hard bubbling with the tears. Marti wondered why he had bothered, but he thought she would have started the even harder bubbling if he hadn't given her the hug. Mam hugged Marti so tight that he couldn't move, and when he even tried there were more tears and little cries like bird noises. Mam hugged him for a very long time and it started to get dark outside. He could feel his eyes closing but his mind was awake and wondering if Mam had the sadness that Dad called the Black Dog.

One time when Mam had the Black Dog Marti asked them what it was. "Sure, it's the curse of the Irish, son," said Dad. This made him confused, because when Dad had fallen in Pete's swimming pool with the leaves in it Mam had said something else was the curse of the Irish. "I thought the drink was the curse of the Irish, Dad?" said Marti.

Mam and Dad had both started to laugh very loudly.

"Sure, we're a very unfortunate nation altogether, son," said Dad when the laughing was stopped, and then he looked at Mam and spoke again. "Haven't we curses just queuing up for us."

When Marti woke in the morning Mam was still sleeping and hugging him tight. He thought maybe he should wake her to get him ready for school. Then he remembered Dad had said it was sometimes better to leave her when she had the Black Dog, because it was a bit like an illness, and when you have an illness, rest is the best thing for you.

He left Mam to sleep. He thought about saying a little prayer for her. That's what they would have said to do at school, but he knew they didn't say prayers in the Driscol house anymore. Dad said they were all a long way from a state of grace and that saying prayers at this stage would probably bring the roof down on their heads. Marti didn't want to damage the roof so he blew a little kiss to Mam and promised to be a good boy.

16

He washed and dressed himself and tried to make his lunchbox up and then Jono, who lived out the back, appeared at the kitchen window. "Shhh, you'll have to keep quiet. My mam's not well," said Marti.

"Okay, is that why you're so late today?" said Jono.

"I've got to make my own lunchbox."

"I wish I could make mine. You could have heaps of choco."

"I don't think we have any choco."

"Well what are you going to do? You can't make a lunchbox with no choco, Marti."

He looked around the kitchen. He could see his Mam's purse sitting up on the counter next to the empty biscuit barrel. He really wanted some choco now Jono had started on about it.

"Jono, you've got to keep quiet about this," he said, and started to reach for Mam's purse.

"Marti, what are you doing with that?"

He opened the purse and took out a blue ten dollar bill. He had never held a ten dollar bill before and it felt strange to have it in his hands. "Wow, ten bucks . . ."

"What are you gonna buy, Marti?"

"Choco!" he said, and the two boys ran out the kitchen door.

At the supermarket they filled their arms with choco bars and the counter woman looked at them like they were trouble. The most Marti had ever bought before was a big box of Froot Loops the time Mam had given him five dollars, and even then he had had to take the change back to her. When the counter woman leaned forward and asked him where the money had come from, Marti froze.

"He's buying for the whole week," said Jono.

The counter woman looked down at Jono and said, "Who's pulling your strings, matey?" Then she started to ring up the money on the till and Marti and Jono smiled. When they got outside the boys started laughing and cramming the choco into their mouths until their cheeks were full and their teeth turned brown. It was a great laugh, thought Marti, watching the choco squelch about in their mouths, and then Jono said they had better run or they'd be late.

School was all about Ned Kelly and his gang who were bush-rangers, which was like outlaws, and they had armour made from ploughs like the kind they used to have in fields in the olden days. Marti liked the stories about Ned Kelly and his gang who went around robbing and shooting in the armour made from ploughs. He had heard all the stories about Ned Kelly and his gang from Dad, who said some people were down on poor old Ned.

"But sure wasn't that just because he had the good Irish blood in him," said Dad, and hadn't he seen the same himself. "No, Ned was just doing his bit. He was stopping the English getting the whip hand on this country, and isn't there many a man would thank him they never did."

Jono told Marti he thought it would be great to be like Ned Kelly and his gang, robbing and shooting and wearing the armour made from ploughs. Marti agreed and they both said they would like to be like Ned Kelly, then Jono said, "Do you feel a bit like a bushranger after stealing the money from your mam's purse?"

Marti felt his head go all hot. "No," he said. He knew he had been wrong to take the money and he knew he had eaten too many choco bars and now he didn't feel very well at all.

He still had four choco bars left, which would get him into trouble when he went home because Mam would say, "Where did you get them from, or do I not want to know?"

He opened up the last of the choco bars and started cramming them into his mouth, one after the other. The first two were hard to eat and the third was beginning to hurt his jaws because he had to chew so fast. When he tried to swallow the third choco bar it wouldn't go down at all, and then there was a funny feeling in his stomach that made him lean over and he was sick all over his jotter and all over his desk.

In the Nurse's Room Marti was told to lie still and wait until someone could be found to sit with him. He didn't know why it was called the Nurse's Room when there was no nurse. There never was a nurse, and then the man the teachers called Mr Spitz and the boys in class called Charlie came in and said he would wait with him awhile.

Charlie always wore the same mustard-coloured coat, except when he was in the playground or on the roof, then he would wear a big hat and a vest with holes in it. Marti liked Charlie because he would always have a laugh and a joke with Jono and himself, and if he found tennis balls or cricket balls on the roof he would sometimes give them to the boys to keep.

"So you're a bit crook are you, sonny?" said Charlie.

"I've got a sore tummy. I ate too much choco and sicked it back up."

"Choco, eh? You can have too much of a good thing, you know." Charlie messed up Marti's hair with his big hand and said, "Well, maybe you had to learn your lesson the hard way." Marti didn't want to learn any more lessons the hard way, and he wished he had never taken the blue ten dollar bill. He wondered if he would be in trouble for being sick all over his jotter and all over his desk and if Mam and Dad would find out. If they ever found out there would be trouble for sure, thought Marti, and he curled over in the bed and groaned.

"Now, now," said Charlie, "I'm sure it can't be all that bad . . . and your dad's on his way to collect you. Doesn't that make you feel better? You can spend the rest of the day at home."

Marti didn't feel better at all. He didn't want to go home either because Mam might say there was a dear price to pay for Dad taking time off from working and earning their keep. Dad couldn't be taking time off to collect him because wasn't it the working and the working alone that kept the roof over their heads, like he said. Mam must be really bad with the sadness called the Black Dog, thought Marti. If she couldn't even come to collect him from school then she might even still be curled up on the sofa.

He didn't know what he would say to make it better. He knew Dad wouldn't give him a row, Dad never gave out the rows. It was always Mam who would shout and say, "That's you for the hot arse." Dad never gave out the rows, or the hot arse, and sometimes Mam and Dad would row because Dad wouldn't give out the rows or the hot arse.

Marti felt the guilt for taking the money now and he wondered, would he be the one to blame for another fight at home? One time when he had been really bad and caused a flood trying to sail a boat in the bath, Mam said he was a bold boy, which is what the Irish say when a boy is bad. He had gone beyond the beyonds and was in big trouble when his dad got home.

When Dad got home he didn't really get angry, though. He only said if he had done that when he was a boy his own father would have taken a belt to him. He said that money didn't grow on trees and that everything had to be bought and paid for and he couldn't afford to be flooding the place for a laugh and a joke. He said if he had so much as thought of causing a flood at home when he was a boy, his father would have made sure he couldn't sit for a week. He said his father played in the All-Ireland Hurling Final and could heft a belt like no man before or since, and if he had a drink in him you never knew whether you were going to get the buckle across your legs as well.

Marti felt sad to think of Dad getting the buckle across his legs when he was a boy and wished he had been good so Dad wouldn't have to tell him the story again, or to take the time off from working and earning their keep. He could see Dad shaking his head sometime soon and saying, "Well, this is a fine state of affairs with your mam sick abroad in the house."

A great lump swelled in Marti's throat, caused by the sadness he felt for being such a bold boy and adding to all the troubles they already had at home, because now he knew there would be more troubles to come.

3

The last straw, that's what it was, thought Joey Driscol. The last straw entirely. Macca was a good man and a grand boss but to be going to him with the begging bowl for more time off was a terrible reddener. Joey knew there would be talk around the place about him not pulling his weight now, or worse yet, he might be called a bludger. They were a grand bunch of lads, or blokes like they said in Australia, but the ore wouldn't move itself about and wasn't working the job you were paid just a man's duty.

"Can ye plant the foot, mate?" he shouted out the car window. "Jaysus, isn't green for go." Two fingers were raised out the roof of the car in front and Joey started to shake his head. "Don't be thinking that's the way, Marti," he said. "Sure, isn't that just ignorance showing. The man cannot accept he's in the wrong. It takes a big man to accept he's in the wrong, sure it does, son."

Joey looked at Marti sitting next to him and started to smile. He was trying to copy his dad's movements, his little arm out the window and his little fingers drumming on an imaginary steering wheel in front of him. Wasn't the boy a dote, thought Joey, and then he felt the smile slipping from his face.

Where was his mother? It should be the mother collecting him from school surely, not the father. Oh no, not the father, who was out doing his bit, working and earning their keep. That's the way it was when he was a boy and sure didn't every boy know that was the way of it; shouldn't the mother be the one there for a child in time of sickness.

He strained his eyes at the hot sky ahead and felt his thoughts shift back to his own childhood. His mother was always there, minding and tending, keeping her brood safe. He could see her now at the back door calling him away in when the light was failing, her cold breath hanging in the air around her like a pall. Joey had come along first, his own mother then added another five children to her lot. Wouldn't she be ashamed entirely at the way Marti, an only child, was being minded? Wouldn't it just break her heart, he thought, if he hadn't already done that himself a long time ago?

"Will you ever stop your fidgeting, Marti?" snapped Joey. Snapping now, is it? Taking your problems out on the boy now, is it, he thought. He looked for a reaction in Marti's face, but the boy only sat very still and looked straight ahead like he was worried about what was coming next, or worse, he was too scared to move.

"I'm sorry, son," said Joey. "Sure you're not in any trouble. Isn't your old dad just a bit touchy this weather. The heat's a grand thing, so it is, but isn't it terrible for fraying the old temper."

"It's okay," said Marti. Joey smiled and roughed the boy's hair with his hand. God, he was a grand lad. Maybe they weren't doing such a bad job with him after all.

"Dad?"

"Yes, son."

"Will you and Mam fight today?"

Holy Mother of God. Joey always heard a voice say Holy Mother of God at moments like this. It was the voice of no distinct person but a voice with a familiar burr of age and wisdom and it always made him think solemnly.

"Marti, why would you say that to me?"

"Mam has the Black Dog."

Holy Mother of God – there it was again – this boy's too old for his eight years, he thought. Hasn't he seen far too much, the Black Dog indeed! Was his wife's problem as obvious to the boy now as it was to himself? Jaysus, it was a sad state of affairs entirely.

They had tried the lot for Shauna over the years, tried it all to get rid of the problem. Doctors. Medicine. Therapists. And more doctors and more medicine and more therapists. Nothing ever worked for her. It was like she wanted the Black Dog. Hadn't she once even stopped with all the treatments because she said she felt more like herself *with* the depression. Wasn't it a desperate state of affairs, he thought.

"So, it's the Black Dog back?"

"She was at the bubbling with the tears again – all night. Will you and Mam fight? You always fight when she has the Black Dog and aren't you taking time off from working and earning our keep again?" Marti started to cry, and then he hid his face.

"Whoa-whoa-whoa there, sonny boy, sure there's no need for the waterworks going on." The boy's tears were a saddener for sure. Joey could hardly watch. He thought there could be nothing worse in the entire world, nothing could ever be worse than watching his son in a state like this. And wasn't it all for no good reason. He knew Marti shouldn't be bothering himself with the likes of this.

His own father, the grand Emmet Driscol, would have beat him as black as a mourning coach for starting with the tears, but Joey was determined to be a better father to his son. He could still see Emmet, could feel his presence. At moments like this he was a boy again himself. He remembered his father, at the height of his hurling days, always close to rage, and closer yet to the whiskey.

Once his father had returned from Molloy's pub in the middle of the night roaring the house down. The baby Clancy cried in his mother's arms but the rest of the children stayed where they were, quiet in their beds. Joey could still remember the noise of his father's roars that night when he called out his name and demanded he raise himself. There was the noise of furniture being moved about, knocked over, and the sound of his father's heavy boots and curses chasing round the house. When Joey presented himself, his father was on the floor, his face scarlet, his hair wet to his brow. There was scarcely a stick of furniture or picture on the walls that wasn't disturbed, and then Joey saw the cause of it flash before him like a ghost.

His father had been given another gift by one of the men in Molloy's. He was always being given things. It was a great advertisement to say the mighty Emmet Driscol was a fan of your tyres or your shoes or your bacon. This time the gift was a lively piglet that had come home with a rope round its neck but was none too happy to see it tightened.

Joey was told to make a grab for the piglet but there was no need, for didn't it jump into his arms the moment it saw him. The rope had been wrapped round its little snout and when Joey loosened it, there were great breaths taken after its exertions. Emmet got to his feet with a struggle, knocking a lampshade about face and said, "Grand, grand. Now follow me. We have a job of work to be done."

Joey followed his father into the kitchen, where he watched as Emmet steadied himself over the sink then reached for his razor strop. The sight of the strop being taken made Joey's heart gallop but not for himself – he had felt its lashes too many times. He wondered what his father had planned now for the piglet. The little creature seemed to sense it too and squirmed in Joey's arms.

"Hold that bastard steady," said his father.

"What'll ye do? What'll ye do to it?"

"I'll cut its throat, what d'ye think?" He grabbed the piglet and hung it over the sink by its back legs. It struggled and squealed and his father had to use both hands to keep from losing it again. All the while the piglet looked at Joey with great black eyes, staring. He remembered them still.

"Joey, get my razor. Ye will have to do it."

"No."

"What d'ye mean 'no'? Ye *will* do it. The razor now. Cut this bastard's throat before it has me on my back."

Joey looked at the piglet, upturned and struggling in his father's great hands. The black eyes pleaded again when he took down the razor and then there was an almighty struggle as though the piglet knew it was on its own. The squeals were the sound of terror and Joey could feel them reaching into him.

"Cut its throat, hear me. Cut it, cut it, now!"

Joey stood with his father's razor in his hand. He was motionless, he couldn't move. He knew he was disobeying and he knew what that meant, but he couldn't harm the animal, and then the razor slipped to the floor. There was a sharp pain in the front of Joey's head when the razor fell and he realised he had been struck by his father. He lay on the floor beside the razor and when he saw his father reach for it he was filled with panic.

As Joey got up he could feel the cold flap of skin where his father's knuckle had struck the bone. There was blood running from his head, going into his eyes and into his mouth. He felt no pain as he watched his father run the open steel across the piglet's throat. The squealing reached a higher pitch for a second and then blood choked its mouth and spilled over its flesh into the sink.

Joey watched the blood pour from the dying animal. Its black eyes were still staring into the heart of him, and when he watched the blood flowing he felt it was his, like the blood he could taste in his mouth from the wound his father had made.

"*But I took the money*. I took the money from Mam," said Marti. He was still crying.

"What money?"

"Ten dollars. I took it out her purse. I had no lunchbox today and I took the money and spent it on choco."

"Is that what made ye crook, Marti? Did ye stuff yourself on chocolate?"

He nodded. The boy was in a fine state now, thought Joey. Robbing money was a cry for help if ever there was one. Bloody Shauna and her Black Dog. It was time she pulled herself together before she was after wrecking the boy entirely. He felt a cool line of sweat run down his back and he shook his head. "You fended for yourself like a good boy, son. I think the ten dollars can be our little secret, what do you say?"

Marti nodded. His eyes were drying now. Joey roughed up his hair again. He'd had a tough time of it. A telling off was only going to make matters worse. "Are ye okay now?" Marti nodded again, and Joey took a deep breath from the hot air that was all around them.

"Dad, I wish there was no Black Dog and no fights."

"Ah now, wouldn't that be grand," said Joey. Wasn't there no end to the ways this boy could make him smile.

"Did Mam always have the Black Dog?"

"No, Marti, there was a time when she had no Black Dog at all."

"When?" he said, and turned quickly to hear the answer.

"A long time ago."

"A long time ago before I was born?"

"That's right."

"In Ireland?"

"Yes, in Ireland."

Marti turned away again and Joey wondered what was going through the boy's mind this time, but he was too scared to ask. It could be anything at all, he thought. Wasn't the boy just full of surprises.

When they arrived home the purse was still sitting on the counter in the kitchen. Marti looked at it for a long time, and then Joey put his hand in his pocket and took out a ten dollar bill. "Here, put that in there, Marti, and no one will be any the wiser."

The boy took the money and placed it gently in the purse, then stepped back from the counter. "Dad," he said.

"What is it, son?"

"I think, I think I'm feeling a bit crook again."

"Well maybe bed's the best place for you. Away and have a bit of a rest."

Marti went through the kitchen door and Joey watched his little frame trudge down the hall. Jaysus, am I all he has now? The poor boy, the bloody poor boy. Marti turned into his bedroom with his head bowed down and Joey felt his throat tighten. "It's like the weight of the world he's carrying on them shoulders," he whispered.

Joey felt the pain of failure. Marti was his son, the one pure and good thing in his life. He could forget about the rest, about Ireland and the past and the fights, but Marti was different. The boy had to be kept safe from harm. Wasn't that a father's duty?

He lit a cigarette. He knew he was in no mind for Shauna now, hadn't all this been her fault, and then she appeared in front of him, dressed in her nightclothes, her thick hair stuck to her face on one side where she had slept on it. She looked messed up. She was nothing like the girl who turned heads back in Kilmora.

"Is he home, Joey?" she said, putting an ear to Marti's bedroom door.

He nodded and folded his arms and then he unfolded them quickly. "Will ye leave him be, sure the boy's crook."

"Is he all right? Should I go in?"

"No, will you get away from that door."

Shauna started to curl her lip, and then raised her hand over her eyes to stop the tears that were coming.

"Go way outta that, will ye," said Joey.

"Is he okay?"

"What do you care?" He grabbed Shauna's arm and led her away from Marti's room and into the kitchen, closing the door behind them. "It's a sin that boy had to leave this house on an empty stomach this morning. Ye obviously expected him to beg in the street for a feed like some class of knacker."

Shauna's eyes started to fill with tears. Joey shook his head. It was all a holy show. Wasn't it a funny thing entirely, verging on the miraculous even, how she could produce herself at this hour, fresh as a daisy after half the day in bed and after leaving himself to collect a sick boy from the school.

"Look, I'm sorry," she said.

"Isn't it a bit late in the day to be sorry? It's that boy of yours you should be saying sorry to when every child from here to the black stump knows it's a mother that should be there for them in time of illness," he said. "It's about time ye pulled yourself together . . . for the boy."

Shauna opened her mouth like she had just taken a shock and then she took a deep breath. She looked like she was about to make a charge. "Is that your considered opinion then?" She leaned forward, poking a finger in Joey's chest. "Well, it might be easy for you to say. It doesn't make it easy in the real world when you have the burden of all burdens to carry around on your own two shoulders."

"The real world, is it now?" He was having none of it. "I'll tell you what the real world is, shall I? The real world is what goes on out there when you're lying in your pit feeling sorry for yourself."

"Well, I wouldn't know, would I?"

"No, probably not . . . sure wouldn't that take eyes in your head and yours are shut most of the time."

"Well, that's rich. At least my eyes are only shut when I'm asleep!"

"Jaysus, when are ye anything else? Don't I deserve medals after having wet-nursed you all these years, listening to your whining and putting up with your sluttish manner."

27

"Sluttish manner, sluttish manner. Well I wondered when you were going to start quoting me from the gospel according to Peggy Driscol. If your mother was half the saint you made her out to be she would never have raised a bastard like yourself. Abandoned as a babe you would have been."

Shauna was spitting mad and Joey didn't know what he had done to bring it on. He'd only pointed out the facts of the matter. "That's not *her* way," he said.

"It was ours," she said softly. "It was mine, a mother, and I turned my back on our child. It was a long time ago and I'm suffering for it still, and will be for a long time yet. Is that not enough for you?"

Joey felt shame for what he had said, but why was she bringing this up again? "You have a child here," he said. The words caught in Joey's throat like jagged little fish bones and started scratching away inside him.

"Answer me, haven't I suffered enough?" Her voice was higher now. She was pleading with him. "You think I haven't suffered enough, is that it?"

"Who am I to judge that?" said Joey. "There's higher powers will have that pleasure."

Shauna's voice went into a wail as she began to sob heavily, and then Joey walked for the door once again.

"Joey, don't walk away. Joey, don't turn your feckin back on me again."

4

Feck was a bad word. Marti knew it was how the Irish said the f-word because Dad had told him. Dad said feck wasn't really as bad as the f-word but when Marti said it he still got asked if he wanted his mouth washed out with soap for using a bad word. Marti heard Mam say the feck word and then she said bastard, which was another bad word. He knew if he had said bastard it would be the mouth washed out with soap for sure, and maybe even the hot arse. Mam and Dad were fighting again. It was probably all his fault, thought Marti. He wished he had never seen the blue ten dollar bill.

There was a big silence and Marti wondered had the fighting stopped, and he stuck his head out into the hall to look. The kitchen door was closed but there was a little gap where he could see in. Dad was staring at Mam and she had a very strange look on her face, like the way people sometimes look on films when they've just been shot and are about to fall over with the bullet in them.

Marti thought Dad's face looked like he had just eaten something that tasted really horrible and he would spit it out, and then he lunged forward and pushed open the kitchen door. Marti pulled in his head from the hall. He could hear Mam shouting for Dad, but Dad was walking down the hall, very quickly, with the big steps. Mam was still shouting when the front door was slammed and then he heard the bubbling with the tears and knew what would be next.

"Marti, come here. Come and give Mam a hug."

29

He didn't want to give her another hug. All this trouble was caused by the hugs. If Mam hadn't made him give her the hugs then he wouldn't have taken the money. There would have been no choco bought and no being sick in class and there would have been no fight with the door slammed again.

"I don't want to," he said.

"Marti, come to Mam. Come on now. Come here."

He walked out of his bedroom and saw Mam. She was crouched on the floor with her head down in her hands. Her hair had fallen forward and was sticking all over the place in a whole mess. She looked very sad crouched on the floor, and when she looked up Marti saw she was ready to start crying all over again.

"Come and give Mam a hug, Marti." She put out her arms, and when Marti walked over she grabbed him round the shoulders and held him tight. "Isn't it you and me versus the world, little man." He didn't want to be called little man. It was just another one of the silly names Mam had for him. Hugs and silly names. She'd be turning him into a Mummy's Boy like they said.

"Look here, my little man. How would you like a special treat?" she said.

"What kind of a treat?" said Marti.

"A special, special one. How would you like to go on a holiday?"

"Where?" Marti was confused again. He wondered, was it a holiday like the time Mam and Dad took him to the place where the whales came in at the sea? He didn't think it was. It was a long way from the school holidays and Dad was away out the front door again, to be back who knows when.

"No more questions, Marti. You can go and get some clothes in a bag – and a toy, and a book, but just one of each," said Mam.

"Where are we going?"

"Far away, Marti. It's a long, long journey. Now hurry yourself."

"But, Mam, where?"

"Marti, now listen." Mam grabbed his shoulders and leaned down to look into his eyes. "You need to move yourself fast because we haven't much time. We're leaving tonight. Now c'mon, no more questions, son."

"But Mam, Dad isn't home."

30

Mam stood up straight and looked away from Marti, then she pushed her long black hair back with both hands and turned around again. "Marti," she said, "that's right, son, but he can meet us later because doesn't he have the ute and we're going on a train."

"A train!"

"That's right son. A long, long journey on a train and then on a boat or maybe even a plane."

"A plane!" Marti had never been on a plane and had only ever been on a train and a boat once, the time Mam and Dad took him to the place where the whales came in at the sea. He was excited about going on a train and a boat or maybe even a plane, but Mam didn't look very excited at all. She still had the big black eyes like a panda from all the crying and looked like there was more to come.

"Now c'mon," she said, "chop-chop. There's a lot to do if we're to get going. Now pack your stuff up. I want out of here in less than an hour, do you think you can manage that?"

Marti nodded and ran into his room and started to pack his things like Mam said. He wanted to ask Jono, who lived out the back, what toy to take, and he wondered if Jono would be excited too when he found out about the journey, so he called Jono with the galah sound. They made up the galah sound after watching a show on television where a boy pretended to be a bird to make a secret signal to his friends. When Jono's mam heard them making the noise, she said, "Stop making a racket like a bloody galah," and they kept the name.

When Marti made the galah sound, Jono's sister Becca came to the window and made a face that was all scrunched up like Dad said was the woman's look for making the milk sour. Marti never understood why a woman would want to make the milk sour and when he said this to Dad one day, Dad said, "Sure, Marti, don't all cats love their milk sour. Sure, the sourer the better. It's a passion for them." Then he laughed, and Marti still didn't know why a woman would want to make the milk sour.

Becca shouted on Jono and he came to the window and waved, then ran to meet Marti. He counted one-elephant, two-elephant . . . Jono usually took about six or seven elephants to get to the door. "G'day, Marti. Are you coming out?" said Jono.

"I'm going on a train and a boat or maybe even a plane!"

Jono looked sad when Marti said about the journey and only said, "When?"

"Now, soon."

Jono looked really sad, thought Marti, even more sad than the time when Dad showed them how to play Battleships with the pencil and the paper and Jono wanted to stay and play all night but his mam said no.

"Marti, why are you going?"

"I don't know. My mam just said."

"Can I come?"

"I don't think so. She has it all planned and I can only take one bag with a book and a toy, but I'd like you to come," said Marti. "Will you help me pick a toy?"

The Incredible Hulk used to be Marti's favourite toy before he started on the television and looked like he was just all covered in green powder. Marti couldn't take the Incredible Hulk seriously anymore when he was just all covered in green powder, because it was a long time since even Marti had got the powder on him and powder was just for babies. When he was much younger he remembered Mam putting the powder on him after the bath and saying, here's the chip going to get some salt, and he would always laugh at that. But the Incredible Hulk just all covered in green powder wasn't even funny, thought Marti, and when he told Dad, he said, "Wasn't that man just making a holy show of himself on the television for the big fat paycheque." Dad said there were some things just not worth making a holy show of yourself for, and television shows was one of them, because there was no dignity at all in being paraded in front of the world like an eejit no matter how fat the paycheque.

"Are you taking the Hulk?" said Jono.

"I don't even like him anymore," said Marti.

"How long will you go for?"

"I don't know."

"Marti, will you come back?"

"Yes, I think so. Dad says this is our home and Australia is God's country and he would never live anywhere else in the whole world. I think it's just like a holiday, Jono, so we'll be back, I think."

Jono sat down on the bed and looked away at the wall. Marti couldn't see his face, so he asked him to turn around, but Jono shook his head.

"What's wrong, Jono?"

"I have a sore tummy." Marti knew there was no sore tummy. It was all a holy show. Jono was just sad because he would have to go back to school tomorrow and have no best friend to talk to and have a laugh and a joke with. Marti was sad too but he wanted to go on the train and a boat or maybe even a plane.

Mam started calling him to bring the bag and pick a toy fast. "I have to go, Jono," said Marti. She had taken the notion into her head, and Dad said once Mam had taken the notion into her head there wasn't a pack of terriers to be found that could flush it out. She was a holy terror for acting on a notion all right, always had been, he said.

"Marti," shouted Mam again, and then the bedroom door was flung open. "When did he get in here?" She had a mad angry look on her and Marti wondered why she would be so annoyed to see Jono when he was forever in and out of his room.

"Jono was helping me pick a toy," he said.

"Well, you can say goodbye to him now. He's off home," said Mam, and she grabbed Jono by the arm and lifted him up off the bed in a hurry.

"Bye, Jono," said Marti. "Bye . . . Bye . . ."

"Will, Marti be back, Mrs Driscol?" said Jono, and Mam turned her head to the side and said, "Back where?"

"Bye, Marti. Bye," said Jono, and he was led away very quickly by Mam.

Marti watched his friend taken home across the back yard to his own house. Mam walked so quickly that sometimes Jono's feet were lifted off the ground entirely but he still shouted, "Bye, Marti, bye," with every step he took.

5

Now that was something, thought Joey Driscol. Sure it wasn't every day you saw three pelicans flying in a row. But there it was, three of the big white fellas up in the sky with their saggy jowls flapping as loudly as their wings against the bright blue sky. It was a grand sight to see, so it was, but sometimes the melancholy Celt came out in Joey and he wondered did he really deserve to be in this place. In Ireland they would have said it meant something. Three of anything in a row would have brought bad news, like a black hat on a bed or an umbrella up indoors. He knew his own mother would have been splashing the holy water around, lighting candles in church and praying to her patron saint at such a sight as three pelicans flying in a row. But there were no pelicans back in Kilmora, and weren't blue skies there only half as rare?

Joey walked into the house and called out, "Marti, are ye home, son?" There was no answer. "Marti, Shauna, are yees home?"

The place was deadly quiet, he thought. He looked in the kitchen and he looked in the living room but there was no soul to be seen. He lit a cigarette, inhaled deeply, and breathed out slowly. Wasn't it the queerest thing? Shauna had hardly raised herself for days and here she was now, up and out. She'd have to be dressed and made up to face the world. Perhaps their little talk had worked. Was she finally shaking off the Black Dog? Joey smiled to himself and put his cigarette back in his mouth.

Jaysus, this could be just grand, he thought, Shauna making the effort now. And mustn't she have young Marti with her, that was grand too – didn't the boy need the attention of his mother. A father could only do so much, what with the working and earning their keep. No, a mother was definitely needed to raise the child properly.

Joey bolted back to the kitchen. He scanned the fridge door for a note from Shauna, but there was none. Maybe that would be asking too much of her. She was only after getting over the Black Dog, wouldn't notes and the like come with time. He was happy to think of Shauna, fully recovered and off treating Marti to some manner of visit or other. He imagined them together, laughing and smiling, Marti pointing at all the new toys in the shops and Shauna saying, "Maybe for Christmas if you're a good boy, son."

Things could be just grand now, he thought, just like they were before it started to go wrong. Hadn't Shauna been a rare one, back in their day. She wasn't like the rest of the Kilmora culchies. There was a wildness in her. All night she stayed out, dancing and drinking and enjoying herself and didn't she care less who knew it. Joey's own mother had said she was a wild one.

"Wouldn't she stick her tongue out at the cross and mind not who saw her."

Joey heard his mother's words and then there were more of her words came back to him, and he remembered why he didn't like to think about the past in Ireland with Shauna. If there was one thing he was sure of it was that the past must stay where it was. That was just Shauna's trouble, didn't she need to lock it all away.

Joey looked out the window into the yard and saw Marti's friend Jono sitting on the back step with his fists dug into his cheeks. The boy looked sad, he thought, upset even. He waved at him. Jono looked up, gave no sign he had recognised Joey, and then he ran out the yard at full pelt.

"Jaysus, who's taken his cake?" said Joey, and when he turned his gaze he saw Jono's mother at the window over the way. He raised his hand to wave at her too, but she turned her back before he could make any further movement. Am I a leper here? No, surely not. There'll have been some falling out had because Jono couldn't go with Marti this afternoon, sure that's what it'll be. Aren't they a terrible pair them boys, inseparable.

Still, it unsettled Joey to see his friendliness rebuffed. They were always so kind with a nod and a wave in Australia, weren't they the nicest people entirely. You had to be a real mongrel like they said to turn the neighbours against you. It was the old mateship thing. You couldn't be falling out with anyone because weren't you always jumping the fence for a bit of a barbie or a look at the footy or such like.

He walked out the back door to see if he could find Jono and ask what the bother was, but the boy was nowhere in sight. Joey was about to come back inside when he noticed the shed door was open, the padlock swinging from the latch, the key still in it. Well, there's been no robbery, that's for sure, he thought, but who would be in the shed? Wasn't there only a bunch of junk kept there, only stuff they never used like Marti's old bikes, a tyre with a puncture and the big old suitcases, brought with them from Ireland back in '68. He looked inside. The shed was still a whole mess, but someone had definitely been in there. He shut the door and slipped the padlock back on the latch. There was something up, something queer.

Joey sat on the back step, watching the sky darkening and waiting for Shauna to come home with Marti. He felt the heat draining out of the day and he heard the crickets starting up. It would soon be night-time. Where were they? He lit another cigarette. He was smoking too many, he knew it. He could feel his throat getting raw, but didn't the cigarettes calm you down, didn't they take your mind off things. His palms were sweating and a moist ring appeared round the base of the cigarette.

"Jaysus, where are they? They should be home by now, surely," he said.

He stood up – *think* – control was needed. Where would they be? He knocked on his head with a closed fist. There was no zoo, there was no bowling alley or even a cinema for miles, and Shauna couldn't drive anyway. The shops would be closed and it was getting too dark to be wandering around parks. Wasn't Marti too old for them now anyway; he was beyond the swings stage, sure. They could be anywhere. What's to be done? Joey's heart was beating faster. "Gordy, that's it. I'll ask Gordy. He's a copper. He'll know what to do."

He ran through the street to Gordy's house. It was dark now. They were never big on street lamps round their way and as he ran he tried not to think about what might have happened or what could happen in the dark.

At Gordy's house he banged on the door. "Hello, hello. Is there anyone home?"

There was no answer and he banged on the door again.

"Hello, hello! Gordy, Jaysus, are ye home, man?"

The porch light came on and then the door was slowly opened. "G'day, Bluey, mate," said Gordy.

"God, am I glad to see ye." Joey was breathing heavily from the running.

"What's the drama?"

"It's Marti . . . and my wife, they're missing."

"What do you mean *missing*, mate?"

"Gone, vanished. Haven't they just disappeared."

Gordy told Joey to come inside whilst he called the station. Joey stared at his feet and ran his fingers through his hair again and again until Gordy came back and said, "There's nothing reported, Bluey."

"What . . . nothing. Well, where can they be?"

"Look, mate, could they be visiting someone or . . . ?"

"Christ no, sure Shauna hasn't spoken to anyone in months. She has the depression. I'm scared out of my wits here, Gordy. She's not fit to be minding the boy."

"Okay, okay. Let's keep calm. Did you have a row?"

"A row . . . did we ever. But sure there's nothing strange in that, a man having a row with his wife."

"No, no, there's nothing strange in that, but if she's depressed and you had a row, well . . ."

"What are you saying here?" Joey's mind was buzzing. He couldn't think straight. All he could think of was Marti, where he might be and what he might be doing. Jaysus, he could be anywhere could he not, and in any state entirely.

"Was everything like normal at home?" said Gordy.

"How do you mean?"

37

"Were any of their things taken – clothes, toothbrushes, that sort of stuff."

Joey jumped to his feet. He had caught Gordy's drift. He felt his eyes open wider than ever, then snap shut like he'd been stunned by a bright flash. "God – the suitcases! That's what she was after in the shed."

Gordy stood up beside him. "Bluey, are you all right?"

Joey's mouth dried over. He wondered was his heart about to jump right into it. He felt like he had just been given the scare of his life, like his entire body was fighting the shock of it. "Christ Almighty, she's taken my boy," he said.

"Bluey, now you don't know that yet."

"She's taken him."

Joey broke for the door and Gordy stood up. "Bluey, what are you going to do, mate?"

"Find them. What do ye think, man? My son is taken, my wife has finally lost it."

"Bluey, don't do anything silly." Gordy grabbed Joey's arm tightly and delayed him where he stood. "Sit down and I'll give the blokes the word, to keep an eye out . . . okay?"

"No chance."

"Joey, you're madder than a cut snake. Stay away from the grog. I won't be there to keep you out the divvy van tonight."

"Gordy, let me go. I appreciate what you're saying, but I have to find my boy."

Gordy released his grip and Joey ran into the street. He ran past his own home and into the next street where he had told Marti not to climb the trees. He ran to the late-night milk bar and he ran over the cricket oval where he had taught Marti to punt a pig-skin. He ran past the stream where Marti caught the frogs that he'd taken home and over the bridge where the stream flowed into a river. He ran through the rushes and the long grass that he had told Marti to stay away from for fear of tiger snakes and red-bellied black snakes that were seen there. And he ran to Marti's school where he grabbed the gates and shook them until they rattled so much that the entire street sounded like it was suddenly filled with machine guns firing.

"Marti, son. Where are ye? Where has she taken ye, my boy?" Joey fell to his knees and started to sob into his chest. He sobbed for only a short while, until his thoughts of Marti made him wonder what the boy might think of him, and then he stood up and started to walk away from the school gates.

The streets were cold and dark, but Joey was miles away. He was lost in despair, numb with wonder at what had happened. He'd had no clue, no inkling this was on the way. Why? Why had Shauna done it? She was at her wildest with a notion in her, always was, but why this? What did it all mean? And worse yet, would he ever see Marti again?

When Joey got back to the house Macca's ute was parked out front. When he got closer Macca's kelpie sat up in the back of the ute and barked, but only once. Macca was sitting on the front step, clutching a cigarette in one hand and shooing mozzies with the other.

"Bloody dunny budgies are everywhere," he said, taking off his hat and waving it through the mozzies. When he was finished he stood up and looked at Joey. "I thought I better drop by," he said.

Joey looked at him but said nothing. His head was sore now, his heart still pounded, he felt like some kind of mentaller – a crazy person out running the streets – sobbing and calling into the night.

"I heard from Gordy," said Macca.

"Did ye now?"

"You've copped a gutful there, mate."

"You don't know the half of it."

"What do you mean?"

"She's not fit to mind herself, never mind my boy, Macca."

"She couldn't have gone far. We'll have a look about tomorrow. We'll get a few of the blokes together, no worries."

"You'll be telling me to put posters up on trees next. It's not a feckin dog I've lost."

"Look, mate, I know. We'll find the boy."

"You've no right to be telling me that. Don't ye read the papers? Jaysus, some of these bloody women just disappear off the face of the earth."

"Bluey, mate . . ."

"No. Macca, he could be anywhere. Anywhere except the one place he should be, and that's here with me."

Joey pushed past Macca into the house and slammed the door so hard it swung on its hinges. The place was in darkness, but Joey kept the lights out and crept into Marti's room where he threw himself on the boy's bed and buried his face in the pillow, then he felt the sobbing start up again.

He was back in his own childhood once more, face down in his own tears, the mighty Emmet Driscol stood over him, berating. It was to be his first stay away from home, the visit to Bunratty Castle with the school. He had never been away on any of the school's visits before and it felt to him like a hard-earned treat. They would take the bus and see the castle that kept out Ireland's invaders and stay over for two nights in a dormitory nearby. Joey was excited about the visit, but he was worried the other boys in the dormitory would laugh at him because he had no bedclothes. His father said he would have to grin and bear it though, because there would be no money spent on the likes. Bedclothes were a vanity only, he said, and if Joey worried what the others would say he could undress under the covers.

For days Joey begged for the jamas, even his mother said it was like a knacker child he'd be without them, but Emmet Driscol's word was final. There would be no money spent on them. Joey's mother couldn't stand the mope on him or the thought of her eldest child being made a cod of – wasn't it the type of thing that would stick with him his life. She got hold of a pattern and made the jamas out of pieces from her rag bag. There were sleeves didn't match and seams all over but a pocket and collar of green velvet that made them look like the best jamas in the world, thought Joey.

His brothers and sisters were sworn to silence about their mother's handiwork, and when their father was out at Molloy's pub Joey gave them a show of the new jamas. Everyone thought they looked grand and Megan said it was like a prince in a book he was and Joey acted the part, parading about in the jamas for all to see. He even laid down on the floor and pretended to be sleeping to show how grand and comfortable the new jamas were. And then, all of a sudden, Emmet came back with the smell of whiskey on him.

"What is this?" he said. "I told ye, woman, no bedclothes."

"'Tis just a few rags, Emmet," said Joey's mother. "Aren't they hardly fit for his back."

"I said, *no*. Did I not, by Christ, did I not say, *no*?"

Joey's father grabbed for him on the floor, clasping his great hand round his ankle and jerking him into the air. Joey was rigid as a branch in his father's hand as he was stripped of the new jamas, torn from his back, returned to rags on the floor below. He could see his brothers and sisters watching, Megan crying into her sleeve. It was a fairy tale being taken apart before her eyes. His mother was silent, slipping her arms quickly round the children and leading them away. When the jamas were in tatters Joey was dropped on the floor beside them, then he ran to his room in his pelt, all bar one cuff of green velvet, and cried into his pillow.

"Up. Up. Get up, Bluey," said Macca. He grabbed Joey's shirt front with one hand and the belt round his waist with the other.

"Get off, man," shouted Joey.

"I'll get off when your boy's back in that bed," said Macca, and he lifted him up onto his feet in one swift move. "Now, come with me. There's only so many places the pair of them can be. We'll find them, Bluey. We will."

6

There was something the matter with Mam, thought Marti. It was the way she kept looking about the train, going all in a panic, and smoking the cigarettes called Majors all the while. He wondered was it because Dad was going to be late, but she said Dad wasn't going to be late and sure didn't it make no difference at all because he could catch them up at any time. Marti said would Dad be on the train and Mam said it depends, but when he asked what depends she got mad and said she'd had her fill of silly questions and not to be bothering her.

Marti wanted a comic from the front of the train where they sold the newspapers and the coffees in the paper cups like they have at parties sometimes, but he thought that he would be bothering Mam with a silly question. She had already said he wasn't too big to be getting his pants pulled down and have everyone on the train shown him getting the hot arse.

He wondered how Dad would catch up with the train and if he'd drive really fast and then jump out the ute and get on the train, but he thought this would wreck the ute and there were no roads in the bush anyway, just the track for the train.

Everything was red and dusty out the window, because it was the outback where Dad said you could fry an egg on a rock. Marti wondered if you really could fry an egg on a rock or if it was just one of the things grown-ups said that wasn't really true. He didn't think he would like to eat an egg that you could fry on a rock anyway, because it would be all dusty from the bush. It would be like the time he dropped a lolly in the street and it had all bits on it when he picked it up and Mam said to throw it away because a dog might have done its business there.

It was really hot on the train but he wasn't allowed to say it was hot because Mam said she knew it was hot and didn't need a reminder of the fact every five minutes of the day. If this was the start of the bellyaching then it had better stop now or it's a sorry boy he'd be. Marti didn't want to be a sorry boy because that was what Mam usually said before she said is it the hot arse you're after?

If Dad was on the train he would give Marti the money to buy a comic and say to Mam not to bate the boy, or is it a broken man you're trying to raise, for wasn't there enough of them in the world already thanks to mothers like you. Mam and Dad were always talking like that. They said all the same words over and over, and sometimes if they didn't think to say the words then Marti would say them.

If it was Dad's words he said then Dad would laugh and say, "Sure, hasn't the boy got the cut of your jib."

But then Mam might hit Marti on the head and say, "Is it a hot arse you're after?" If it was Mam's words he said then she would say, "I don't need a parrot," and Dad would shake his head.

"Well, is it a picture you want?" said Mam. She was flapping the collar of her shirt for a bit of a breeze to cool down and she had the woman's look for making the milk sour.

"No," said Marti. "Are you very hot, Mam?"

"Well, what do you think? No, Marti, I'm not. I'm froze to this seat, this bloody great uncomfortable . . ." Mam started to slap the back of the seat and a big cloud of dust came out and made her cough. "That's it, that's it," she said. "I've had enough, enough do you hear me?" Mam's face went all red, even her eyes started to go all red, and then she started to cry into her hand. Marti wondered what was so bad about asking her if she was hot to make her start to cry into her hand. He felt bad, like he was in bad trouble, but he didn't think he had done anything really very bad.

"I can't take another minute of it, I swear I can't, I can't, I can't," said Mam. She was roaring shouting and Marti was worried about the noise she was making and if the guard man in the blue jacket with the gold buttons who took the tickets would tell them off, or maybe even say leave the train.

Marti looked about to the other people in the train to see if anyone was going to tell the guard man. Everyone was looking at Marti and Mam, but some of them looked away or out the window when he looked at them. There was an old lady with a fur coat and a big bag who smiled at Marti and then she tugged a man's sleeve and whispered something and they both walked over.

"I bet you'd like to come with me to find a nice comic, sonny," said the man.

Marti walked down to the front of the train with the man and picked a comic that he hadn't seen before, but he liked it because it had a free soldier with it and the soldier had a parachute you could throw in the air. The comic looked like it cost a lot of money, and he wondered if the man would really buy it for him because Mam would have said she wasn't paying extra for a bit of tat because didn't they just stick that type of thing on the front to put the price up.

The man had a big red face and Marti wondered if he was very hot or if his collar with the tie on it was very tight. The man looked very hot but Marti thought maybe he wasn't really because he had a big green coat with checks on and if he were hot wouldn't he take the coat off and open the collar and tie?

"Are you happy with your choice now, sonny?" said the man.

"Yes," said Marti.

The man was called Larry Lally and he was a funny big man, thought Marti.

"And what might your name be?"

"Marti Driscol."

"Ah, Driscol, a good Irish name. Sure Briney wasn't wrong when she said she was after hearing a brogue on your mam there." Marti wondered what a brogue was, but he didn't want to interrupt the man who was happy because he had a good Irish name like Driscol.

"My, you're a serious looking fella, Marti Driscol. Is it the weight of the world you're carrying on them shoulders?" Marti didn't know what to say so he stayed quiet, and then Larry Lally said, "Sit yourself down. We'll get back to your mam in a while. Sure Briney will be having a grand time with her chatting away and talking about the movies and Elvis Presley and the like."

"My mam likes Elvis," said Marti, and the man nodded and looked happy to hear it, "but not just before he died last year because it was a crying shame the way he let himself go towards the end." Larry Lally laughed and his face started to go the bright red colour again and Marti wondered if it might pop like a big red balloon.

"Sure aren't ye a ticket," he said. "It's a ticket ye are. My, aren't we blessed with the gift of laughter?"

"I suppose," said Marti, and Larry Lally started the laughing again.

"God, it's a comedian we have here I think."

When it was time to go back and see Mam and Briney, Marti thought it was hard to walk on the train but not as hard as it looked for Larry Lally. He was too big for the little gaps in the seats and had to turn sideways to get through. Sometimes when he turned sideways to get through he had to go up on his tippy-toes and hold his breath, which made him have a big sigh afterwards. One time when Larry Lally went up on his tippy-toes he flicked out the tails on his jacket and said, "It's a ballerina you have to be for this job," and Marti laughed.

Mam had stopped crying and smiled at Marti when he got back to his seat. She looked like she did at birthdays when the cake was brought in with all the candles lit up on it. "Marti, son, where would you most like to go in the whole world for a visit?" she said.

"I don't know," he said.

"Wouldn't you like to go to Ireland, where your mam's from?"

"I wouldn't like to go to Ireland."

"Marti," said Mam, and then her face changed. She started talking very quietly. She was trying not to get mad, he thought. "Wouldn't you like to go and visit Ireland, way on the other side of the world, because sure wouldn't that be exciting?"

Marti remembered when Dad had said there was no sun at all in Ireland, and he had thought it must be a terrible place with everybody walking about the streets in the hats like miners wear with the light on the front. "I wouldn't like to go to Ireland."

"But why not, Marti?"

"Dad says it's always wet and dark in Ireland and Australia's our home."

"Oh, so that's the reason. *Your father says*, is it?" said Mam, and she had the anger on her. Marti thought he was in trouble again and Mam was going to say he wasn't too big to be getting his pants pulled down and have everyone on the train shown him getting the hot arse again.

He didn't want to go to Ireland because Dad would never go back. He had told Marti Australia was God's country and he would never leave for the days soaked through and feeling grateful for a bit of digging in a ditch, because wasn't that the only work you could ever find in Ireland. Marti knew Dad loved Australia and the sunshine and driving the trailer because there was no sunshine and no work entirely in Ireland. Dad said Ireland had gave us the Guinness, and wasn't the soda bread something to be grateful for too. But if you could tow the entire country to anchor off Sydney then he would still have to seriously consider setting foot on it, and even then it would be a temporary affair.

Mam grabbed Marti by the shoulders and led him away. She walked very fast and didn't look at any of the people who were staring at them as they went.

"Mam," said Marti.

"Shut up."

"But, Mam," said Marti. She was walking him really fast by the shoulders, and when Mam walked him really fast by the shoulders it meant the hot arse. "I didn't do anything. I didn't."

"Marti, be quiet."

"But, Mam." She stopped walking and turned to look down at him. Marti was sure he was going to start crying and when the tears came Mam looked around and then she sat down and took out a little blue handkerchief.

"Marti, now listen to me. You need to be a big brave boy for me. Do you promise to be a big brave boy for me?" Mam started to wipe tears from Marti's cheeks with the little blue handkerchief.

"I do."

"Good, that's good, son," she said, and stroked his hair. "Ireland's to be our new home, do you hear me? Our new home, Marti." He didn't understand because earlier Mam had said it was just for a holiday and he started to cry harder. It made him all sad, and he wondered why Dad never came and if he was ever really coming, but he didn't want to ask Mam because he didn't want her to say he was a bold boy and Dad didn't come to get him because he was a bold boy.

Marti wanted to see Dad and to have the laugh and a joke that he always had with him and to hear him tell the funny stories and show him the green flower thing on his arm that he could make dance in the wind. He wondered if he had never taken the blue ten dollar bill from Mam's purse and never eaten all the choco bars and never been sick in class if Dad would have come. He kept wondering and wondering why Dad never came and if he might come yet, before they left for Ireland, but Mam never said another thing, just kept stroking and stroking his hair.

7

Joey Driscol did something he hadn't done in a very long time. He knew entering into a church was what people did every day of the week but the fact didn't make it any easier. He had promised himself he was through with churches, he was finished with them the day in Kilmora when the priest asked Shauna and himself to rise and depart from the Lord's House for offending the congregation with their very presence.

"And how would we manage that?" Joey had said to Father Eugene, who was stooped and nervous before them, his top lip twitching and sparkling with the sweat on it.

"Now, Joey Driscol, we need have no trouble from the likes of ye in front of these good people," he said.

"Good people? *Good people*, is it? There's not one I would call good among them, haven't they had the knives out for us."

Shauna touched Joey's arm but said nothing. She was usually the fiery one, the first to start wagging the finger and shouting, but wasn't she done with the lot of them too. Wasn't she more done than she deserved to be. She still looked beautiful to Joey, the black hair flowing out behind her, but her face had hardened. She was no longer a carefree young girl. She was a woman, searching for courage. "Come on, Joey," she said. "Let's just go."

"I will not. Haven't I every right to be here?"

Father Eugene straightened his back and raised his voice. "Ye cannot seek forgiveness here, not now, not ever. Go."

They rose to leave and there was a flutter of tongues about the place, then Joey glanced back and saw his mother and father sat at the front of the church. His mother flinched uncomfortably where she sat and turned towards him, but his father laid a hand on her shoulder, jerked her round, eyes front, away from the son who wasn't fit to look at.

"And ye can stay away," shouted the priest at their backs, his voice emboldened. "The Holy Mother weeps at the sight of the likes of ye in the Lord's House."

Joey wanted to turn round, but Shauna grabbed his arm again. He wanted to shout, to show the blackness of their hearts, the falseness of their piety, but Shauna led him outside. "What did they want, us ruined?" she said, her courage vanished now. "Me barefoot and you begging to feed us? I cannot take it anymore. I cannot, Joey."

The memory of that day in '68 was a fierce one. He remembered how the priest had made him feel. The hate, even though he tried to bury it, was still there. In the days soon after, Australia was decided upon and Shauna had agreed. They could be happy yet, sure, hadn't she said it herself.

The church Joey entered now was quiet, wasn't it deadly quiet, he thought. He was lost for words; he knew what to say, all the prayers were printed on his soul in childhood, learned first in the Irish and later the English, but none came to him. He looked up to the cross. The church was small, much smaller than any he remembered in Ireland, but the cross was huge, it dominated the wall.

Joey kneeled and blessed himself. Coming into the Lord's House and asking for help was fine work now but sure wasn't he really up against it. It was lovely hurdling the job the Church had done on him in the past but, before Christ, wasn't he prepared to beg. "Please," he said, "*please*, God, give me back my boy."

He moved towards the stained-glass window where the rows of candles were perched beneath in their wiry little racks. He raised a taper, lit it and selected a candle for Saint Anthony, the finder of lost things. "And if ye see Saint Jude up there," said Joey, "ye could tell him I might be onto him myself soon enough."

Outside the church Pando the Greek and his brother were waiting, leaning on the side of their dusty Kombi. When Joey appeared Pando stepped forward, raised up his arms and shrugged his shoulders, then he shook his head. They had been out since the night before searching for Marti and Shauna. They both looked tired and beat, but far from ready to give up.

"Bluey, mate," said Pando, "we've been out to the highway servo – that's nearly two hundred ks. No one's seen them."

"Did ye talk to the truckers? They could have got a lift from a trucker, sure," said Joey.

"No one's seen them, mate. If they hitched a ride from a trucker they could be in *Woop Woop* for all we know."

"Did you ask them?"

"Mate, we asked," said Pando's brother. His voice was weak, going on tetchy. The men were tired. Joey was tired. They had been driving all night, stopping strangers, asking questions and all they had got were headshakes and strange looks, sometimes hostility when they pressed too hard.

"Bluey, let's go home," said Pando, "make some calls or something. We're getting nowhere pounding the streets."

"I know. Look, sorry I snapped. It's just . . ."

"No worries, mate, we know, eh." Pando patted Joey on the back and smiled, then got into the Kombi with his brother and started the engine.

Joey watched them leave then got in his ute and started to drive slowly back home. It was early morning and there were a few signs that the world was starting to wake up. Orange-bellied parrots pecked and scratched about for breakfast on the nature strips by the side of the road and houses winked when a curtain was pulled back. It was warming up everywhere. It was like every other day, thought Joey, but different. Something was missing from the picture. The sky was still there, still blue; the gum trees were still shedding their bark; gravity was still keeping the wheels on the road; but nothing was as it should be.

Joey saw Marti everywhere. He was running down the main drag. He was jumping the gate to the plaza pathway. He was walking to school, running to school, roller-skating, cycling. He was wading through the stream, picking up coins, getting his sleeves wet, getting shouted at. He was kicking a ball around the footy oval with Jono, on his own, with a group of boys. He was everywhere. But he was nowhere, really. He wasn't with his father anymore.

Joey's chest felt empty. He wanted to fill the space quickly by smoking a cigarette, but he was all out. He had gone all night without a smoke. In all the driving and frantic searching he had forgotten he had the demon of all tobacco addictions. He pulled into a servo to buy some cigarettes and put some petrol in the car. The tank was just about empty and took a long time to fill up. When the cap clicked he took out the nozzle and went to pay the attendant.

"Howya," said Joey, and handed over a twenty dollar bill. He scanned the boxes of cigarettes behind the counter: no Majors. There never was. They were *the* Irish cigarettes and could only be got from the shipping blokes who sold them on to the men from the transport section. The Majors were Joey's one concession to his past life, his one reminder of Ireland he couldn't cut out. "Oh, and I'll take a packet of smokes as well . . . the blue ones will do, I suppose."

"No worries," said the attendant.

Joey took his cigarettes from the counter and thanked the youngster, then a thought came to him. "Were you working here last night, son?"

"Sure was. Don't you remember?"

"*What*?"

"You were in . . . at about three, looking for a boy and a woman."

"Ah, sorry."

"Not a problem. You didn't find them, then?"

Joey shook his head. He felt his chances had slipped below even desperation level.

The rest of the journey home passed in a haze. He tried to smoke hard and fill the void in him, but it didn't work. Macca had said to be strong. Life goes on, he said. But did it really? Marti was his life. What did he have without the boy? Shauna had taken him, that said what she thought of their marriage, surely. But the boy was all that was left, the one good, true thing in his life. He knew when he looked

51

at Marti nothing else in the world mattered. Marti was the world. He couldn't imagine it without him.

Joey turned into his street and immediately felt his pulse quicken. Jaysus, it was him. It was Marti. Holy Mother of God, he was back. Joey planted his foot and the car lurched forward. The boy was sitting right outside the house.

The car screeched to a halt and Joey leapt into the street. "Marti," he shouted.

The boy looked up. "No," he said. It was Marti's friend, Jono. "I forgot he was gone."

"Jaysus lad, you near ended me there," said Joey.

"Sorry, Mr Driscol," said Jono. "I came to get him for school. I thought it might have been a dream, but he's really gone, isn't he?"

"Yes, Jono, he's gone all right." Joey put his foot on the little wall in front and leaned over, expelling the air from his lungs like he had been winded by a jolt to the chest. When he gathered his strength he watched Jono walking to school by himself, his little head down, looking sad like the night before, and then something hit him. "Hold on, Jono, hold on there."

The boy stopped in the street, stood still. "What is it?"

"What do you mean a dream? How did you know he was gone? Who told you?"

"Marti."

"What . . . when?"

"Before he left, he told me."

"What?" Joey bowed down and looked into Jono's young face. He was so like Marti, weren't they all alike at that age, he thought. They all had the same bag of tricks and this one knew something for sure. "Jono, now you must concentrate and tell me everything."

The boy scrunched up his nose. "He said he was going on a train and a boat, or was it a plane?"

"Oh God, where? Did he say where, son?"

"No."

"He didn't tell you?"

"No."

"Shit," said Joey. He stamped his foot in the red earth and cursed the heavens.

"But I know where he's going. His mam told my mam. I heard her say yesterday."

Joey grabbed Jono's shoulders and looked deep into his eyes. "Where?"

"I don't think I'm supposed to say . . . she was mad at me for even knowing about the train already."

"Look, Jono, this is very, very important. You must tell me where they went. You won't get into trouble for telling, I promise you that."

"She said they were going to Ireland."

Joey raised his hand to his mouth and spoke through his fingers, "Never . . . I'd never have believed it."

The boy looked confused. Joey patted him on the head and said, "Thank you, Jono. You're a grand lad, a real grand lad."

"Can I go now?"

"Jaysus, yes, sure ye can go, son. Off ye go to school, and thanks, thanks a million. You're a real little lifesaver, so ye are."

Jono smiled for a second and then turned to go to school. Joey watched him walk for a while, saw his little head sink into his shoulders again, and he felt his hurt. Something awful had happened – people were hurting all over the place. He couldn't bear to think how Marti must be feeling, on his way to Ireland.

Joey went inside the house and sat in silence. What had happened here? Ireland, it was the last place she would take him surely. Wasn't she through with the place ten years since? Wasn't Ireland nothing but bad memories and broken hopes? Wasn't Ireland where her family was, and his, Christ, his that he hadn't heard hide nor hair of for the best part of ten years. Wasn't it the last place *he* would go for that reason alone. Holy Mother of God – it was the voice again – maybe that was *her* plan. Sure, wasn't Ireland the one place Shauna knew he would never go.

There was a rap on the door, and then Macca shouted, "G'day . . . Bluey, mate, you home?"

Joey was up, rummaging in the bottom of his wardrobe, tipping out boxes and shoes and clothes, throwing them behind him in frantic panic.

"What's the game, mate?" said Macca.

"She's taken him to Ireland, the one place she knows I cannot go. The bitch, the bad bitch."

"Joey, she's ill, mate. She's not thinking, you said that yourself."

"Exactly, Macca. How can she look after my boy? Like I say, she cannot mind herself. Ah balls, I cannot find it."

"What are you looking for?"

"Bank book, she must've taken it. It was for Marti's education, the college like."

"*Fair Dinkum.*"

"If it wasn't bad enough taking the boy and depriving him of a father now she's depriving him of an education and a decent life too. Ah, it's too screwed for words, Macca."

Joey slumped back on the floor and held his head in his hands. His thoughts wandered off again. One second they were on Marti, the next on his own desperate situation. This couldn't happen, not twice. His own father had put a stop to any thoughts Joey might have had of college, sending him out to Gleesons Bakery at sixteen. It couldn't happen to Marti.

Joey remembered his early days at Gleesons, going home with the burns from the ovens all over his arms, the rows of men flooding into the place, then the lot of them, fluthered drunk every Friday when the wage packet came. He didn't fit. He knew he hated the place, saw his life unfolding before him. Only the fella the men called Old Nelson because of his one eye sensed his anxiety.

"Always with the books, Driscol," he would say. "Have ye ever thought of the college?"

Old Nelson opened up a new world to Joey. He would bring in books and tell him what he should be reading. Joey felt special because hardly anybody spoke to Old Nelson, who would always sit with the books himself, and here he was making a friend of him. It was Old Nelson told him to get the night classes started and it was Old Nelson who pointed him on the road to Trinity College.

It was Shauna's dream as much as his. The education was to be their way out. With the right education there could be a proper job with proper wages and a home for them some day filled up with books galore. There would be nothing but struggles ahead without the education, begging and borrowing from Joey's family, sharing rooms with his brothers and sisters; forever and a day under Emmet Driscol's roof. Hadn't they even made the one sacrifice that they would never forget, and never be free of, for the education. It was Shauna herself who had said it. It was her notion.

"What would ye be then if you gave it up?" she had said. "What would ye think of me then?"

They did what had to be done and Joey prayed to God for forgiveness, begged absolution for the grand sin they had committed, but nothing would cleanse the guilt. All Kilmora knew what they had done and soon enough their dreams for Joey's education were ended. The Bishop no less had called a halt to their grand plan. "It would only give ye notions," he had told Joey. "Sure, the world has a place for the working man and ye must know yeer place." That was the end of it, as with everything else. The Bishop's word stood unchallenged.

The same couldn't happen to Marti. His life had to be different. Joey knew it, he was sure Shauna knew it too, and when he closed his eyes he could almost taste the rancour inside him.

"Bluey, mate, keep calm. You've gotta be strong at times like this. At least you know where they are now."

"So?"

"So . . . so you can go to Ireland, get the little tacker back."

"Macca, there's no way I can do that."

"Why not?"

"I just can't. I'm finished with Ireland. She knows that. That's why she's gone there. Marti knows it too. Jaysus, he must be terrible worried, desperate he'll be at the thought of going there. He'll know I'd never go."

"Bluey, mate, you have to prove them wrong."

"I can't. There's things you know nothing about, Macca, things we came over here to get away from, to escape from. I could never do it, I just couldn't . . . sure, I'd be disgraced entirely if I even tried."

"*Bluey, Bluey, mate.*" Macca placed a hand on Joey's arm. "If you want to see your son again, you're going to have to go back there." He leaned into Joey's face, shook him at the shoulder. "There's nothing else you can do. You have to go, for Marti's sake."

8

Ireland was not like anywhere Marti had ever seen. It had started off with the rain coming down in little specks and then there was the sun, but the sky was still a grey colour and looked very low and close to people's heads. He remembered the sky in Australia always looked very blue and very far away and not at all like it did in Ireland. Everyone walked very fast around the streets and Marti had to stay close to Mam's back or be knocked down. Sometimes there were buildings with colours painted on them and sometimes there were buildings that were only grey and he wondered why they didn't have the colours. When there was rain coming down Marti wanted to go into one of the buildings with the colours, but Mam said if they stopped every time there was a bit of rain they'd be lucky to get a yard.

He wondered was Mam happy to be in Ireland, but he didn't think she looked very happy the way she kept lifting the big bag from her shoulder, staring at people and saying, "Ignorant bogtrotters, the lot of them."

It had been a long flight from Australia and not as much fun as Marti thought it would be at all. It had been difficult to sleep on the hard seats that were very straight and he was always being told off for fidgeting. Mam had dragged him straight from the airport into the rain and when they arrived at the train station Marti thought they were both very wet but Mam said it was only damp. There was steam coming off their clothes and going into the air and he wondered if this was what Mam said was only damp. Then a man with a pointy black umbrella came and shook all the rain off and said, "Is it a drowned rat ye have there, missus?"

Mam smiled and said, "Ignorant bogtrotter," but nobody heard her when she said it like a whisper.

The train was long and empty and Marti and Mam had to queue behind a man in a vest with a whistle and wait for him to blow the whistle and let them go on. When the queue moved everybody made the chatter noise and went to have their tickets ready. A man was singing really loudly, and when Marti turned round to look at him he saw the man was leaning on a wall and had a big messy beard and messy grey hair. He was singing really loudly, but Marti couldn't understand the words and wondered why anyone would be singing really loudly waiting to go on the train.

"Why's he singing, Mam?" said Marti.

"That's Arthur Guinness singing, son," said Mam. The man behind them in the queue laughed and said, "Tis. Tis."

"Do you know him, Mam?"

"Jaysus," said the man in the queue, "that's a card ye have there, missus."

Mam smiled and shook her head and said, "No."

When the train left the station, the outside looked very different to when Marti was on the train in Australia. The ground was green instead of red and the sky was grey instead of blue and it made him think of Dad back at home with the red ground and the blue sky. He missed Dad and Australia and driving about in the ute and even going to school with Jono. Ireland seemed a very strange place compared to Australia, which was always warm and bright and felt like home. Marti felt the sadness growing inside him when he thought about the home he had left and he wondered what was going to happen to him and Mam in Ireland with no Dad there to look out for them.

"Mam," said Marti.

"Yes, son."

"Do you think Dad will be sad all by himself in Australia?"

Mam said nothing, only looked out the window, and Marti saw she had the cross face. Marti didn't want to be asked if it was the hot arse he was after again so he stayed quiet, but he didn't stop thinking about Dad. He was very sad when he thought about Dad and he wished he could see him again. He wished Dad was with him, but wouldn't that only make Dad more sad because he didn't like Ireland, he liked Australia, which was God's country. Marti decided he wouldn't like Ireland either because he wanted to like what Dad liked and because he thought that would make Dad happy. More than anything in the world Marti wanted to make Dad and Mam happy, but he couldn't see how anybody could be happy so far away from the place they called home.

When the train stopped Mam said this was the country now and they could be thankful they were well away from the city that was called the Smoke, for the fresh air was everywhere in the country just waiting for you to take a big gulp for yourself. Marti took a big gulp of the fresh air that was everywhere and then Mam said, "Would ye ever stop acting the maggot."

The town they were headed for was called Kilmora, said Mam, but it wasn't a proper town. It was just a village, really. Marti didn't know what she meant until she said it was like a town, only smaller, and in the country. He wondered if it was far away and Mam said no, because the distances between places were less in Ireland than in Australia, and weren't Australians great for suffering the old tyranny of distance malarkey and there would be none of that here.

Mam said Aunt Catrin and Uncle Ardal mightn't be home, but if they were then surely there would be a bed for the night and maybe even longer.

Aunt Catrin and Uncle Ardal's house was very small and grey and made of stones all piled up on top of each other right to the roof. There was a little wooden shed that made a *coo-coo* noise and when Marti asked what was that, Mam said it was Uncle Ardal's pigeons. There were rabbit traps hanging on the shed that Mam said were to keep the cats away from the pigeons, and Marti felt sorry for any cat that might get caught in one of the traps.

When Mam knocked on the door there was the sound of footsteps and then the door was opened and a woman in a long grey coat with a scarf on her head appeared and said, "Saints preserve us, tis yourself."

Aunt Catrin was older than Mam and had the big staring eyes when she looked at them with the surprise. When she sat down she didn't sit back on the chair, which had a little white patch for your head to rest on. Aunt Catrin had a very straight back when she sat down and when she took off her scarf she touched her mouth with it. "I don't know what to say. Would you ever look at yourself, sitting there in my own home," she said. "And this'll be the boy, is it?"

"Tis, Catrin. This is Marti. Say hello to your Aunt Catrin."

"Hello," he said.

"Would you listen to him, sure he's an Aussie." Aunt Catrin sounded as though she didn't like him, thought Marti, and he wondered if she hated only him or all children and was that why she hadn't any herself. "And the father, where's he?" said Aunt Catrin.

"Will I wet some tea, Catrin?" said Mam.

"Tea, yes, tea. It will help me gather my thoughts, sure won't the whole town be in shock at the sight of ye."

When she had her tea Aunt Catrin said it was hardly cause for a sing-song but there was a caravan sitting empty outside. It was just a bit of tin and paint, she said, but then beggars couldn't be choosers, especially the type that turn up on yeer doorstep unannounced after a lengthy absence.

When it was bedtime Aunt Catrin said if yees were cold then there were some good thick coats just hanging there doing no good to no one. There was a heater that ran off the gas but wouldn't you pay through the nose for it because wasn't the price of gas a crime. Mam said the coats would be fine and it was good enough of Aunt Catrin to give up the caravan.

"Quite," said Aunt Catrin. "I'll get them coats . . . and will yees take a hot bottle?"

"That would be grand," said Mam.

Marti had never had a hot bottle before and he wondered what to do with it when Aunt Catrin gave him the old lemonade bottle in a brown sock. There was boiling water in the bottle and the sock was tied at the bottom. At the top of the bottle the cap poked out through a hole. Mam got a bottle too but her sock was grey and there was no hole. The bottle was lovely and warm, thought Marti, but he didn't like the sock and wondered whose it had been.

"Marti, what are you doing?" said Mam.

"I'm smelling the sock."

"Marti, will you stop making a show of me. Now say thank you to Aunt Catrin."

"Thank you for the sock, Aunt Catrin," said Marti. "It doesn't smell."

Aunt Catrin shook her head and said she knew the sock didn't smell, for sure hadn't she washed it herself, and then she said, "Don't be messing with the bottle because there's hot water in there and it could do you an injury to get it on your skin." She walked away very fast, and Marti thought Mam would say it was a hot arse he had earned, but there was only a sigh from her.

In the caravan Mam said it was only proper knackers that lived the like, there was no respect in it at all, she said, and then the bubbling with the tears was started and Marti was called for a hug.

When they settled down to sleep there was no noise beyond the caravan and Marti wondered why there was no noise when in Australia there was always the mozzies and the crickets and sometimes even the maggies to be heard, moving about on the roof, looking for spiders. Marti found it easy to fall asleep when there was no noise but he wasn't sleeping a very long time when Mam woke him.

"Did you hear that?" she said. Marti had heard nothing, but Mam said there was definitely a noise. "There, did you hear it?" she said. There was a little noise like footsteps and Marti thought he heard a laugh or maybe a whisper and Mam said, "Oh God, it'll be the knackers. They come for the washing off the lines."

Marti knew the knackers were the tinkers or gypsies or sometimes the itinerants. Mam said you were never to go near the knackers because they carry all manner of diseases, and fleas especially. He wondered, if the knackers were nearby, would he get diseases and fleas and should he maybe hide under the coats. Mam said she could hear them coming and Marti was very frightened and could hear his heart beating when he hid under the coats. He wanted to run out of the caravan and into the house, but Mam said to be quiet and don't move a muscle. He was too scared to even breathe and he heard the footsteps that might be the knackers right outside. Somebody was leaning on the caravan and making it move, and Marti wondered if they were maybe going to take the caravan away with them inside it. His heart started to beat even faster and then the door swung open and Mam sat up in the bed and screamed out, all in a loud panic, "What do ye want?"

A strange woman came in the caravan and she started the screaming too when she saw Mam in the bed. When the screaming noise was made, a light went on in the house and Marti saw the strange woman was wearing a long coat with no clothes on underneath, only big white panties. He thought she must be very cold standing there with the coat all flapping open and her hands up on her head with the shock and then a man came in behind her.

"Janey Mackers, it's yourself, Shauna," he said.

"Jaysus, Ardal," said Mam, and then the strange woman stopped the screaming and became mad angry.

"Who the feck is this?" she said.

"Ahh, now," said the man, who Marti thought must be Uncle Ardal.

"Ah, now . . ." said the strange woman, and then she started to hit Uncle Ardal on the head. Uncle Ardal tried to grab her and stop the hitting but his great big black pants with buttons on all the way up over his big round belly fell right down onto his boots. The woman was very mad, thought Marti, and she was wailing and hitting out at Uncle Ardal and trying to scratch him with her nails, and when she scratched him on the face, he called her a mighty hoor's melt and gave her a slap. She fell on the floor with the slap and Uncle Ardal bent over and pulled up his pants.

Aunt Catrin was behind him when he bent over and when he fastened his buttons Aunt Catrin spoke at him in a very slow voice. "When your slut's put her diddies away the pair of ye can go."

Uncle Ardal said nothing, and when he walked away the strange woman tried to stand up but fell over, then she tried again and got up and followed after him.

Aunt Catrin had a look Marti had never seen on anyone before. Her lips were held together like a tight little knot, then she closed the caravan door and Marti heard her go back inside the house.

"Mam, will anyone else come in tonight?" said Marti.

"No, Marti, there'll be no one else."

"But how do you know, Mam?"

"Marti, I know. Did you see your Aunt Catrin? She could stop a clock with that look. There'll be no one coming within a mile of this caravan for a long time. Now get to sleep."

Marti wondered how Aunt Catrin could stop a clock with a look and then he thought it was just one of the things grown-ups said that wasn't really true.

"Mam, I'm cold. My bottle's gone cold," he said.

"I said get to sleep."

"But, I'm cold . . ."

Mam sat up in bed, her voice was raised. "Marti Driscol, cold is the very least of our worries. I'd say your Aunt Catrin will scrap this caravan tomorrow and we will both be a damn sight colder then, I can assure ye of that. Now get to sleep, whilst we're lucky enough to have any manner of roof over our heads."

9

Joey knew all the blokes at the transport section had been too good to him, but wasn't this going farther than far enough. Macca had told Joey that he was no use to anyone the state he was in. People were too used to seeing him grinning like a pork chop, the stories flowing out of him, but he was a changed man. He knew it himself, sure hadn't he a face on him as long as today and tomorra since Marti was taken. But what these men were after doing was a heart gladdener.

Macca and the men from the transport section had the house tightly roped. When the winch was in place Macca gave the say-so and it was raised from its stumps. Joey heard the loud crack of it lifting up and felt the noise like a jab at him. He watched it raised higher, then he watched it lowered on the trailer and every sag and every creak was a blow to him.

Marti had loved the house. Joey had loved it too. It had been their home, but now that was all over. Marti was gone and the house was going too. When Macca nodded, the men started to throw more ropes over. They slid off the roof and were quickly snatched and tightened under the trailer, front and back. Joey thought his home looked like some manner of giant beast, snared and about to be slaughtered. He could hardly watch.

"Wait. Wait there," he said.

He ran to the trailer and the men stopped to watch him climb onto the white rails and into the house through a window. Inside all was roped and tied, everything from the beds and chairs to the television and the fridge closed tight, the morning's milk still in it. It was Macca's idea to auction it all together in one lot. Joey walked into Marti's room and took down the Superman picture. It had hung there since the day they picked out the house. There was no way he could leave it.

On the way out he had an urge to take one last look at the room he had shared with Shauna, to say goodbye to that life forever. It was as it always had been, the bed unmade, the curtains closed to keep out the light. He had crept in a million times to see if Shauna would raise herself, come out of her cocoon, but she never had. The scene set him back. Wasn't it as it always had been, beyond change, like a trap that had caught the pair of them. He lashed out, kicked the bed, again and again, then there was a dull thud and when he looked down he saw a little book had landed open on the floor.

Joey picked it up. It was a little leather-bound diary, thick pages broken down into days and months. Shauna's writing filled the pages, little blocks of words squeezed into tight paragraphs, a day apart. What was all this? She had never kept a diary, Joey knew it was the last thing she would do – sure she wasn't able for it, for a start. He turned to the first page. "Hell no. I cannot read her diary," he said, and closed it quickly. It would be snooping. He put it back on the bed then headed out the door. He got as far as the hall when he realised his wife's diary might hold some clues for him, might be some use in finding Marti. He ran back, snatched the book off the bed, and tucked it inside his shirt.

When Joey climbed back out the window and onto the white rails, the men from the transport section were still watching him; he knew they were wondering what it was he was after rescuing from the house.

"Bluey, mate, what's the go?" said Macca.

"I had to get this, the boy loves it." He held up the Superman picture. "The rest can go. Not this, though. Marti will have it back one day."

"Are you done now, mate?" said Macca.

Joey nodded and his friend waved the driver on.

"There she goes," said Joey. "No going back now."

"Not now, mate."

"Tell me, Macca, once it's sold, what do I bring Marti back to?"

"To you, mate. You bring him back to you."

"It's not going to be easy."

"You'll be right, wait and see."

Joey watched the house move slowly down the road. It was his life being uprooted and taken from him. None of it made any sense, 'specially not what he would have to do now, what he would have to go back to. It would be a grand homecoming, would it not, he thought. Could he really face it? Could he feel those eyes on him again? He remembered when he was Marti's age and his own father was the talk of the village and the entire country. Emmet Driscol had played in the All-Ireland Hurling Final, on the winning side. He was a hero.

Nobody had even heard of Kilmora before Emmet Driscol raised a hurley. If anyone knew about the worth of a man, it was Joey's father. The day the mighty Emmet Driscol had returned to the village with the medal there was traffic stopped in the street. Joey stood watching the car with his father inside being surrounded by people. They swarmed to him, clapping and shouting, banging on the roof of the car and screaming for a look at the medal, a word from the man himself.

How could he compete with that? How could he have ever? His own father had been a mighty hard act to follow, impossible in Kilmora, sure. Joey remembered his own efforts on the hurling field as a boy. He was a worthless coward, his father had said so. He had cost his team the game. Joey didn't care about the game. He hated hurling, he hated being watched by his father and he hated hearing people laughing and saying there goes the next Emmet Driscol. They would laugh long and hard after this day, he remembered. His father had said he would never forgive him for the shame of his actions.

It had all happened like a dream, the ball floating down from the heavens, landing at Joey's feet. There was no one between him and the goalie. It was a clear run. He had only to cross the field, then hit the ball. There were cheers and roars when he took off with it, the rest of the players behind him could only watch. He ran for goal and when he ran he looked up and saw all that stood between him and mythic success was the scrawny frame of the goalie, Callum Madigan . . . and then he froze.

Something had stopped him. He raised the hurley above his shoulder but hesitation held it there. He could hear his father shouting for the whack of the stick to follow, but he couldn't move. He looked at the ball, black and muddied below, but no matter how hard he stared Joey couldn't summon the force to move it, and then the moment passed. The scrawny Callum Madigan appeared before him, running, a raised hurley already making its way to the ball, which he cleared back into the field of play.

Joey was never to play hurling again. He was too much of a worthless coward, too yellow to face a runt of a boy like little Callum Madigan, a streak of a lad without the strength even to hold up his own socks.

"My, he got the better of ye," said his father. "It's ashamed to show your face in Kilmora ye should be after this."

Joey still recalled the scorn in his father's voice then, and when he left for a new life in Australia it was still there in the last words he uttered before his son went to the other side of the world. Emmet scoffed and reminded him of the day he had faced the scrawny Callum Madigan on the hurling field. "He is in London now, a big job in the government so he has, the English working for him. And here's ye, running away to nothing. Aren't ye worthless yet."

Joey felt a wince. He sensed the eyes on him already, but when he turned his head he saw it was only Jono watching him. The boy was crouched over; his face was in his hands again. Joey knew he was upset at the sight of his best friend's home being roped and dragged away.

"Howya, Jono," he said.

"Hello, Mr Driscol."

"That's the house off then."

"I guess." It was like something a kid in a movie would say, thought Joey.

"We'll both miss it, I think."

Jono looked up, but said nothing. Joey thought the boy was checking his expression for honesty or sarcasm, but he seemed to have passed the test.

"Jono, I know you're missing Marti," he said. "Sure, we all are, but it does ye no good to be sad. You have to brighten up, have a play. There's lots of boys your age about here."

Jono looked up again. Joey recognised it was the same expression on him. "I have something for you. Do you like the comics?" he said.

"The super-hero comics?" said Jono.

"Yes."

"*Superman*?"

"Eh, no, Silver Surfer, I think." Joey handed him the comic and the biggest choco bar he had found in the shops. "Here ye go. Let's see a wee smile, eh?"

Jono took the comic and the choco bar and gave Joey a smile. It was the weakest smile he thought he'd ever seen in his life. The trailer was well down the road now and could hardly be heard anymore, but they watched together until it had disappeared into the distance. Joey wondered where the house would end up next, who would live there and if they would be sadder than him when they had to pack it off. He knew there had been precious few good memories in the house of late. He could only think of the fights with Shauna and the times he got back to find the curtains closed and the air thick with the Black Dog's presence. He ached inside. Was this how she felt? Was this what the Black Dog felt like? Was this what she wanted: to make him hurt too?

"Bluey, mate. C'mon, the blokes have got a bit of a farewell planned for you down at The Bushman," said Macca.

"A bit of a do, eh?"

"It's not much."

"It sounds grand, Macca. Just grand."

The Bushman pub was packed with men from the transport section and men from the mines. There were even some of the girls from the wages office and every worker's wife had brought in a tray full of pies or little sausages or sandwiches or cakes. Joey felt overwhelmed. He felt he deserved none of it, but wasn't that just the mood of him, he thought. He knew he couldn't feel as bad as Shauna – if he could work that out for himself – but realising it was no victory when she was the one with Marti.

"I was sorry to hear about, you know," said a woman with a floppy lilac bow in her hair. She was one of the miners' wives.

"Thank you," said Joey. Jaysus, he thought, wasn't everyone sorry. He didn't want sympathy. He'd lavished enough of that on himself already.

"It's so, so sad, isn't it?" she said.

"Tis," said Joey. She'd had a good drink, he thought, didn't know what she was saying.

"You must miss him . . . your boy."

"I do," he said. For Chrissakes, woman, would you leave me be, he thought. She was talking like Marti was dead. He wanted to scream at her, he's not dead, he's not dead, this is temporary. A temporary affair and no more. Sure, wouldn't he have the boy back in no time at all, wasn't that the plan anyway.

"I don't know what I'd do if one of my children was snatched like that, but still, he's with the mother, that's not so bad, is it?" She poured out a large glass of cold beer for herself. Beer, now there was a thing not touched in a while, he thought. Could he possibly handle this pain in the arse and all the sympathy with a beer in him?

"Will you pour a glass for myself?" he said.

The woman tried to pour another glass of beer and the liquid frothed up and over the sides. "Oops," she said with a giggle, and then her floppy lilac bow slipped over her eyes.

Joey smiled and tried not to laugh. "Here, let me."

The first beer he took went down smooth and fast and he remembered how much he liked the taste. The second beer he poured went down even faster and then he remembered the effect was the thing he really enjoyed. Beer followed beer and Joey soon found he was forgetting about Marti and Shauna and the house vanishing off into the distance forever. It had been a long time between drinks, he thought, but wouldn't he make up the time now. He could hardly remember a drink ever tasting better and wasn't it a mighty hit he was getting. It never worked like that in the past.

"Bluey, what are you doing?" said Macca.

"I'm enjoying the wonderful hospitality of my good Aussie mates," said Joey, "and Jaysus, is it not grand. Are these your wife's pies? They're grand pies, Macca, just grand."

"Good on you, Bluey, you deserve a few beers. Just don't do yourself any harm, mate. You know we all want to look out for you."

"That I do, that I do, and sure my days of soaking it up are long by. I might fall back occasionally but – *but* – I am a far cry from the soak I once was." Joey held onto Macca's shoulder for support. "They knew me as a rare soak in the old country, Macca."

"Did they, mate?"

"That they did. Now wouldn't that be a thing, if I were to roll back there soaked the gills through. Christ, the tongues in Kilmora would have something to wag about then, would they not?"

"Bluey, have you somewhere to go when you get there?"

"No."

"Nowhere? What about family?"

"No words have passed between us these last ten years now."

"Jeez, sounds like you've some fences to mend there, Bluey."

"Not a chance. Hell would have to freeze over first!"

Macca shifted Joey's arm to his other shoulder. "Look, Bluey, mate. The blokes had a bit of a whip-round. We've . . . well, here it is." He handed over a little package. It was wrapped in tissue paper with a ribbon. The tag read: *Good Luck, Bluey*. Joey opened it up. Inside was a boomerang and a plane ticket. He read the flight details that told him he was leaving the next day, for Ireland.

"You gotta take the boomerang with you, mate, to make sure you come back," said Macca.

"I don't know what to say. This is too much."

"Thanks would be a start."

"Oh Jaysus, thanks, Macca." Joey held up the boomerang for everyone to see. "Thanks, fellas. I don't know how to thank you all."

"Try getting a bloody shout in," said Pando the Greek, and the room laughed and cheered with Joey.

Cold beer was shifted about in big pitchers and the bar and table-tops started to fill with glasses, empty and full. People moved in lurches and bounds to greet newcomers, fresh from the street and with no idea a farewell party was in full swing. There was dancing and singing and jokes and stories told, even some by Joey. Nobody seemed to give a thought to the time or how much the drink was flowing and soon even the people fresh from the street were dancing and singing.

"Tis a grand hooley, Macca," said Joey.

"We know how to send off a mate, Bluey. Bloody oath, we do."

Joey slapped Macca on the back and said thanks again but he could tell Macca's attention was drawn off to the bar. An Aboriginal family had come in, a tall black fella and a woman carrying pots and three young children. They were all barefoot. The family stood silently, their mouths closed. They were covered in dust and thirsty. They looked to all like they had just walked in from the bush.

"They want their pots filled, Macca," said Joey.

"I know, I know." Macca put down his beer and walked over to the family. The barman told them he wouldn't fill the pots and there was a crowd of men poking and prodding at the black fella, telling him to go back out the door he came in.

"Fair go, blokes," said Macca. "Let him have his water. It's dry as dust out there."

Joey didn't recognise any of the men in the crowd. They weren't from the transport section for sure. They were all bush pigs. He didn't like the way they were poking at the black fella and he didn't like the way they were looking at Macca. The children were frightened. Wasn't their father only trying to do his best for them. It was too much for Joey to bear. He drained his glass and strode to the scene at the bar with his shoulders back.

"Here, mate, give me your pot." He took the black fella's pot and then he jumped over the bar to fill it from the tap. "See, simple as that," he said. "Isn't there more than enough to go around. Now another pot I think."

The black fella smiled, showing a row of great white teeth. He took the pot full of water from Joey and then he handed over another one.

"That's the way, Bluey," said Macca.

"The way it is," said Joey, and he smiled at the crowd of men but there were no smiles back. "There, another one full for ye, mate," said Joey when the second pot was passed over, and then one of the bush pigs grabbed it and tipped the water over Joey's head.

"You feckir," shouted Joey. He went to jump back over the bar but the pot was already being swung at him and crashed across his ear. There was a loud crack came from the side of his head where the pot hit and then he fell back and landed behind the bar in a loud crash of breaking glass.

10

Aunt Catrin said there was room enough for Mam and Marti in the house now the lousy feck was gone and wouldn't be back. Mam said she was terrible sorry for the way things had turned out, but Marti wasn't sorry because he was glad to be out the caravan, which was very cold entirely.

It was lovely and warm inside the house with the big fire going and there was bread for toasting on the fire if you couldn't take it a bit hard, or there was porridge instead, said Aunt Catrin. Mam said she would take the porridge because there had been no porridge in Australia, only oatmeal, which wasn't the same thing at all, and Marti said he would have the bread for toasting.

"I don't want you going overboard with the butter," whispered Mam when Aunt Catrin went to get their breakfast. "Sure, doesn't she put it on with a razor and take it off with a feather . . . and she can have a savage tongue in her when she thinks she's seeing waste at her table, so you clear your plate too."

Marti wanted to know why Aunt Catrin would use a feather in the butter and Mam got really mad and said, "Don't you be making a holy show of me. You'll mind yourself, do you hear?"

Marti nodded and then Aunt Catrin called out to him from the kitchen. She said she couldn't get over the accent on him but she would bet a pound to a pail of shale he'd be talking like a regular once they got him down to the school.

"What school?" said Marti. He didn't care about the feather in the butter anymore when Aunt Catrin said about the school.

"The school, Saint Joseph's. You didn't think your mam was going to keep you home every day, did you? There'll be the school for you soon enough. Where would you be without the schooling? You need to learn about the maths and the life of Our Lord. Ah sure the brothers will do a grand job."

Marti started to get the lump in the throat when Aunt Catrin talked about the school because he could only think about his school in Australia and Jono, who was his best friend. He had tried not to think about Australia and Jono and Dad because Mam had said the second he stopped the thinking about them then the lump in the throat would go away. It was very hard not to think about them, especially Dad, who was forever coming into his head. Marti was always seeing pictures of Dad, telling him the funny stories and making the green flower thing dance, just for him.

"Marti, would you ever make yourself useful," said Aunt Catrin, "and get that porridge out the drawer there for your mam?"

There was a dresser with four big drawers and the top drawer was just a little bit shorter than Marti. "Aunt Catrin, who's the brothers?" he said. The drawer was very stiff to open and Marti pulled and tugged very hard and even tried to waggle the drawer about, but it wouldn't open.

"The brothers are the brothers. Here, lookit," said Aunt Catrin, and put her hands under the drawer. There was a thick layer of hard, grey porridge in the drawer that was filled all the way up to the top. Aunt Catrin put in a knife and cut out a slice. "There now, wasn't that just a perfect slice of porridge there? I think I'll have a slice m'self. Will ye have a slice?"

"No thanks," said Marti, and started shaking his head. "Who's the brothers, Aunt Catrin?"

"The brothers teach at the school – don't ye like porridge?"

"Do you cook it in a drawer?"

"Ah Jaypers, no ye don't cook it in there. That's where you put it to set. Sure a drawer is the best place for a slab of porridge. Keeps it lovely and cool, and wasn't it there fine and handy for you in the morning."

73

"I don't think I'd like it."

"Suit yourself," she said, and pushed the drawer closed with the front of her legs and wiped the handles with her apron. "It's the brothers are needed to educate the likes of ye, Marti Driscol, and you would have a puck in the gob for frowning at a good slice of porridge in front of them brothers, sure ye would."

"They could try, Catrin," said Mam. She had brought in some letters from the postman and sat them on the table.

"Are them bills?" said Aunt Catrin. "If them's bills they can go to the lousy feck."

"Catrin, is the brothers still running the boys' school?" said Mam.

"They are so."

"Ah Jaysus."

"What's the matter with the brothers there, Shauna? Sure the brothers will do a grand job of educating the young fella."

"They'll do a grand job of filling his head full of bigotry and nonsense, you mean."

Aunt Catrin widened her mouth like the shape of an egg and told Mam to take that back, but Mam said she never would and then Aunt Catrin touched her head and made the signs that were the cross.

"Lord forgive ye, Shauna Driscol," said Aunt Catrin. "Them brothers are a fine and blessed manner of men."

"Bollix," said Mam.

"Oh Jaypers, Shauna, stop the cursing. You'll have us knee deep in the filth of Hell." Marti thought this was a very strange thing to say, but Mam said don't be worrying your head about the likes, because no son of hers was being raised under the Catholic Faith which had done enough damage to her family already.

"Shauna Driscol, I don't believe what I'm hearing. How can ye deprive the boy his religion?" said Aunt Catrin.

"The boy has no religion. He's an agnostic, like his mam."

"Oh, Lord save us all," said Aunt Catrin, and her eyes rolled up in her head towards the ceiling.

Mam got all fidgety after the talk about school and the Catholic Faith and she pushed away her porridge without even taking a taste of it. Marti knew the porridge would be wasted and he wondered

74

would Aunt Catrin be angry because hadn't Mam said waste put the savage tongue in her, but nobody seemed to care.

"Right," said Mam, and the table was shaken when she stood up quickly, "we will settle this school business today. Come with me, Marti."

"Where . . . where are we going?"

"The brothers. We have to see the brothers."

Saint Joseph's All Boys Catholic School was a very big building, all painted white, with a big white cross on the front. The man who was in charge was Brother Michael, never Father Michael, because father was what you said to a priest and wasn't his lot different entirely, said Brother Michael. There were lots of boys running around the school and they would all stop running when they saw Brother Michael and say, "Good morning, Brother," but the brother would only frown.

Brother Michael was very old and had to sit down a lot because the walking was a terrible, terrible strain on the old legs. Mam said there was no need to be giving them the grand tour because wouldn't the boy find his way around fine, and if he gets lost then he's a good Irish tongue in his head, which it would be no harm to use. Brother Michael said he would be happy enough showing Brother Aloysius's classroom, where Marti would be placed, and then they could go back through the main hall where the boys take rosary.

"Brother there is no need for that," said Mam.

"Ah, no, there's plenty of puff left in these old gills yet," said Brother Michael, and started the walking again. The corridors were very long and there was coloured glass on the windows with pictures of men and women and sometimes babies. Marti knew the pictures were from the Bible and the man on the cross was Jesus, but he didn't know the names of the others. There were lots of pictures of a lady in a blue hood with a baby, sometimes with a heart, and sometimes with rays of sunlight all around her. Marti wondered who the lady was and why there were so many pictures of her, but he didn't want to ask Brother Michael, because he was a teacher and might start talking for a long time about who the lady was.

"Now, Mrs Driscol," said Brother Michael, "this here is the main hall where we do the assembly every morning and the games – that's Brother Declan's boys now. Ah, and the rosary at the lunchtime like I say – sure aren't its uses multifarious."

Brother Michael smoked cigarettes all the while and blew the smoke off into the air and said wasn't he just a slave to the craving, so he was. Brother Michael said the cigarettes were a terrible, terrible bad habit but Our Good Lord surely turns a blind eye to the occasional vice, wasn't that so?

"Now, Marti, don't we have all manner of details to be collected for your enrolment," said Brother Michael, "but sure, I'll set ye up with a spectator's seat in there and ye can feast yeer eyes on the athletic largesse of Brother Declan's boys."

Brother Declan was very tall and had a wild red beard that was wet at the whiskers. He was a lot younger than Brother Michael and there were no black robes on him and there was no white collar and no cross like Brother Michael had. He wore a green tracksuit with very thin white stripes down the sides and he had a whistle round his neck. All the boys sat very quietly when Brother Declan blew the whistle and all the boys looked at him when he said, "I'll have your full attention for I will not be repeating m'self this day."

Some of the boys had bare feet and Marti wondered why they didn't have their gym shoes on like the other boys, and some of the boys had no shorts on, only their jocks and a vest, and Marti thought they looked very cold. Brother Declan had proper gym shoes like the tennis players wear, and when Marti looked at them Brother Declan smiled on the side of his face.

"Now, we have a spectator here from Brother Aloysius's class," he said. "Could be a spy no less, after our tactics maybe. Stand up, boy. I'm only having a cod with ye now, no need to look so serious. Sure it's a fine spy you'd make, is it not?"

"I don't know," said Marti.

"Janey Mackers, where's the accent from – it's never an Aussie we have here, is it?"

Marti didn't speak and Brother Declan said, "If it is, then it's the quietest Aussie I've come across. Name, boy?"

"Marti Driscol."

"Marti Driscol! Well, that sounds Irish enough. Are you back from the New World with a fortune? Was it a gold rush ye were at, Marti Driscol?"

"No, I've no fortune." The boys laughed when Marti spoke and one of them said, "He's like Skippy," and there was more laughing.

Brother Declan smiled on the side of his face for a little while until the laughing was too loud, and then he said, "Shut it. Well, Marti Driscol with the lilt of the antipodes, if you've no fortune I hope you've learnt to jump like a kangaroo, for we've precious few who can clear more than a toadstool among this rabble."

Brother Declan blew his whistle and all the boys were told to do headstands against the wall; if a boy's legs weren't straight enough he would shout, "Close your legs, ye hoor," and slap the boy to make him fall over. Marti thought Brother Declan looked mad angry with all the boys. Some were even slapped on the head and some were dragged by the collar, but when there was no collar to grab then an ear or the hair was grabbed instead. None of it looked like fun at all, and when Mam and Brother Michael appeared at the door of the hall Marti was very glad to see them.

"Marti, Marti," said Mam, "will you come over here?"

There were lots of boys running around outside the hall and when Marti got near to Mam and Brother Michael all the boys stopped running and said, "Good morning, Brother."

"I have what ye might call the Moses effect in these situations, Marti," said Brother Michael. "Ah, but sure I won't bother ye with Moses, for hasn't yeer mam explained all about your agnosticism." Marti wondered what agnosticism was because it sounded like a bad thing, maybe a disease.

"Thank you, Brother," said Mam. "I hope it's not a trouble at all for yourself and the brothers. Like I say, tis a personal belief I have."

"Ah now, Mrs Driscol, it's no bother at all, at all. Marti isn't the first boy the brothers have educated outside the sacred bosom of the Church and he will not be the last, but, I will be praying that God leads the boy to Divine Faith in his own time, his own time, Mrs Driscol."

Mam had the look she sometimes had when Marti was a bold boy after Brother Michael said he would be saying the prayers, then she looked down at him and the look was gone very quickly, and suddenly she looked very worried entirely.

"Now, Mrs Driscol ye can be off and leave the young fella here with me," said Brother Michael. "I'm sure he will be no trouble at all, at all. Isn't that so, Marti?"

11

Joey Driscol knew it. Things had gone from bad to worse. He had woken with a desperate throbbing in his head and a ringing noise like an electric drill in his left ear. Worse yet, he was in a hospital bed, the heavy white linen sheets strapped across his chest telling him he was going nowhere in a hurry.

All he remembered of the night before was Macca's warning about the grog which stabbed at him with the guilt of it. Jaysus, he was bad for the drink. Fluthered, he was. A fine state for a grown man and father to be in, was it not? When he thought about Marti, miles away in Ireland, he felt the guilt stabbing again. He could see his mother shaking her head at him, saying, "Hell mend ye, haven't ye only your own self to blame."

Hadn't he entirely. It was his own stupid fault. He had let the bockety-arsed old witch with the bow in her hair get to him. He was mad with himself. He had put up with worse than her before, ones that would talk the teeth off a saw sure, but he had let this one drive him back on the drink. God, thought Joey, this had better not be the start of it. That was the way of it usually, one drink . . . then a thousand to follow.

Wouldn't it be grand rocking back to Kilmora with the thirst on him – they would all have a gas at that. Joey was scarlet at the thought of people he knew pointing and laughing, filling in the gap of the last ten years with all manner of ideas about himself foostering away in the pubs of Australia. The thought made him mad. It wasn't him at all. He had done all the right things for long enough now, and compared to the way he was, didn't he feel ready for a sainthood.

In the week before he had left Ireland, his father had told him he was a living disgrace; wasn't he just doddering his days away on the dole. "Gee-eyed once a fortnight at the expense of the hardworking, God-fearing, proper, decent Irishman who wouldn't cross O'Connell Street to piss down the likes of yeer leg if your trousers were on fire." That's what he had said, the mighty Emmet Driscol. His father had no clue to why he was drinking in the first place – sure that would have taken eyes in his head and having a look at himself, which he'd never do.

Joey eased himself up in the bed and started to feel dizzy. He touched his head. There was a bandage round it. Holy Mother of God – the voice was back – that's some bandage, he thought. He felt round his head to get the extent of his injury. He could feel lots of bandage but little of himself. Almost his whole head was covered. There was a mirror beyond the bed, away off down the ward. He wondered would he make it? He'd try. He was unsteady on his feet. He felt like he was floating, his usual sense of balance gone entirely. With every step the noise in his ear got louder until he found himself standing in the middle of the floor, clutching his head and gnawing his jaws together with the pain of it.

"Sir, you shouldn't be out of bed," said a young nurse. She looked angry, not at all how nurses should look. "Have I to call the doctor?"

"It might be a start," said Joey. "What's the matter with me, anyway?"

"You have a head injury, sir. You shouldn't be out of bed."

"Out of bed . . . I have to get out of bed some time."

"Look, get back to bed now. The doctor will be around soon to see you, Mr . . ."

"Driscol. Could ye tell him to make it snappy? It feels like some manner of bomb's gone off in my skull." Joey looked away, caught sight of a big clock above the ward door. "You can tell him I've a plane to catch in a little while."

The nurse took him by the arm and guided him back to bed, cursing and tutting all the way. She was what they call a right scanger in Ireland, but he tried to let her comments float away from him. It would be good practice for going back to the old place would it not, he thought.

When the doctor arrived he said nothing, just picked up the chart hanging at Joey's feet and started reading. Joey said a soft hello but the doctor said nothing in return, only leaned over to put a thermometer in his patient's mouth.

"You have a perforated eardrum . . . a mild concussion and a possible hairline fracture," said the doctor. He seemed to be talking to himself. It was like he was speaking into a tape recorder, taking notes to go over later.

"Excuse me?" said Joey.

"I think you heard."

"What?"

"Look, I'm not about to repeat myself to you."

"To me . . . what do you mean by that, fella?" said Joey. He was on the receiving end of some pretty obvious hostility here and he wanted to know why.

The doctor took the thermometer back and sighed, "We have more worthy patients in need of that bed."

"Aren't ye just after reeling off my list of ailments."

"Injuries – self-inflicted, I might add. You bloody Irish are all the same, have you no shame?"

Joey was up. The room was spinning again. He wondered had his feet actually reached the floor or were they as numb as his head. "I have plenty of shame, Doctor, more than I would wish on even you."

The doctor took off his thick glasses and looked closely at him. "Sit down. You can't get out of bed."

"Oh, I wouldn't dream of taking up your bed a moment longer, fella. I have a flight to catch – back to Ireland, you'll be glad to hear."

"You're not going anywhere."

"*What?*"

"There's no way. Not in your condition." The doctor put his glasses back on his nose, scribbled on the chart, then turned to leave. "Now get back to bed. There's a good *fella*."

Joey sat back on the bed, his head was spinning twice as fast now. Thoughts of Marti and the ringing noise competed for space inside his skull. What now? Could he risk a move by himself? He touched his head and felt the size of the bandage once more: there was no chance, surely. The doctor turned away and started striding down the ward. He was sneering out the back of his head, thought Joey.

"Doctor," he shouted, "how long . . . till I can fly?" The ward fell silent. Everyone looked at Joey like he was a mental patient.

"Weeks, at least a month, maybe two," said the doctor.

This wasn't happening; it couldn't be, thought Joey. He had to get to Marti, had to find him and make sure he was safe. Didn't the boy need his father now more than ever. He had to get to him soon. Even if he were still okay in a month, he could have forgotten about his father entirely, wasn't that the way kids were.

He looked about for his things. He found his shoes sticking out from under the bed, then in a cupboard nearby he found his clothes. On top of the neatly folded pile was Shauna's diary. The sight of it gave his conscience a wince.

He dressed slowly, like an old man, saving his shoes until last, slipping in his feet and leaving the laces undone. I must look a sight, he thought, walking into the middle of the ward, laces flapping below him like litter in the street as he tucked the diary inside his shirt.

The hospital was a vast tangle of corridors, clogged up with old giffers in dressing gowns, bright white lights and the rank smells of antiseptic and disinfectant. Nowhere else conjured up the same feeling of despair like hospitals for Joey. There was the air of death lingering in every nook and cranny. There was the general air of death and there was the specific air of death. The specific was by far the worst. The specific was memory, reality that had to be shoved to the back of the mind, forgotten about and defeated, replaced with thoughts of better times.

Death was everywhere, Joey knew it. People died all the time but that just happened, nobody had any say in it. When someone had a say in death – had decided to take a life – that was the worst. He could never face that. He knew he would have to though. He had to go to Ireland and face it, for Marti. If he didn't, then wasn't he as good as taking the boy's life from him.

He staggered to the pay phone and dropped in some coins. His hands were trembling, his one unbandaged ear hot against the cold receiver. "Hello, Macca, is it yourself?"

"Bluey, what's up?"

"Macca, I need your help."

"No dramas . . . what can I do?"

"I need a lift. The flight, it's going in an hour or so."

"I thought they were keeping you in, Bluey."

"They could try. Macca, I have to get that flight, do you understand?"

"I do, but, Joey . . ."

"No buts, Macca. I have to get it."

"Okay. Okay. Hold tight, mate."

The call was brief. Joey knew he had no need for histrionics, his voice said it all. He was desperate to go. Desperate to get to Marti, whatever the cost, however he had to pay it. He had no idea where Marti was. Ireland was a small enough country compared to Australia, but wouldn't it be a job and a half, like finding a needle in a haystack, sure. He felt for Shauna's diary inside his shirt. It went against his morals to read another person's diary, but these were desperate times indeed. If there was some clue, some hint or other about where they might be, he had to try it. He opened the first page.

Well here we go, I suppose, don't quite know where to begin really, but Dr Cohn says I should try writing down my thoughts . . .

Dr Cohn was the fella that treated Shauna when she had her last bad bout with the Black Dog. It was the time she really slumped and Joey remembered it clearly.

. . . I feel a bit silly, really. I've never done anything like this before. Joey would be laughing at me but Dr Cohn says he shouldn't know about this diary anyway. It's to be for me alone, to help me work through my thoughts and get myself better in time. He says I can write whatever I want about anybody so long as it feels like it's helping.

Joey closed the diary. He had seen his name mentioned once already and that was enough. It was Shauna's thoughts she had put down for herself, it was her therapy. He knew he had no place reading any more. He put the diary back in his shirt and tried to forget about it.

When Macca arrived he pulled up outside the hospital and Joey saw his ute was streaked with rust-coloured flashes where the tyres had screeched in the dry earth. Macca's kelpie barked and jumped about in the back of the ute like he had just finished a rollercoaster ride. But Macca ignored the dog's cries and ran quickly towards the hospital, passing Joey on the front steps and dashing through the automatic doors.

"Macca," shouted Joey. "I'm here."

Macca twisted on his heels. "*Bluey?*"

"Who did ye think it was, the Invisible Man?"

"Sorry mate, it's the bandages. Strewth, you look like some old digger back from the trenches."

"Well, I feel like shit. Thanks for asking."

Macca scratched his head and squinted at Joey's bandages. "Jesus, you got bashed pretty bloody bad."

"I hate to sound ungrateful but could we go, *please*."

"Sure, sure," said Macca, and then he shook his head and muttered, "*Fair Dinkum*," as he eyed the bandages once more.

When Macca had driven them a safe distance from the hospital, Joey reeled off his list of injuries, cursing and punching at the dashboard in front of him. "So that's it. They said I had no shame taking up a bed, they can have their bed."

"Bluey, these blokes know their stuff."

"Bollix."

"Mate, you could end up in a worse state, just running out and jumping on a plane." Macca looked at the bandages round Joey's head again. "If that's possible."

"Look, I have the ticket . . . and wasn't Marti bound to be worried beyond belief already. I cannot leave it any longer. I'm flying today, sure."

"Hang on, mate, there's got to be another way."

"Like what?"

"I don't know."

"Exactly."

"Well . . . maybe you could go by boat."

"Takes too long, five or six weeks. Tis madness, the idea."

Macca eased the ute through the traffic. It was light for the hour of the day and they made the highway towards the airport in quick time. Joey stared out of the window at the dusty landscape, the patches of sand spinifex and ironstone rocks lining the roadside. He wondered when he would see the harsh reds and blues again. He was heading for a very different place entirely. He loved Australia, which had given him an honest living and good friends like Macca there, but it was time to leave. Marti needed him.

The flowering gum trees crowded together on the edge of the sand plains that stretched all the way to the huge red mountains, as they got nearer to the airport. Red and yellow banksia bushes flashed by the car window in a haze and Joey felt his throat tightening as he took in the view for the last time.

"So, this is it?" said Macca.

"It is so."

"I don't want you blubbering on me when we get up here."

"No fear."

When they reached the car park Macca took Joey's things from the back of the ute. He stood in front of him and painted a thin smile on his face but couldn't hide the long sigh that forced its way out when he looked into his friend's eyes.

"What about Superman?" said Joey.

"*What?*"

"The picture, Marti's picture."

"Oh yeah. It's here." Macca put down the luggage and reached into the ute again. His kelpie lunged a slobbering tongue at him. "Get off, you silly bugger," he said.

"Thanks," said Joey. His voice dipped. "This really is it, then."

"Good luck, Bluey." Macca's brows were creased against the brightness of the sun, the thin slits of his eyes below looked very far away. "Just remember your job is still here when you want it."

"Thanks." Joey and Macca stared at each other for a moment and Joey wondered should there be a handshake or a hug given, and then the moment passed as Macca broke for the ute's door with rapid chatter breaking on his lips.

"You can't be going in there like that," he shouted. "But don't worry, I've got just the thing."

Macca rummaged inside the door of the ute and pulled out a brown woolen hat. "Here, get that on you! Might not be the weather for it, but it'll stop heads turning, I reckon."

Joey took the hat and stretched it over his bandaged head. "I'm going to look a right bogger in this."

Macca stood back and watched the hat forced into place, then reached out to hide a few stray strands of white bandage that hung around Joey's ears. "It's a tight enough fit, but you might just get away with it."

Joey didn't want to think of the alternatives. "I better had."

This time there was a handshake and smiles. When Joey turned for the entrance Macca raised a wave and gave a smile that looked altogether more convincing, thought Joey. He was lucky to have such good friends here in Australia, he knew it, and with any luck he'd be back to see them all again some time soon.

Inside the terminal the air conditioning blasted cool bursts that chilled the skin on contact and shrill voices fired out departure times like squawking gulls. Joey felt his stomach churning as he searched the crowded lounge for the airline desks. The pain in his head had reached a new high and the drilling noise in his ear had been turned to full. Jaysus, he scolded himself, why didn't ye take some pain relief from the hospital?

The shrill voices came back again and Joey recognised the flight. This time it was his. It was the last call, they said, and his heart jumped inside him. He tried to run but failed, then he fell into a jog, and finally a fast walk. He felt unwell, like his head was filling up with gas, the light gas that makes balloons float, he thought. He was starting to stoop over with the bag and the picture; his one free hand that held the ticket was sweating, then his airline counter loomed ahead of him. Joey passed over the ticket – it was damp now – to the girl on the counter. She seemed nice, no scanger this one, sure hadn't he had enough of them for one day. She checked the numbers on the ticket and tipped her head towards the counter like she was going through the motions of a job she'd done a million times.

"That's fine, Mr Driscol . . ." When she looked up, the girl on the counter seemed to take an awful interest in his head, her eyes widening up at the sight of the hat. "Do you have any baggage, sir?"

"Just the one," said Joey, "and the picture – tis hand luggage, really."

The girl on the counter took his bag and weighed it on a set of scales, smiling all the while but still staring at his head, then she attached a sticker to the handle and returned to Joey's passport. "I'm afraid I'll have to ask you to take off the hat, Mr Driscol."

Joey's heart stilled. "You *what*?"

She held up the passport. "I have to check your likeness to the picture in here."

Joey felt a tremble pass over him. There was a hot flash like a firework had gone off behind his eyes, and then his heart started to pound. He reached a hand up to the hat and that's when he felt the bandages falling about his ears. "Oh, God . . ." He felt more bandages falling as he removed the hat.

"Ouch! That looks like a bad knock you've had."

He started to feel dizzy. "Tis nothing. A minor bump only."

She made an inverted smile. "Sir, we have strict rules about head injuries because of the cabin pressure on the plane."

"*What?*"

"Do you have a safe-to-fly cert' from your doctor?"

"*What?*" Everything started to move wildly. Joey felt his eyes rolling.

"Are you all right, sir?"

"I am . . . yes . . . fine."

"Sir, are you sure? You look unwell." The girl moved out from behind the counter as Joey felt his knees begin to buckle and then the lights went up. As he fell backwards he thought he heard the girl on the counter scream, but he wasn't sure because everything went so quickly to utter blackness.

12

Being alone with Brother Michael in his office scared Marti. There was a big old desk and a cross on the wall and a picture of the lady in a blue hood. She was holding a baby and had the sun shining all around her. There were lots of shelves with books and silver cups and little wooden cups and little silver crosses. There was a very big picture of a man in olden times with lots of men around him and a devil with a big stick. The devil was poking the big stick in a man's back and the man was screaming with the agony and the pain of it, and Marti thought it was a very scary picture to be hanging on your wall.

"Tis the Last Judgement," said Brother Michael, "the picture. Do ye like the picture?"

"It's scary," said Marti.

"Ah, now, the Last Judgement was never meant to be a day at the races, Marti. Lookit, that's Christ in Glory and those are the resurrected souls around him, with the Devil himself there, on his right, with . . . is it a trident? Sure it looks just like a pitchfork. Anyway, himself's ready to chase the damned souls into Hell. Do you know what Hell is, Marti?"

"It's a bad place."

"Oh, it's that all right. It's a very bad place," said Brother Michael, "but that's enough about Hell on your first day. Sure and haven't I my orders from your mam to be keeping well away from the religion altogether. Now you be minding yeer mam, d'ye hear, Marti? She has the look of one not long for this world herself."

"I will."

"Good, and don't be telling her I'm after talking about Hell the minute her back's turned."

"I won't."

"Good. I'd have my eye dyed for that, so I would. We'll stick to the curriculum I think."

Brother Michael told Marti to sit down and then he took out one of his cigarettes. The room was full of the smell of cigarettes already and when Brother Michael blew out the smoke Marti thought he could taste the grey and white wisps that were everywhere.

A knock sounded on the door and a boy was called in by Brother Michael. The boy had very straight black hair combed over his eyes all in a straight line like it was a black curtain he had on his head. "Ah, Pat, I have a job for ye," said Brother Michael. "I want ye to take young Marti here under your wing. Mind him through the lunch and back to class."

"Yes, Brother," said the boy, and then he raised his thumb and smiled at Marti.

"Fine so, Pat. Ye can give Marti the grand tour and save my legs, which are a terrible, terrible affliction I have these latter years."

Outside Brother Michael's office Pat said only the senior boys and the prefects could leave the school at the lunch if you didn't have the pass. The brothers didn't give the pass when all you were after was a bag of chips and a bit of craic up the town. The chips were great, amazing, all dripping in the vinegar and with the salt running down them. Marti wanted to get the chips and followed Pat through the gap in the railings where you could get out the school. Pat said the prefects would kick the shite out of ye if they caught you, but wasn't it a torture to spend the whole lunch doddering about in the school.

Pat wanted to know all about Australia and asked if Marti had ever shot a kangaroo or if there were any wars in Australia. Marti said he hadn't shot a kangaroo and he didn't think there were any wars, but Pat said it didn't matter anyway because he wanted to go to Italy and get the scooter like they have on the films and ride around Rome giving the two fingers to the Pope. Pat said he was for leaving Ireland because everyone in Ireland had the name Pat Kelly and there were no great footballers called Pat Kelly and all the great footballers were from Italy with names like *Giorgio*.

Pat said he wanted to go to Italy and see all the great footballers and get the scooter and didn't he have the hair for it too because everyone in Italy had the black hair. Marti had the black hair too, just like Mam, and Pat said he could go to Italy too, and Marti thought it would be grand fun to get the scooter and ride around Rome.

Pat said they had to go the long way over the cobbles and keep off the roads. The brothers take the roads with their cars and didn't the prefects take the roads with their bikes and wouldn't they both have their guts for garters if they caught them out on the roads just parading about without the pass. Pat said the guards were okay and didn't they never mind you, because Billy Finneran's father was a guard and he said they were too busy looking out for the criminal element to be minding young boys who were just needing a good fong in the arse most of the time anyway.

"There c'mon, Marti. That's the chipper," said Pat and started running and Marti had to run too. The chipper was very small and all painted green on the outside with a word Marti couldn't read because it was in the Irish. All the green paint was peeling off and there were boys all in a queue outside waiting to buy the chips.

"Arrah, Mick," said Pat when they got inside the chipper, and a man with a sweaty brow said, "Howya, Pat, is it the chips?"

"Tis," said Pat, and then he said, "this is my new friend, Marti Driscol from Australia."

"Howya, Marti. Australia, is it? Well, I've no prawns for yeer barbie, but I could do ye a haddock," said Mick, and started the laughing.

"I'll have chips," said Marti.

"All right so, the chips it is," said Mick, and rolled up the two bags of chips in newspaper very quickly.

Marti followed Pat out of the chipper and round to the back of the street and there were lots of boys from Saint Joseph's All Boys Catholic School eating the chips and Pat said howya to some of them. The chips were lovely, all dripping in the vinegar and with the

90

salt running down them, thought Marti, but he couldn't cram them into his mouth as fast as Pat.

"Aren't the chips mighty, Marti?" said Pat.

"They are," said Marti, and when he spoke one of the boys from school said, "Ah look now, it's Skippy," and there was laughing from the other boys.

Pat kept cramming the chips into his mouth and said, "Don't mind them, Marti, aren't they Brother Declan's class. They're all eejits." The boys stopped laughing and when Pat was finished the chips he started to roll up the newspaper.

"*Please, please*, the paper," said a boy to Pat. He had a very dirty face and very dirty old clothes.

"Feck off, knacker," said Pat and the boy said, "*Please, please*," again and Pat threw the newspaper away into the back of the yard behind the chipper. "Ye can't be encouraging them, Marti," said Pat. "The knackers would never leave us alone if ye gave them so much as the one chip, I swear it."

The knacker boy ran after the newspaper and there were big old brown rats at the newspaper before he could get to it. The rats were very quick running about until the knacker boy picked up the newspaper and started to unravel it, and then he flattened the newspaper out and started the licking of it to taste where the chips had been.

"I'm for a lemonade. Will ye have one, Marti?" said Pat.

"No, I'm not thirsty."

"All right so, I'll go get one. Will ye wait for me?"

"I will," said Marti, and he tried to eat the chips but the hunger was gone and he threw them into the back of the yard. There were chips spilled out and then rats came out again and there were lots of them all over the place and coming from under stones and behind fences. The knacker boy had to shout and stamp at the rats to make them stay away from the chips. Some of the rats grabbed at the chips and ran off with them, but the knacker boy got most of the chips and started cramming them in his mouth very fast.

"Hey, stop feeding the knackers," shouted one of the boys from Brother Declan's class, and Marti looked at the boy who was very big and fat and had lots of little marks on his face that were like freckles but were really little holes.

91

"I didn't. He just took them," said Marti.

"*I didn't. He just took them,*" said the fat boy. He was trying to sound like Marti with the Australian accent and all the other boys started the laughing again. "Ye talk like Skippy," said the fat boy.

Marti felt his face get hot and he wanted to hit the fat boy right on the nose but he was very big and there were lots of other boys with him. "Skippy's a kangaroo, he can't talk," said Marti.

The fat boy grabbed him round the neck and said, "I'll kill ye."

Marti felt his face go from hot to cold. Nobody had ever said they would kill him before. He started to shiver and then Pat came back with the lemonade and said, "Leave him, Dylan."

The fat boy let Marti go and started to look at Pat instead. "Are ye fighting his battles, Kelly, are ye? C'mon then?" The fat boy started to jump about with his fists up like he was going to fight Pat. "Ah, yeer chicken, Kelly." Pat stood beside Marti and there were no words and all the boys from Brother Declan's class waited to see if there would be a fight. "Give us yeer lemonade, Kelly?" Pat handed over his lemonade, and the fat boy took a big drink and started slugging it all down. Then he filled up his cheeks and spat all the lemonade out over Pat's face.

There was cheering and there was jostling and then the boys started shouting, "*Fight. Fight. Fight.*"

There was lots of shouting and the noise made people look out windows round the back of the chipper and then Mick came running out, waving his hands and said, "What's all this? Is it the guards I've to call?"

"He's after taking my lemonade off me, Mick," said Pat.

"Give him the lemonade back, Dylan," said Mick.

"I will not, sure he was messing with it, tormenting the knacker."

"Mick, he's lying so he is. Lookit, he's only after spitting a load of it over me," said Pat.

"All right now, Dylan, hand the lemonade over or it's the guards for ye and the last time you set a foot in my shop," said Mick.

The lemonade was handed over to Pat. "Now, drink it up, Pat," said Mick.

"It's my lemonade. I can drink it when I want."

"Drink it up, I say. We'll have no retaliations this day."

Pat started to drink down the lemonade and the fat boy and the boys from Brother Declan's class watched until he had finished and tipped the lemonade bottle upside down to show it was empty.

"All right now, that's grand," said Mick. "Now shake and make up." Pat and the fat boy stood looking at each other. Marti wondered if Pat was even breathing because he looked so mad. Then the hands went out and there was the shake and Mick smiled and said, "Grand so. Now about yeer business and we'll have no more altercations, d'ye hear?"

There was nodding and the fat boy said, "Yes, Mick."

"Pat, I say we'll have no more altercations. What say ye?" said Mick.

Pat didn't answer, and when everyone looked at him to see if he would speak he puffed out his cheeks to show there was still a full mouth of lemonade inside and then he spat the lot of it all over the fat boy.

"Run, Marti," shouted Pat. "Run for yeer feckin life."

13

It was five weeks in a floating prison he was facing, but hadn't he no choice entirely, thought Joey Driscol. It was take the boat or wait, maybe even longer, until his head was healed fully. No one would believe the run of bad luck he was having, but wasn't Marti the one who would suffer the most? The boy was over in Ireland, a strange country to him, with a mother who was unfit to mind him. Sure, Marti could be in any state now and wouldn't he be cursing his father for allowing it. How did it happen? How did he get into this whole mess?

Joey paced up and down the few steps that lay between the tiny cabin's bunks. Five weeks. Jaysus, couldn't anything happen in five weeks. Marti could be taken from Shauna, placed in care. She wasn't well sure. Or couldn't the boy run off, mightn't he be desperate to get back to Australia. He pictured Marti on the run from home; he saw him in an orphanage, crying and hungry, and then he saw him taken by knackers and forced out into the cold to beg for a feed. It was too much. With five weeks of this, he would be mad entirely.

He had no idea where Marti was. He knew Shauna had little family left. Her mother and father were dead long before their daughter's own troubles started. There was a brother Barry who went in that terrible suicide business after they left, and a sister Catrin – Old Kiss the Statues, they called her. Was she still back in

Kilmora? Joey remembered she had a diabolical mouth on her, so full of religious chatter that ye wanted to say *Amen* whenever she finished a sentence. Hadn't she plenty to say before they left for Australia. If Marti was living under her roof . . . Jaysus, it didn't bear thinking about. He felt his stomach churning at the thought. He kicked out at the bunk in front of him and the flimsy article shot into the wall like a rabbit diving for its warren. "Ye dirty feck," he said, and then the door swung open behind him.

"Sure, that's grand chat, me old segotia," said a round man standing in the doorway. He was ruddy faced, burnt in the sun, and panting from the effort of lifting a great bag at the back of him.

"Who are you?" said Joey.

"Tiernan's the name. I think we're bunk buddies."

Joey took in the sight before him. There was little or no light from the hall breaking behind the man. How would they both fit in the cabin?

"Paddy Tiernan," he said, dropping his great bag and stretching out a sweaty palm, "from Dingle. Jaysus, I never thought I'd be travelling with a fella from the old country."

"Why not . . . sure there's a lot of us about, ye know."

"Ah, yeer right there, the old diaspora. Sixty million Irish the world over. You've as much chance of meeting an old boyo strolling along the Amazon as the Liffey!"

"I suppose yeer right," said Joey, and took the hand he was offered. "Joey Driscol's the name . . . from Kilmora."

"Driscol, ye say . . . from Kilmora. You're no relation to Emmet Driscol, the hurling player, are ye?"

Joey dropped his head. Was there no escaping the man. "Tis my father."

"Stop the lights! Aren't I travelling with royalty."

"Ah, go way outta that."

"Emmet Driscol's boy, eh? They'll never believe this back home. I saw him play once. Christ, he was fierce."

"I know it, sure."

"Jaysus, I'm flabbergasted. Here, how is he these days?"

"I don't know."

"*What?*"

"We don't talk, haven't for ten years past. You know . . . *families*." Joey looked at Paddy. He had a droop on his lower lip, confused at the thought of a great Irishman like Emmet Driscol having led anything less than the perfect existence.

"Oh," said Paddy, and his tone was changed. "Well, Joey, my man. I'm glad to make your acquaintance, and to show how glad I am . . ." Paddy unzipped his bag and pulled out a bottle of Jameson whiskey, the seal already cracked, a good drop taken. "I'll drink yeer health."

"Ah, no."

"Come on, now a little drop never did a man any harm." Paddy leaned over to the shelf above the little sink and stuck two fat fingers in as many cups. "There," he said when the whiskey was poured. "*Sláinte!*"

"*Sláinte*," said Joey, taking the cup. There was no harm in one, sure enough, and wasn't this Paddy fella all right. He could have teamed up with worse, so he could, and hadn't Paddy ignored the bandage on his head, or at least resisted the mention of it so far, and that was something to be grateful for.

The two men talked away, though Joey was mostly forced to listen to Paddy's tales. It was a relief to be entertained instead of doing the entertaining, he thought, especially the way he felt, though there was more than a touch of the Blarney in Paddy's talk. Sure if bullshit was music he would make a grand brass band altogether. He was what they called a redneck back in Ireland, the type of country fella that gets a slap on the neck and told go and find some work in the city. He was rough and ready, sure, but there wasn't a flitter of badness in him. Paddy had toured the world, always by boat for fear of flying, but had rarely saw more than the latest site of some grand new building, usually carrying a hod full of bricks over his shoulder.

"Ye know there's some grand craic to be had on a boat, Joey Driscol," said Paddy.

"Is that so?"

"Tis . . . you get some characters travelling by boat, so ye do. Tis the romance of the sea."

"Ah go away, it's not *Love Boat* now."

"Ha-ha, ye haven't seen the nurse will be looking after the bandage there, and don't they say there's only two sure things in life – one is death, the other a nurse."

"Cop onto yeerself." Joey felt the reddener flushing over his face and picked up the whiskey bottle.

"Don't worry, I won't be asking how ye managed it," said Paddy.

"I look a sight, don't I?"

"Not at all . . . sure yeer like some manner of Sikh gentleman."

Joey laughed. There was no craic like the Irish – wasn't Paddy a gas entirely. Even though Joey's thoughts were full of Marti he was almost enjoying himself. "Right . . . shall we go and find a bit of this romance yeer on about, then?"

Paddy said it was a powerful idea, the travelling by sea. Didn't you have the relaxation that came with it into the bargain. He said all the great explorers and adventurers travelled by the sea, and though there were some mighty aviators in time of war, and so on and such forth, wasn't the sea the thing for a fella with a bit of pluck about him? If he had his time again, Paddy said he would love to be setting out on a life at sea and maybe even becoming a salt into the bargain. Your average salt had a constitution blacker than a rat's guts, said Paddy, and a mind at least twice as dark. A good salt always knew where to find the craic on a ship like this and they only need keep their eyes peeled for the right one.

The ship was busy and there were lots of people walking about when Paddy suddenly pointed to a salt and said, "Now, Joey, there's a fella who's seen a bit of the world. Hang on, I'll have a word."

Paddy and the salt stood talking together for a while and then there were a lot of gestures from the salt, like he was giving directions. When the salt stopped with the gestures, he nodded at Paddy and then the two men shook hands and Paddy flicked back his head to beckon Joey to him.

"Right, me old segotia, have I a night planned for you."

"What is it?" said Joey.

"What is it? Only the grandest of craic known to man."

"*What?*"

"Five card brag."

"Poker?" said Joey.

"Shhh . . . Jaysus, don't be broadcasting it."

"Oh come on, tis only a game of cards."

"Tis not matchsticks we're playing with here, Joey now, tis bigger than that."

"Lollypop sticks?"

"Stop now. It's big money. We can clean up, sure. Come on, game's starting in ten minutes. What do you say?"

"No way."

"Ah, now. Don't be dismissing the idea, sure I know a thing or two about the old five card."

"Forget it." Joey turned round and walked away from Paddy and his idea of a bit of craic. Funds were tight. Since Shauna emptied the bank of Marti's college funds Joey had worried about building them back up. He had never known money, what he had – which wasn't much after the usual parasites took their bite out of the house sale – he had worked for and now he had no work. Every penny would be needed to find Marti, make him safe and keep him that way.

"Joey," said Paddy, walking after him.

"See ya."

In the cabin Joey pulled out the bunk and flattened his pillow. The bunk was hard, rock solid. He wondered how he would manage five weeks of it, and then the door was opened again.

"Look, haven't I a system," said Paddy. "Tis a sure-fire system and all I need is a bit of the folding stuff. See I'm what ye might call embarrassed financially."

"Forget it. Anyway, what makes ye think I have a bean?"

"Well, ye would be flying if ye were counting pennies."

"I have hardly a pot to piss in . . . and anyway, all I have is accounted for. I have a boy needs looking after."

Paddy leaned over and placed a sunburned hand on Joey's shoulder. "What I am about to tell you now I have told no other man, tis my secret but I'm desperate, sure. I'm broke."

"Shame," said Joey.

"That's not it. I have a talent." Paddy went to his bag and took out a deck of cards. "Now watch." The deck was shuffled faster than Joey thought possible, and then the cards were sprayed into the air and collected one after the other in Paddy's hands.

"That's impressive," said Joey.

"Fluff. Watch this." Paddy dealt out four sets of five from the pack and told Joey to take one. He reached out. "Uh-uh," said Paddy.

"You said *any* one."

"Try that one instead."

Joey picked up the hand: a flush. He was surprised, curious. He turned the others over: a pair of aces in one, three eights in another and an ace high. "Amazing!" said Joey.

"It's all in the deal. Sure a great dealer can deal everyone at the table a hand to die for . . . and a better one to himself!"

"Christ, this is dynamite." Joey's mind filled with the possibilities. Was this his chance to come out ahead? To turn the little cash he had left from the house sale into a real nest egg? Marti could be taken proper care of – mightn't the college money be replaced entirely. The whole sorry slate could be wiped clear with a win at the table. Joey saw rows of books bought for Marti, a whole set of encyclo-paedia, tutors paid for and the best of exam results. He saw his dream realised. Marti would go to Trinity, sure no Bishop could deny the boy like they had done him.

"Count me in," said Joey.

Paddy smiled. Joey recognised the wild optimism of the gambler in his face, but sure wasn't this a cert. Paddy was like a firm tip for the horses. It was bet-the-house time entirely.

"How much are ye in for?" said Paddy

"Everything."

"Grand so, I'll drink to that."

The two glasses were filled once more and Joey drained his in one shot. "Paddy, you could be just the break I needed."

"What do ye mean *could*? Aren't we invincible. Just one question, how much are you carrying?"

Joey dipped into his breast pocket. "Tis all I have."

Paddy eyed the bundle of notes, then reached out for it.

"Not so fast. I'm trusting ye with my life here. If ye lose it I lose more than money, Paddy. I lose the chance of finding my boy."

Paddy looked at Joey, "*Finding your boy?*"

"My wife's disappeared with him."

"Jaysus, tis like something ye would read in the papers. Your money's safe with me, my friend," he said, taking the bundle.

It was the strangest thing, thought Joey. As soon as the money was given over his hopes evaporated. But sure, it was probably just the fear of losing, was it not? This Paddy fella was a magician with the old cards – he had never seen anything like it, never in all his days. He checked his thinking, told himself it was money in the bank. There would be a win at the table and he would rock back to Kilmora like some manner of flashman, spraying gifts on Marti. There would be a power of cash set aside for the boy's future and maybe more to tide them over until he found work enough to get them both back to Australia. Jaysus, wasn't the forecast brightening up entirely.

Paddy stripped to the waist and started to douse himself in water at the little sink. He had a small leather case full of all manner of soaps and talcum powders and lotions which he used to spruce himself up before the big card game. Joey tried not to watch whilst Paddy readied himself but it was hard when he didn't stop talking all the while.

"I always get a bit jittery before a game, so I do," said Paddy.

"Not too jittery, I hope."

"No way, sure tis all superficial – just nerves." Paddy covered his body in a cloud of talc. "Sorry, don't I sweat like a rapist."

Joey started to cough when the talc floated over his head. "Ye have a lovely way with words."

"Sorry, tis the nerves again."

"I wish ye would stop talking about your nerves. You'll have me thinking you're not up to this . . . and the game is underway now, you realise!"

"Sorry."

"And stop saying sorry. Are ye ready yet?"

Paddy buttoned up a sky blue shirt with coconut palms swaying all over it. Joey thought the shirt looked more suited to the beach; he hoped it wouldn't attract attention to Paddy, but he didn't want to mention it for fear of rattling his nerves any more.

"Okay, I'm set," said Paddy.

The pair left the cabin, Paddy in front, Joey following behind in the bigger man's shaky steps. The card game was to be held in one of the luxury cabins at the front of the ship. It was a long walk and before they were even halfway Paddy was taking a seat and gasping for air.

"Are ye okay?" said Joey. He thought about calling the whole thing off, taking his money and running back to the cabin.

"I'm fine. Maybe a glass of water."

Joey led Paddy into a nearby toilet, filled the sink with cold water and told him to get a grip. It was no good. The second Paddy leaned over the sink, he vomited.

"Holy Mother of God," said Joey.

"Sorry."

"Stop that. In fact, I'll stop it. The money, get it over."

"No, Joey I'm fine. Better out than in, like they say, eh."

"I swear. If you mess up."

Paddy stood and grabbed Joey in a handshake, gripped him tight. "Trust me. It's just the way it always takes me. I'm fine, sure."

Joey looked him in the eye. "Then let's feckin do this," he said.

14

Marti and Pat took off running over the cobbles and Marti was the fastest and had to slow down for Pat, who had the stitch with the laughing. They ran and ran for a very long way, but when they could see there was no one following and they were tired with the running, they stopped and sat down with their backs to a wall. They were miles from St Joseph's, said Pat, and wasn't that the reason Dylan and the boys from Brother Declan's class had given up.

"They're too scared to mitch off the school. Sure Brother Declan's a mentaller," said Pat.

"What's mitch?" said Marti.

"It's going on the hop, sure – missing the school."

"Oh."

"Oh, indeed. Sure it's mitching we are now," said Pat. Marti wondered would they be in trouble?

The brothers would know they were missing for sure, because wasn't he just a new boy and new boys were always looked out for. Marti knew his mam would say he had earned a hot arse for mitching, but he didn't care because St Joseph's was a terrible place. Sure, the hot arse would be better than the rest of the day spent at school with the brothers and the likes of Dylan Gillon, who wanted to kill him.

"Come on," said Pat. "Ye can have a grand time on the mitch, aren't I forever at it?"

It was wet out on the streets and when Marti stood up he felt his backside was damp, but he didn't mind because it felt like an adventure he was on. When they started to walk he felt his feet squelching and saw his shoes were sodden after running in the wet streets. When he looked underneath the shoes there was a hole in one and a big crack in the other that had split the sole in two. Marti said he couldn't be walking anywhere now, but Pat said there were bicycles galore left outside Gleesons Bakery and weren't they there for the taking. They could borrow one and go for a burl, which would be showing Marti the sights into the bargain.

"It's stealing," said Marti. "We'll get into trouble."

"It's borrowing only, sure. I'm always at it. We just have to put it back in one piece and nobody's the wiser."

At Gleesons Bakery there were lots of big old heavy black bicycles lined up in rows. Some of the bicycles had bars on the front and some of them had a basket. Marti watched Pat creep in and grab a bicycle with a basket on the front and then he wheeled it away with the *squeak-squeak* noise following him. When Pat got beyond Gleesons Bakery he jumped on the bicycle and told Marti to get on the back. Pat's legs were too small to reach the pedals properly, so he had to sit on the bar and slide sideways about. The bicycle was very shaky until Pat got the hang of it, and then it was going like the clappers they were.

They rolled down Quay Street on the bicycle, with the basket on the front sometimes catching the wind and nearly knocking them off balance. At the end of Quay Street there was a street of cobbles and there was bumping and rattling and Marti and Pat were nearly off the bicycle entirely until the course was straightened miraculously, and then they were in flitters with the laughing.

The two boys had turns about with the bicycle and when they both had the hang of it, racing around the village like skylarks, Pat said it was time to go down the old railway. He said that down by the old railway was the best of places to go on the mitch and they would have themselves a grand old burn up with the papers that were dumped by the boys who were too lazy to do the deliveries. It was very quiet with no one to be seen. The tracks and the bridges of the old railway were silent, only the long grass and the bare trees made a noise when the wind passed them. Pat had a little yellow can with a white swan on it hidden under a rock at his favourite spot to go on the mitch. He said the can had lighter fuel in it, which was needed for the burn up.

The papers that were everywhere were collected up and the top ones and the bottom ones that were wet were thrown away, and then Pat splashed on the lighter fuel and took a box of matches from his pocket. It would be a grand old burn up in no time, said Pat, but wasn't it a shame they had none of the marshmallows like they have on the films. Pat said if it was Huck Finn he was there'd be marshmallows galore for roasting on the fire, and wasn't it a mystery where he always got them when they were as scarce as hobby-horse manure about these parts.

"Where did ye learn to make a fire like that?" said Marti.

"My dad showed me," said Pat. "Well, I saw him, really, when he was at the rubbish burning in the summer."

When Pat said about his dad Marti felt the lump in the throat coming because he hadn't seen his dad in a long time and things were very different now. He kept thinking about his dad and missing him. Mam had said the second he stopped the thinking then the sadness would stop too, but Marti didn't want to stop the thinking. Sometimes Marti would think as hard as he could and hope that Dad would catch the thought like it was a special message and come and get him, but he never did. When Mam had taken him past the fountain where the coins were thrown, he had made a wish for Dad to appear but the wish hadn't come true, and Marti wondered if wishes ever came true.

"Your old fella must have shown ye some tricks in the bush now?" said Pat.

"We were never in the bush. We had a proper house on a proper street," said Marti. His voice was weak and cracking with the lump in his throat. He didn't want to talk about his dad. He had got used to just the thinking about him because Mam didn't like to hear him talking about Dad and would start with the moodiness whenever he did.

"Ye sound homesick, are you?" said Pat.

"Maybe," said Marti, and he started to poke at the fire with a long stick.

"What do ye miss the most?"

"My dad."

"*Your dad* . . . didn't he come with ye?"

"No, was just my mam. He's still there."

"Is he coming?"

"I don't think so. He says Australia is God's country and he would never leave. He says he would never come to Ireland for the days soaked through and digging the ditches."

"Oh," said Pat.

Marti could tell Pat was confused. He had the eyes rolled back in his head like he was trying to think what to say next but had no idea entirely.

"My mam says it's just us for now . . . and Aunt Catrin, I think, because we live with her."

"Is that Old Kiss the Statues?"

"Who?"

"That's what they call her, Old Kiss the Statues. Sure that woman's a bockety-arsed old witch. They say she's mad entirely . . . couldn't she just be going through the old change of life business though, like all the women do," said Pat.

The old change of life business was new to Marti. Pat had surprised him. This was something strange altogether and Marti wondered what it could mean. It sounded very dramatic and he wondered why he had never heard of it before. "What's the old change of life business?" he said.

"You're codding. Ye don't know?" said Pat.

Marti shook his head.

"Man alive, it's a sheltered life ye had in Australia. Lookit, it's when a woman's after drying up down the way." Pat pointed to his mickey and Marti laughed. "Do ye want to stay ignorant of the ways of the world?" said Pat.

"Sorry," said Marti.

"All right so, but you better listen, for it's for your benefit I'm telling," said Pat. He was very serious and making all the hand movements to show how serious he was. Pat said the old change of life business was when the whole plumbing goes dodgy after a while and it turns the woman a bit mad because she cannot have any more children.

105

The old change of life business made Marti worried. Aunt Catrin was mad enough already and if she was to get much worse like Pat said then there could be all manner of troubles ahead. If it happened to all women like Pat said then couldn't Mam go well and truly beyond the beyonds when it was her turn. It didn't sound good at all and he wished he had never asked Pat because there were some things in this world that were better not knowing about.

"*What the feck was that?*" said Pat.

"I don't know," said Marti. "Someone is shouting."

"I know it's shouting," said Pat. "Shit, I'll bet it's the guards. Someone will have seen smoke from the fire." Pat started to kick soil onto the fire and there was lots of smoke and then there was coughing and hacking at the smoke that came up from the fire.

"Come on, Pat. We should run," said Marti. The shouting got louder and louder and then Pat spotted Guard O'Dowd down the way, waving his fist and shouting.

"Stop. Stop. Stop where ye are."

Guard O'Dowd had his hat off and was holding it in his hand, and Marti could see his shiny bald head bobbing up and down when he tried to run through the thick grass and the ferns and the bramble bushes down the way.

"Come on, Pat, leave the fire and run now. Come on," said Marti. There was still lots of smoke coming from the fire when Marti got hold of the bicycle and started to push it along the old railway tracks. Pat ran behind and when Marti started the pedalling fast Pat jumped on the seat.

The bicycle wouldn't go very fast at all on the old railway tracks, and there was lots of shaking and swaying and the noise of Guard O'Dowd shouting.

"He's very close," said Pat, and Marti said he was going as fast as he could but the bicycle didn't like the railway tracks. Pat said they would be better running and Marti said there was a hill down the way and wouldn't they be fine if they made it there and got a bit of a speed up.

"Go. Go, Marti. Go for the hill," said Pat. He pressed hard into the pedals and there was rocking and swaying to get the speed up. "We're nearly there, quick," said Pat, and there was more rocking and swaying and Marti pressed harder into the pedals but they would only spin very fast this time, and the bicycle was thrown out of control when they went over the hill.

"Oh, Jaysus, Marti," said Pat, "we'll be killed entirely." Marti couldn't talk at all with the bicycle racing out of control. There were branches and bushes flying past very fast and he gripped onto the handlebars as hard as he could. The basket started to crash and clatter about and then it went flying up into the air and when it came down there was a loud crash as it went bouncing on very fast right to the bottom of the hill. Everything seemed to move very quickly and there was a green blur from the grass and a blue blur from the sky and then there was the noise of the bicycle reaching the bottom of the hill and thumping into a mound of earth. Marti and Pat landed on their backs, and when Marti looked at Pat there were daisies in his hair and he started the laughing.

"Ha-ha, look at the flowers," he said.

"What about you with the brown face? Aren't ye like a grotty old knacker." There was hard laughing and then Marti noticed the bicycle had a buckled front wheel and the handlebars were all pushed to the side.

"Oh, Pat, look at the bike."

"Ah sure it's banjaxed."

Marti sat looking at the bicycle and he felt the sadness because he knew he had been bold and would be in trouble again. He wanted to run away very far and never have to see anybody in Kilmora ever again, and then he started to hear Pat shouting, "Run, Marti, run," but it was too late when Guard O'Dowd reached down and grabbed him round the neck with his very big hand.

15

Joey couldn't take it anymore. The strain was too much. Another whiskey was called for. It wasn't Jameson but it tasted fine enough – it could have been the crystal decanter it came out of. The cabin was luxury all right, sparkling it was, even the ceilings looked like they'd been polished. The air conditioning was wafting out a cool breeze that filled the place, but Paddy Tiernan was sweating, the sky blue of his shirt turning to black where sweat soaked the fabric.

What had he done, thought Joey. This Paddy fella was as crooked as two left feet, sure he was. Holy Mother of God, gambling the last of his money away, did it get any worse? If the money was lost, what then? Jaysus, it didn't bear thinking about. He closed his eyes tight and tried to shut out the scene in front of him.

"Raise," said one of the card players. Joey opened his eyes and looked at a man of forty with wiry little glasses, the air of a bank manager, an eye like a stinking eel.

"Jaysus, I'm folding," said Paddy. He was scanning the deck and shaking his head, sweat gleaming on the wet ends of his hair.

Joey stared at Paddy. He looked like a bogtrotter that was lost in the city, way out of his depth, so he was. "Paddy, would ye get out?" he said.

Paddy's face was beaming, beet red. "Deal me in, fellas," he said. "Deal me in."

Joey's heart pumped so hard he wondered would it burst out of him. He turned his back on the game. He couldn't watch another hand. There was more laughter at the table, another quick hand had finished. He looked over his shoulder to see the man with the look of a bank manager scooping money from the middle of the table towards him. He thought he recognised some of his curled-up notes sliding across. They were the same notes he had carried, tightly bound and close to his chest, for days. It was the money from the house sale, all he had to find Marti, all he had to sort out the mess his life had become. Without the money he knew he was finished, done for entirely.

"Right, that's enough," said Joey. He swung Paddy around on his chair. "The game's over. I'll have what's left of my money."

"Joey, man. Calm down," said Paddy.

"I'll give ye calm down. Having a rapid time losing my money, are ye?"

"Is there some problem here?" said the salt. He stood up and fastened the brass buttons on his jacket. It was a look Joey had seen on many a doorman, many a time.

"And you can feck off, ye bollix," he said.

Paddy stood up. "Tis all right, tis all right. Joey, come on now." Paddy placed an arm round Joey's shoulder and walked him away from the card game towards the door of the cabin. "Joey man, ye cannot be disrupting a game like this. They'll have us both chained up for the rest of the voyage."

"Paddy, you've spun me some wide shite here . . ."

"I cannot deny I've had a bit of a losing streak – tis the luck ye take. These fellas are good, so they are."

"How much is left?"

"Not much. It doesn't matter."

"It doesn't matter. Get what's left of my money."

"I cannot, that's what I mean. I'm in till I'm out – tis the rules."

Joey felt his stomach start to turn over. "Christ above, Paddy, what have ye done to me?" He slumped in the jamb of the door and Paddy placed a hand under his arm for the support that was needed. Joey saw him glance over his shoulder at the game as he did it.

Wasn't the man hooked entirely. He couldn't get the game out of his mind for a second even.

"Joey, I'm still in there, sure," said Paddy. His voice was rising. He had no clue at all of the circumstances they were in. "Go back to the cabin and calm yeerself down. I could be back with some winnings yet." Paddy's face was shining and he was breathing hard, but he placed both his hands under Joey's arm and eased him out the door. "My luck is bound to change, losing streaks never last long."

"Don't kid yeerself," said Joey, but he could tell Paddy never heard a word of it. He was miles away, imagining himself some grand hero of the green baize, piles of winnings stacked up before him. The cabin door closed shut and Joey heard a key turned in the lock. He fell back on the wall, slumped to the ground, his stomach turned over once more, and then he vomited.

The smell was vile, tinged with whiskey, and forced him to his feet. He walked through the ship's corridors – wasn't it desperate entirely, he thought. It was headed for poor street, he was, for sure. His hopes were destroyed. He'd been a bloody fool, an eejit, what the Irish call, an *omadhaun*. Taken in by Paddy he was, a Dingle redneck that anyone with half a brain in their skull could see was as wide as a gate. Oh, it was a grand plan, was it not, the gambling. Double your money, triple it maybe and rock back to Kilmora like he was the cat's whiskers. It was blown now, so it was. Wouldn't he be going back in a worse state than he left. Penniless, with a wife deserted him and a son, ruined already, probably.

He kept the cabin light off and lay on his bunk in the darkness for what seemed like hours. He was looking at some trying times ahead, so he was. Jaysus, had there been any other class of times, he wondered? It was never supposed to be like this. He tried to think of good times from the past, before Marti even. There had to be some, it wasn't all like this was it? Shauna had said life was what you made of it. They would have grand times together, so they would. She had told him this when they were younger, when they had only their hopes, and hadn't they plenty once. Joey could still see Shauna, the way she was before their hopes were dashed and the Black Dog caught up with her.

He managed a smile when he thought of Shauna, sitting on the wall outside Gleesons Bakery, waiting for the whistle to blow and himself to come running. He would stride with his chest out and raise her off the wall and she would shriek and scream when the flour got onto her dress. The young lifter boys were all mad jealous, nudging and pointing when they saw her waiting at Gleesons with the wide smiles and the long black hair. Even the old men who worked the ovens were forever cracking toothless grins and saying, "Tis a fine mot ye have found for yeerself, young Driscol, a fine mot indeed."

He had wondered why Shauna would choose him when she could have chosen anyone at all in the whole world. He wondered why she would be interested in him at all, with only the job at Gleesons, got for him by his father, the great hurling player, who thought his son was fit for no better. He wondered if Shauna would leave him eventually and he decided then that it was only a matter of time before she did. He could still see his picture of Shauna in his mind, the way she was. It was still so real he felt as if he was with her yet. Why did she never leave him, then? Why did she wait until it was least expected, after they had been through so much together that he thought she would never leave him now.

The ship's swaying made Joey feel like he had arrived at some strange place between the past and the present. He knew he couldn't hate Shauna for leaving him and taking Marti away from him anymore. There was too much had passed between them for that, but wasn't it all a mighty saddener. He tried not to think about what her reasons might be for leaving now because there was no reason at all. It was the Black Dog was to blame surely, and the cause of that was something Joey could do nothing about.

He rummaged through his things for Shauna's diary. There would maybe be some hint there, some kind of pointer to what she was thinking. He wanted to understand her. He wanted to know what could make her think taking Marti from him was the answer. He found the little leather book and skipped a few pages from the last entry he had read:

Dr Cohn thinks I have issues with everything, he thinks I want to just hide from them all, but he's so wrong. I want to face them down. Joey's way is to run, to hide from everything, he locks things away in his head and thinks they don't exist anymore. But they do. They always do, and I'm sick of hiding from them . . .

Joey knew what Shauna was on about, the thing she wanted them to face, but he couldn't. It was all a shock to him seeing Shauna's thoughts for the first time. The picture he had in his mind of her vanished. He felt like he was getting to know her all over again and she wasn't the same person. He didn't want to know this person. This person was a stranger. Shauna was ill sure, and this person was trying to blame Joey for it.

As he threw down the diary, the cabin door started to creak slowly open and Paddy crept inside. He carried with him a smell of whiskey, sweat and smoke.

"Tell me," said Joey.

"We lost," said Paddy. "Joey, I really am very, very . . ."

"Save it. I don't want to hear your voice." He turned over in the bunk – wasn't he worthless like his old fella had said. He buried his face in the pillow, but Emmet Driscol's words came with him. Worthless he was. He'd amounted to nothing, right enough. That's what his father had told him when he left for Australia with Shauna, fleeing the scorn of the whole village, and now wouldn't he be back in just the style to prove him right.

Joey felt like he was a boy still, facing the prospect of his father's disapproval again. He could see his father's eyes, the large whites and the darkness of the centres that looked into the marrow of you. Emmet Driscol never flinched when he set his eyes on anyone and Joey could feel the power of his father's glare still watching him, still disapproving, still judging him lesser than himself.

When he woke in the morning the air of the cabin was thick and odorous. Joey's head throbbed. He thought for a moment he had gone to Hell, and then he saw Paddy sitting over him, perched like a gargoyle waiting for him to waken. "I'm so sorry. It was the money for yeer boy," he said.

"It's gone now."

"I feel like such a . . ."

"Loser?"

"*Worse.*"

"Well, join the club." Joey sat up in the bunk, touched his head and found the bandage still in place.

"Joey . . . I expected you to be roaring like Doran's Ass, at least giving out at me."

"What would be the use?"

"Look . . . I've decided. I'm going to pay you back, every penny."

Joey laughed in Paddy's face.

"I mean it, Joey, every penny."

"How will you manage that, a loser like yourself?"

"I don't know, but I grant ye this: I will stick by your side till this debt is paid. I can help ye get your boy back too."

Joey looked at Paddy with disbelief. Was this man a complete and total mentaller? He knew he should be angry with Paddy, should be belting him round the head, knocking sense into him, but wasn't his type beyond learning. He was somewhere between a child and a dumb animal, a hapless kind and as ignorant as a bag of arses, for sure and certain.

Joey stood up. The air in the cabin was making it hard to breathe. He wanted out. He was already fully dressed, sleeping in his clothes like a right knacker. He reached for the door handle and brought in the morning light. "I want nothing more to do with you. Save your promises for the next eejit ye can con into handing over his last penny."

"Joey, come on, you don't mean that."

"I do."

"No ye don't. I can tell you're a good fella, aren't ye just a bit messed up?"

"I was fine before I met you." He walked through the door of the cabin. Paddy followed him into the corridor. "I have enough worries without a jinx like you following me around. Now would ye ever feck off and find someone else to annoy."

"Joey, stop, would ye. I feel bad enough. Don't I only want to make it up to you."

"You cannot."

"I can. Sure, I can get yeer money back with interest. I just need a bit of time. Let me help you find your boy, sure aren't two heads better than one."

"Usually, I'd say they were, but in this case I think I'd make an exception." He strode back into the cabin and pulled down his bag.

"What are ye doing?" said Paddy.

"Packing. Tis you or me."

"No, ye can't do that. The ship's full. They'll not allow it."

"I'll sleep in the corridor, then."

"Joey, see sense, man. You'll be chained up – haven't they your card marked already for yesterday's showing."

He lifted his bag and Marti's Superman picture was placed gently under his arm. "I'm outta here."

Paddy stood in front of him and stretched his arms apart to try and block the way, but Joey barged past and he was nearly knocked over. "Joey man, I thought we were friends."

"Friends like you I can do without," he said, and kicked the door shut when he left.

16

Guard O'Dowd said he was marching Marti up the road to Mam, where if there was any sense left in the woman she would belt the b'Jaysus out of him with a riding crop or some manner of painful strap. Guard O'Dowd still had his very big hand on Marti's neck when he walked. When Marti didn't walk fast enough there would be a squeeze on his neck and the guard would say by Christ it's a whipping such as never was seen in the world I'd deliver if ye were a son of mine. The bicycle made a squeaking noise from the buckled front wheel and Marti could hardly steer at all with the handlebars all pushed to the side. He felt bad when he looked down at the bicycle, but Guard O'Dowd made it hard to look down at all when he was forever at the squeezing with his very big hand.

There were far too many boys about the place acting the giddy goat for Guard O'Dowd's liking and wasn't his job like throwing apples into an orchard morning, noon and night on account of their antics. It would never have been countenanced in his day, said Guard O'Dowd, when a man would be thanked for giving a young cur a wrap in the snot locker and the streets were a quieter place and safer entirely. These days it was desperate, verging on the diabolical, with all the carryings on about the place making old ladies scared to come out of their homes, afraid of a mouthful of cheek or worse. Guard O'Dowd squeezed Marti's neck hard when he said a mouthful of cheek, and then there was a shove and a jolt and he was told, "Move yeerself."

"I am moving," said Marti.

"And I'll have none of yeer lip," said Guard O'Dowd. "Oh yes, it was a fair old gas at the time, was it not, a fair old hooley ye had to yourself with the fire."

"Ah, you're hurting me."

"That's the general idea, boy. I bet there's not a minute, not a second nor a millisecond of thought ye gave to the people you could be hurting with the fire, now was there?"

"There was nobody there."

"Ye had the whole place in a state of fear and panic, so ye did. Old ladies worried in their homes, their poor hands trembling with the thought of the fire approaching, not knowing if they were to be burnt out of house and home."

Marti didn't believe it when he said about the fear and panic and he thought it was all just a holy show to make him scared, but he was scared enough anyway. He had never been taken home by a guard before and Mam was sure to be mad angry and say it was a hot arse he had earned. Hadn't he only just started at Saint Joseph's All Boys Catholic School and here he was mitching and stealing, lighting fires and being taken home by a guard already. It would be the hot arse for sure. It might even be worse, thought Marti, but he didn't know what worse might be because he had never been in so much trouble ever before.

When they got to Aunt Catrin's gate Guard O'Dowd took away his big hand and said, "Hold up there a minute, boyo." He stared at the rabbit traps hanging around the shed where Uncle Ardal kept the pigeons. Guard O'Dowd was in a fury and said he'd told Uncle Ardal about the traps he didn't know how many times. He pulled away at them and threw them into a big pile on the ground and then he said it's lucky yeer Uncle Ardal is there's no cats trapped and calling for dear life, and wasn't a cat the only companion some old ladies had in the whole world.

Guard O'Dowd knocked very hard on the door of the house and called out. He started to write something in his little black book and said Uncle Ardal had seen the last of the traps. "By Christ, he has. As sure as there's a breath in me he's seen the last of them traps this day."

There were lights came on in the house and when the door was opened Aunt Catrin stood on the step and folded her arms. She had the woman's look for making the milk sour and even when Guard O'Dowd spoke to her about the traps she kept her eyes on Marti.

"Ye can take it up with Ardal yeerself. Do I look the type to keep pigeons?" said Aunt Catrin, and Guard O'Dowd was quiet in front of her, staring at her eyes. "Now what are ye doing with this boy?"

"'Tis the mother I'm after."

"Ye can take it up with me. The mother is unwell."

The guard's voice was different when he spoke to Aunt Catrin. It was like he was frightened, thought Marti. There was a quieter tone about him altogether and the anger was all gone. "He's after having a bit of a burn up down the old railway . . . had the whole place in a state of panic, old ladies calling the station so they were . . ."

"Is that all?" said Aunt Catrin. "I thought it was the Houses of Parliament he burnt to the ground the way ye were talking."

"Ah now, ah now."

"Ah now nothing," said Aunt Catrin. "This boy has a sick mother, I told ye. Now don't be bothering us with the like of this when we have real problems to deal with under my roof." Aunt Catrin grabbed Marti by the ear and pulled him into the house, and Guard O'Dowd was left with an open mouth and one foot on the front step.

"But . . ."

"Go way catch some proper criminals. I'll deal with this one myself," said Aunt Catrin, and the door was slammed shut. Marti was glad it was all over and that there were no questions asked about the bicycle or about Pat, and then Aunt Catrin looked down at him and he knew he was in big enough trouble without mention of other things.

"This is a fine display, is it not?" she said. "Brung home by the guards when yeer own mother is lying through there with some manner of illness."

"I'm sorry," said Marti. He felt the shame when Aunt Catrin said Mam was ill, but he knew she was always ill and it was just the sadness Dad called the Black Dog. Marti knew he had been a bold boy and had well and truly earned the hot arse like Mam would say, but he wanted her to say it and not to hear Aunt Catrin giving out

117

at him. He didn't like to look at her when she was like this because she scared him with the look on her. It wasn't like when Mam was giving out at all because she seemed like it was all a cod, but Aunt Catrin seemed like it was real.

"Oh, it's sorry ye are, is it? Well, sorry isn't good enough when ye have a sick mother lying there in need of the love and comfort of her only son."

"It's only the Black Dog. She always has it," said Marti.

"Oh is that what it is *only?*" said Aunt Catrin. "Well let me tell you there's people have died of less in this family, yeer mother is very sick and may be going up the hill soon."

Marti knew up the hill meant the Cabbage Farm because Pat had told him that was where you went to get your head looked at. He didn't want Mam to go up the hill and leave him all alone with Aunt Catrin, and the thought made him sadder than he was already.

"My own brother, yeer Uncle Barry, was the same way, but then I'm sure you've never heard of him, have ye?"

"I haven't."

"No I didn't think so. Sure yeer mother ran off to Australia and left me to mind him. I'm sure she didn't tell ye that either." Aunt Catrin trembled when she spoke about Mam and Marti wanted her to stop the talking, but she just kept on and on about Mam sunning herself in Australia whilst she was left to pick up the pieces of a shattered family, but hadn't it caught up with her now and no mistake.

"Ye with a sick mother and acting the maggot . . . having guards at the door. I will have to be taking a very close look at how you are brung up from now on in, Marti Driscol. Now take those wet things off by the fire and get to yeer bed. There will be no tea for ye this night. You can take an empty belly to bed, will match yeer empty head."

When Marti went through to the fire, Mam was lying sleeping on the sofa wearing the baggy jamas with the very long sleeves over her hands. The fire was nearly out and Aunt Catrin put a clod of peat on to burn and keep Mam warm and heat the place in general. There were little sparks when the clod of peat was placed on the fire and there was a hissing sound when the wetness on it started to turn to smoke which smelled nice but stung the eyes.

When Marti looked at Mam sleeping she had a very peaceful and happy face. It made him sad to look at her lying there because she only ever looked that way when she was sleeping. He felt like there was a very tight little knot inside him when he looked at her and he thought about Aunt Catrin's words. He knew he didn't ever want to be bold again if it would mean Mam had to go to the Cabbage Farm because he didn't want her to go anywhere. Marti knew he had no dad now and when he looked at Mam lying sleeping with the very peaceful and happy face he didn't want to lose his mam as well.

He wondered why she couldn't look that way all the time and he wanted to know but he didn't know who to ask, or if there was anyone at all in the whole world who would ever be able to tell him. He couldn't ask Aunt Catrin because she was a bockety-arsed old witch, like Pat said, and he couldn't ask Pat, even if he was his best friend, because he didn't want Pat to know Mam might have to go up the hill to the Cabbage Farm.

He could think of only one person who would know why Mam couldn't have the face all the time and that was Dad. He thought about the times Dad made Mam laugh when they were in Australia and it seemed like such a very, very long time ago that he wondered if even Dad would still be able to make her laugh. Marti wondered if there ever had been a time when they were all together at all or was it really just a dream, and the very tight little knot inside him got tighter and tighter and he felt the tears coming.

Marti scrunched his eyes up because he didn't want to see Mam lying sleeping anymore and when he put his hand up to his face there were salty warm tears rolling down his cheek.

"Oh ye can bubble away," said Aunt Catrin. "You'll get no sympathy under my roof. Tis changed days ye are facing, Marti Driscol, changed days entirely."

17

The Captain's Bar was a sorry affair with all manner of polished brass about the place, ropes tied in knots and a big old bell sparkling for all the world to see. A man with a duster in his hand was rubbing away at the bell so hard that little chimes were heard in time with the jerk of his elbow. The place was empty of customers but that wasn't going to put him off, thought Joey. The thirst was back with him – wasn't he pure blue mouldy for a drink.

There were people heading off for breakfast all over the ship, happy people on their holidays. The sight of them put the heart cross-ways in Joey. If he heard one more "Grand day" or "Fine morning" he was liable to kick someone's arse into their neck. A drink was needed and all he wanted was a quiet spot to get down to business alone.

"Howya?" he said.

The man with the duster turned round. He looked at Joey like he was something else that needed cleaning in the place. "Hello," he said, and his eyes went up to the bandage.

"I was wondering, could ye pour me a little one?"

"Certainly." The man was what they call a hard neck in Ireland. He had no respect in him but sure wasn't it a free bar, open all hours, and he would serve drink now whether he liked it or not.

"On second thoughts, make it a large one," said Joey. He dumped his bag and sat down at the bar, gently placing the Superman picture in front of him. "Wouldn't it be grand to have superpowers like yeer man," he said, trying to lighten the heavy atmosphere.

The hard neck served the whiskey and rolled his eyes, left to right. "Yes, I'm sure it would."

"Would be mighty, would it not, to have the old superpowers?" Joey threw back the whiskey. "Same again, fella."

The glass was taken and a refill brought back to the bar.

"What would you go for, if ye could have any of yeer man's powers?" The hard neck narrowed his eyes and glowered. "Jaysus, I am only making conversation," said Joey. Hadn't this one the old laserbeam eyes on him already.

From the mirror in front Joey saw the hard neck go back to the bell with his duster. He could see him taking glances at his bandage from time to time. He'd almost forgotten it was there. It was dirty now, ragged bits of it fraying all over. It would have to come off. He had noticed people were staring more than ever but he thought nothing of it, sure wasn't it the look of a waster they were after checking, that's what he thought. It was how he felt, anyway.

"Hey there, laserbeams . . ." Joey felt a bit drunk. He was drinking doubles on an empty stomach. "Can I have another?" The hard neck said nothing, walked behind the bar and poured out another double whiskey.

Joey quaffed the drink and slammed it on the bar. "Another." The glass was quickly filled and handed back to him. "Another." It was becoming a rigmarole, but was repeated until the third request when the hard neck shook his head.

"What, yeer refusing me?" said Joey.

"You've had enough," he said, and then he leant forward over the Superman picture and added, "I don't want to see you flying like your friend there."

"I have things to do anyway," said Joey, and got up to leave. A route of narrow, winding corridors was followed to the ship's infirmary. There were passengers along the way who stared at him and he tried to avoid their eyes. He felt the shame of what their thoughts might be. The world seemed different with the money gone and Joey thought his place in it was a fragile thing. How could he keep an eye out for Marti now when he was returning to the life of a knacker himself?

121

At the infirmary door he pressed the buzzer for the nurse and stepped back. He wanted to lower his head, point, say nothing – the shame of it all was too much – and then a face appeared, smiling wildly in the doorway. For a second he wondered was he seeing things? With the long black hair and the impatient look in her eyes she could have been Shauna's double, but then she laughed and the vision was shattered.

"You look like you've been in the wars," she said.

"Oh, tis my head."

"Well I didn't think it was your arse." The nurse laughed again, putting up her hand to hide the giggles. "I'm sorry. I shouldn't tease you."

"Ah go way, don't they say laughter's the best medicine."

"Well we've plenty of that here. Come in."

The nurse sat him down on a stool and walked away to the other end of the room. He watched her movements as she hunted for the proper scissors, cursing all the while. She had no cares in the world, thought Joey. She threw herself about the place, laughing and joking, every once in a while flicking her long black hair back and looking to see if her patient was watching.

"These will have to do," she said, picking up a very long pair of scissors with a bend in the end of them.

"Say what you mean," said Joey.

"I always do. The truth is a beautiful thing, that's what my father told me – that there's no point gilding the lily."

"Sounds a grand fella, your father."

"He was. He's dead now . . . but don't worry, I didn't nurse him," she laughed again when she spoke and then she placed a hand on his face. "I'm going to have to tilt you a bit, sir."

"It's Joey's my name." He pulled his face away from her. The cold touch of her hand made him fearful, nervous somehow, he couldn't explain it. "Call me Joey," he said.

"Okay, Joey. Pleased to meet you." She stretched out her hand for him to shake and when he took it the fear was suddenly gone. It was like the threat of touching her was all he was scared of. "Is that drink I can smell on you?" she said.

It was still early in the day and he felt embarrassed. "Eh . . . it is, yeah. But, I'm Irish, I can be excused."

"I hope I won't be offered whiskey for breakfast when I get there."

"Ah no, tis an acquired habit, whiskey at this hour . . . and ye don't look the type to acquire it."

The nurse smiled and let out a little laugh. There was something about the way she laughed reminded Joey of his youth. She didn't laugh like Shauna. Her laugh was louder. It seemed more forced by comparison. But then hadn't it been so long since he heard Shauna laugh, he might be wrong, he thought.

"So you're headed for Ireland?"

"Aren't we both . . . It's where the ship goes."

"Ha," Joey laughed himself. "I mean, are ye going to stay there for a time, in Ireland?"

"My dad always said travel was important, real travel and travel of the mind. When he died I thought I should follow his advice."

"He died recently, then?"

"Last year. He left me some money – he was never big on possessions. I thought it would be better to spend it on something he approved of."

"Something ye would have forever."

"Exactly." She cut through the bandages and let them fall to the ground, then tried to ruffle Joey's hair where it had been flattened beneath. "There, you're done."

"No stitches?"

"I've taken them out, silly!"

"God, ye were gentle. I never noticed."

The nurse laughed and Joey stood up to leave. "Thanks a million, I think I owe ye."

"It's okay," she said.

"Well, maybe I can buy ye a drink in Ireland – a whiskey for breakfast, perhaps."

She lowered her eyes. "Eh, no thanks."

"Oh Jaysus, what have I said . . . sorry, I didn't mean that the way it sounded." Joey felt his face start to burn and when he backed out of the infirmary in a fluster he heard the nurse's laughter again.

He carried his bag down the hall – he felt like an itinerant – wandering and wandering with nowhere to rest, then he found himself back at the Captain's Bar. He peered through the glass in the door. The hard neck was still inside, the bell abandoned, his attention turned to a tabletop now. There were other bars on the ship but to get to them meant walking past the cabin. He didn't want to bump into Paddy Tiernan again but he thought it was a risk he would have to take. On the way there he passed the cabin fine, and then he thought he saw Paddy heading towards him, and ducked into a gents toilet.

When he looked in the mirror Joey saw his hair was all over the place. He looked filthy, a thick growth of stubble adding to the look of a desperate bogger that there was about him. He soaked his hair in water and slicked it back with his fingers but the effect was minimal. His eyes were blood red, little vessels running into the corners. One was worse than the other, but they both had a yellow tinge to them. They looked like they'd been dipped in mustard, he thought. It was the drink, sure it was; he knew it. But now wasn't the time to get off it. You don't kick the crutches off a man with two broken legs.

He stuck his head out of the toilet to check the passage was clear and caught sight of Paddy ambling down the way. "Jaysus, he'd be a good messenger to send for death," said Joey quietly to himself and closed the door, putting his weight on it until Paddy's heavy footsteps were heard going past.

When he made it to the Flamingo Lounge there were one or two tables left in the lunchtime rush. He sat himself behind a large cocktail list and hoped Paddy would stay clear of the place. It didn't look like his type of bar anyway. It was full of old ladies drinking from tall glasses with lumps of fruit and little umbrellas in them. He ordered up a pair of double whiskies and pretended he was waiting on company. He kept up the pretence until all the old ladies had left and the bar was just about empty. He was starting to slouch and he could feel something beginning to dig into the side of him. He touched it – it was Shauna's diary. He figured he felt so bad about himself now that he couldn't feel any worse, so he read on:

I hate feeling like this. I feel all alone. Dr Cohn said I should try talking to Joey again, huh, what does he know? I told him Joey doesn't talk about things and the great doctor told me I was being defeatist. Defeatist! I'm not that, not me. Defeatist is running away to the other side of the world to avoid your problems. Defeatist is diving to the bottom of a whiskey bottle to avoid your problems. Defeatist is giving up on your own life and piling all your hopes onto your only child's shoulders. Defeatist is watching your family fall apart and saying nothing. I'm not defeatist . . . Christ I'm the only one left fighting. So why do I feel so bad? Why am I the one in therapy? Why does none of this mean anything to Joey?

He put his head down on the tabletop. Holy Mother of God, who was it writing this stuff? Was it the same Shauna that lay curled up crying, day in, day out? It didn't sound like her, sure this one sounded together, a damn sight more together than the description she was giving of himself, thought Joey. What was she on about? That wasn't him. He wasn't the bad guy she was making out. He just wanted the best for Marti, better than he had. What was wrong with that?

He jammed the diary back in his shirt and then he drained his glass, and slipped onto the floor. There was a loud crash when he landed and then a man in a red waistcoat and black bow tie ran over and tried to raise him. "Come on, sir. I'll take you back to your cabin."

"Feck off," said Joey. "I have no cabin. Get yeer hands off me."

He let him go and when Joey fell to the ground again the man raised his hands in the air and said, "Irish."

The ground was spinning. Joey wondered was he on some manner of roundabout, being pushed faster and faster, and then he heard a woman's voice. "He's okay. You can leave him with me." It was the nurse again. "Can you get up, do you think?" she said.

The nurse and the man in the red waistcoat lifted Joey to his feet and walked him to the door of the Flamingo Lounge. "I can manage from here, Phil. Thanks a lot," she said.

"Where are we going?" said Joey. "I have no cabin . . . no money, no wife, no son – he was taken by her, you know."

"Okay, I hear you. There's a bed in the infirmary you can have. Do you think you can make it there?"

"No problem."

Joey walked holding onto her, occasionally lolling from side to side, sometimes keeling right over entirely, always profuse with apologies and gratitude. When they made it to the infirmary he felt the brightness of the lights burning his eyes – the room smelled so clean it made him feel faint – then he crashed on the bed.

125

The nurse stretched a blanket over him, tucked it in around his sides and then she sat down, staring at his face. She put a hand on Joey's forehead, then removed it as though it felt nothing special. She brushed his hair from his eyes, and then she said, "Why do you drink like that? Why would you do it to yourself?"

18

Mam didn't work or have a job and would wear the baggy jamas with the very long sleeves over her hands all the time. Sometimes after school when Marti came home Mam would still be in the jamas and he would know she had had a day spent in bed or curled up on the sofa with the sadness Dad called the Black Dog.

Aunt Catrin said it was a trip up the hill was needed and wouldn't that see an end to the days spent curled up with the sour puss. She said their brother Barry had left it too late to get himself up the hill. He was beyond the beyonds by the time they took him in, and look how he ended. Aunt Catrin said she wouldn't suffer another indignity of the like and she would see the rest of her family laid to rest in consecrated ground for sure. It would be the Cabbage Farm for Mam soon enough if the Black Dog stayed, thought Marti.

Aunt Catrin brought him a slab of porridge out of the drawer for breakfast. It was cold and hard with no taste but when Marti pushed it aside Aunt Catrin said boys who brought guards to the door had no call to pick and choose. He took the slab of porridge back and when he was finished Aunt Catrin said it was time to be making tracks to the school or it's late he would be and wouldn't the brothers tan his hide a darker shade of red for every minute past the morning bell he was.

Marti put on his coat and scarf and then the shoes with the crack right across the sole that let in all the water. They were very damp and made him pull a face when he put them on.

"Why with the face?" said Aunt Catrin.

"No face."

"You've a face on you as long as today and tomorra. Is it them shoes?"

"No, the shoes are fine," said Marti, and he forced his feet into the dampness. One of the shoes seemed bigger and colder than usual and when he looked down there was a little puddle on the floor, along with an entire shoe sole.

"Oh Jaypers, ye have burst the shoe," said Aunt Catrin. Marti looked at the shoe dangling over his foot and thought it was quite funny and started to laugh, but Aunt Catrin said it was no laughing matter. "What are ye going to wear now?"

"I could stay home," said Marti, "till they're mended."

"That will be right. You'll go to school barefoot before I'll have them brothers knocking on my door like the guards."

Marti didn't want to go to school barefoot like the knackers who begged for chips at lunchtime and would follow you around if you had an apple saying, "*Please the core, mister. Please the core, mister.*" The barefoot boys were always being teased and bullied and nobody ever had a knacker for a friend, apart from Colm Casey who was soft in the head and would cry if the ball hit him on the leg or if he didn't get to pee down the hole at the end of the toilet row in the boys' jacks.

"I could wear my runners," said Marti.

"Ye can't wear plimsolls. It will have to be something else."

Aunt Catrin said her friend from the bingo, Dora Foley, had brought round some shoes that were never worn because now she had the gout and couldn't get them on. Aunt Catrin said they were grand shoes for a boy and nobody would know they were ladies shoes because weren't they lace-ups and black like every other pair of boys' shoes in the entire school.

"I'll be teased," said Marti when Aunt Catrin brought out the shoes from the hall press.

"Try them on," she said.

He put his feet into the shoes and said they were too big, but Aunt Catrin kneeled down and pressed the front of them to find his toe. "Won't ye grow into them."

"But they're ladies' shoes and they don't even fit." Marti started to curl up his lip and breathe hard down through his nose when he thought about having to wear the shoes to school.

"Let's see ye walk up and down there," said Aunt Catrin, and Marti did as he was told. He walked up and down with the heels of the shoes flapping down onto the carpet and making a noise like there was a big old sniffing dog about the place. "Pick up them feet," said Aunt Catrin.

"I am. They're too big. I told you they were too big."

"Now stop the bellyaching, sure sacrifices have to be made." Aunt Catrin told Marti to collect an old newspaper from the kitchen press and bring it through and when he brought it she started to tear up strips of newspaper and poke them into the toes of the shoes. "There now, aren't they a grand fit," she said.

"I don't like them," said Marti.

"Well, I didn't ask if ye liked them. Do they fit or don't they?"

Marti walked up and down and the heels of the shoes weren't flapping onto the carpet or making a noise anymore.

"My toes are in the middle and the shoes are all curling up, look," he said.

"Ah sure that's a minor sacrifice now."

"But look, *look,* they're curling up."

"Ah, sure now, a man running for a bus would never notice that."

"I don't like them."

"Won't they just have to do. They will be a sight warmer than the last lot with the gaping big hole in them. Won't they do ye grand for the school. Now get a jig on and get off to the school or it's more complainers I'll have at my door."

Marti walked out on the street in the ladies' shoes all curled up at the toes and had the red face from the shame that was in it. When he walked past the post office shop on the corner he tried to see what the shoes looked like in the window's reflection, but the window was too high up to see his feet. He tried to jump up to see the reflection but he could only catch a glimpse and decided he would have to stand up on his tippy-toes and look that way. When he stood up on his tippy-toes the shoes started to slide off his feet and fold over

129

in the middle, and when he put his feet flat on the ground again they were even more curled up than ever.

Marti hated the shoes and wanted to take them off and throw them in the rubbish bins, but he just stood there staring at them until a man in a dirty cap came out of the post office shop and lifted the dirty cap off to scratch his head.

"My, that's a fine pair of shoes ye have there, sonny. It'll be off picking winkles ye are." The man started laughing, and Marti wanted to kick him right in the shins with the pointy end of the shoes but he just walked away and left the man laughing in the street behind him.

He knew all the boys at school would be at the laughing when they saw the shoes and he didn't want to go at all.

When he got to Pat's house his brother Brendan said he didn't know the circus was in town and won't the clowns be wanting their shoes back. Pat didn't laugh when Brendan said about the shoes, but his brother Kenny said them shoes were screamers by Christ and got a puck from Pat's mam for taking the Lord's name in vain and a clout from Pat for messing.

"Come on, Marti, sure aren't they only jealous," said Pat.

"Feck off," said Kenny, and then Pat's mam gave him another puck, for the cursing this time, which she would have none of in her house, which wasn't known for its dirty talk and never would be while she could still draw breath.

At school the boys on the gate laughed at Marti and pointed at the ladies' shoes all curled up at the toes, saying it was like Ali Baba he was and could we have a go of yeer magic carpet? Pat said don't mind them, Marti, because weren't they all eejits. Some of them didn't even know who Ali Baba was anyway and were only making the joke to get in with the crowd. It's like sheep they are, said Pat, but Marti was mad at the boys and shouted and pushed them away when they came running over to point and jeer. Pat said that was making them worse and then the boys who were banging out the brothers' dusters on the school wall came running over to see why there was a big crowd all of a sudden.

"Is there a fight?" said one of the boys who was after banging out the dusters and had chalk dust through his hair and on his clothes.

130

"There's no fight," said Pat. "Now feck off." The crowd kept coming and coming and soon there were so many boys around Marti and Pat that no one could even see the shoes. The crowd moved about very slowly and nobody knew what was happening at all until there was a big gap made all the way through the middle right up to Marti and Pat, and it was Dylan Gillon.

"Now then lookit who we've here, lads," said Dylan, and he grabbed Marti by the collar. "I've been meaning to have a word with ye, Skippy."

Dylan had a very tight grip of Marti's collar and he could feel his face getting very hot and then his whole head and he wondered if he was going to be able to breathe soon. Dylan was very big and fat, thought Marti, and when he grabbed him by the collar he felt all the fat up against him and saw the lots of little holes on his face. When Marti looked at the holes on Dylan's face he remembered Pat said they were the chicken pox scars but didn't they make his face look just like a dartboard, and Marti started to laugh and splutter. Pat and Marti always called him Dylan the Dartboard after that, but they never told anybody else because they knew Dylan would be mad if he heard it.

"What the feck are ye laughing at, Skippy? I don't think there's anything to laugh about, do you?" said Dylan, but Marti couldn't stop the laughter coming.

He tried to speak but Dylan's grip was too tight and then Pat spoke for him, shouting in a very loud voice, "Dartboard . . . your face is like a dartboard, Dylan." There was laughing and jeering and all the boys pointed at Dylan and shouted, "*Dartboard. Dartboard. Dartboard.*"

"You're feckin dead, Kelly," said Dylan, and he pushed Marti onto the ground. There were too many boys in the crowd and Pat had nowhere to go when Dylan grabbed him and started the punching and Pat was knocked over.

"You're dead, Kelly. I'll kill ye for that, so I will," said Dylan.

The crowd pushed each other round and round to try and see Dylan punching at Pat. When Marti got up he had to fight his way through the crowd to get to his friend. When he saw Dylan sitting on top of Pat and the punching he was very mad and ran over,

131

screaming and wailing with no words at all. When Dylan turned round to see who was at the racket, Marti swung back his foot and brought it down with a kick. The ladies' shoes made no noise at all when they landed in Dylan's very fat belly, but Dylan let out a cry and Marti kept at him, kicking and kicking until Dylan got up and tried to run away into the crowd. Dylan was at the crying when he ran away and all the boys of Saint Joseph's shouted, "*Dartboard. Dartboard. Dartboard*," after him.

"Marti, them shoes are mighty," said Pat.

"Do you reckon?"

"I do so. Yeer the best fighter in the entire school with them shoes on. There'll be nobody messing with the likes of you now."

There was cheering and shouting and the noise of Dylan's crying, and Marti thought he was a great hero to every one of the boys. Pat had a big old smile on his face and pointed with all the others and there was whistling and clapping, and then there were boys running off in all directions and Brother Aloysius and the prefects appeared.

"Driscol," said the brother, "and Kelly. Well I might have known, isn't it a fine pair ye make together."

Brother Aloysius grabbed Marti and Pat by the ears, one in each of his hands, and led them back to the very big building, all painted white, with a big white cross on the front.

19

The nurse was called Helen and on their first meeting she had talked about her father into the night, which made Joey embarrassed. She would say something about how grand her old fella was and then she'd look over at Joey as if he was supposed to say something similar about his father. It was never going to happen, though, come hail, rain or high water. He had nothing good to say about Emmet Driscol, that was for sure and certain.

The weeks had flown by with him staying in the infirmary's spare bed and only venturing out to eat a couple of times a day. With so many happy people about, he didn't want to put his miserable features on display for any longer than he had to.

Helen became Joey's one source of proper contact for the remaining weeks of the voyage. He felt like a prisoner in a cell, counting off the days until he could see his son again. The nurse became more like a priest then, listening to all his tales of woe and nodding away with that sympathetic smile of hers. She wasn't one to pry, she was too well mannered and too nice for that, but she would hint. It was like she sensed there was some mighty tension between Joey and Emmet, something she thought was wrong and should be fixed. She said that Joey should speak to his father, for his own sake. But she didn't know him, she was mixing him up with her own old fella, who sounded all right. With a father like hers, thought Joey, he mightn't be in this fix; with a father like hers, with a wife with no

133

Black Dog, with no memory of . . . well, sure there were a lot of ifs, were there not.

"Do you not miss him? He's your father after all," she said.

Joey knew this old song. He had heard it sung to him many times before, but the tune of it coming from the nurse's mouth still caught him off guard.

"God, I far from miss him . . ." The idea rattled him. Hadn't he more important things to be thinking of – his own son for starters, who he did care about.

Helen folded her arms and wore a seriously concerned look. "Don't you think you should try patching things up? This could be your ideal chance."

"No way." Joey simply wasn't having it. "That man can rot in Hell for all I care."

"Why have you so much hostility towards him? He's your father."

"It might come as a shock to you, but the entire population of the world isn't blessed with the best of fathers like your own self."

"My father's dead," she said. Her voice cut into Joey.

"I didn't mean anything . . . I'm sorry. Look, I'm only jealous, sure I wish mine was dead too." It was a bad attempt at mending his mistake, the wrong place for humour entirely.

"That's not even funny."

"Sorry." He knew it was the stress he was under – joking was his way of dealing with it – but he would have to keep it together a bit better than this. She was only trying to help, wasn't she grieving as well and trying to help herself, sure. He knew he should try to give her a little sympathy. "I have what you might call some issues with my old fella . . . It goes way back, there's nothing you could do about it and it's beyond me turning up at his door with a pouch of his favourite baccy and a glad hand."

"What issues?" Her voice was low and attentive. Her eyes never moved. She was doing the old bedside manner bit. It was effective, thought Joey. She did it well, he'd give her that.

"It's not something I think we should be dredging up now."

"No, tell me. These sorts of things are best out in the open. You can't lock away your scars, forget they exist. They have to be resolved

134

or they haunt you forever – whether you admit it or not – it's the truth."

Joey paused, thought about what to say. He'd had a lot of time to think about things like this just lately, but he didn't know where to start – sure wasn't it all an issue. "Well, for starters . . . he never accepted me as his son. I was a mighty disappointment to him and he never tired of letting me know."

"How do you mean?"

"He was this grand hurling player and, ye know . . . a drinker, a hardman. And I was this kid with his nose in a book the whole while. I was no use to him. He wanted another little Emmet Driscol to mould."

"All parents try to mould their children . . . in their own way."

Joey resented being lobbed in with the likes of his father. "Rubbish, I would never treat Marti the way he was with me." He jumped to his feet. "I don't want to talk about this any more."

"Joey."

"No. I mean it. Conversation over. Leave me be."

Her eyes were wide. Her mouth was frozen in an arrow point. Joey had seen this face before, it was hurt. Hadn't he managed to bring some more hurt into the world.

"I'm sorry," she said.

"No, tis me. My wife has taken my son from me. She took the boy to hurt me. I don't know what manner of fiery hoops she'll make me jump through when I find her and I'm all wound up."

Her look suddenly changed, turned glacier cold. "I don't believe you."

"What . . . It's true. It's all true," said Joey.

"I don't mean that . . . I mean your wife has nothing to do with it. It's you. Maybe she took the boy to wake you up, not to hurt you, to make you look at yourself."

"What . . . what are you saying?" Joey felt mixed up inside. He had thought he was doing the right thing talking to her – wasn't that what she wanted? It should have made her feel better to see she wasn't the only one with problems, surely. No, he was in the right here, and unless he was missing something, really missing something, then she had no right to be going off at him. "I think you should leave now," he said.

Helen leaned back from him, then stood up. "You need help."

"Help. Is that what I need, is it? And that would be help with what?"

"That I don't know. I'm only a nurse. Goodbye, Joey."

In the morning when he woke Joey checked his face in the mirror. There was no way he was heading out of the infirmary looking like a knacker. He ran a comb through his hair, smoothed down some stray ends on his crown and smiled. It was on instinct, there was no thought or feeling behind it, and then he realised that he wanted a drink. He stared at the smile on his face for a moment. Then the smile slipped away as he remembered why he was on the boat in the first place, to find Marti, to make sure the boy was safe.

He felt a sinking inside of him. He was codding himself. He knew what they would say back in Kilmora – Joey Driscol, wasn't he fond of a few scoops, lick it off a scabby leg, so he would. He couldn't face the look of himself in the mirror, wouldn't he find out soon enough what they would say in Kilmora. The boat was getting in tomorrow. He slapped himself on the head. "Eeejit. Get a grip, man."

There were parties going off all over the ship. Women in evening dresses smelling like the perfume counter at Clerys, men in dinner suits, rivers of drink running wild. Joey didn't share their enthusiasm. Tomorrow would be judgement day for him.

He fought his way through the crowd of dancing bodies to the bar. People were lined up three or four rows deep, calling for drinks. It was like New Year's Eve. He couldn't grudge them a celebration on the last day of their voyage, but he didn't feel like joining them. His mind was full of fears. His head felt like a jar of wasps had been released in it, every now and then a sting landing on some nerve or other.

It had been ten years since Joey had left Kilmora on that wet May morning in '68 but it could feel as close as yesterday when he thought of it. He had tried not to think about the day Shauna and himself set sail for Australia, looking for a new life. He remembered the tears in her eyes as she watched the land turn to a speck on the horizon. He had wondered why she was crying after what they had just been through and he still wondered yet. There could be nothing worse than returning to Kilmora, he thought. There could be nothing worse than facing the very people who had poured scorn on the pair of them, people like the mighty Emmet Driscol, who had as good as cast them out himself. But wasn't that just what he was facing now?

He remembered things had worsened in the days before they left. The whole village knew they were going and had decided it was the time to speak their minds. Wherever they went people stopped in the street, staring and shaking their heads; it was Joey's way to face them down but Shauna wanted none of it. His blood was curdling with them but Shauna was the strong one. Even when there were cigarette butts thrown down before them, or names called out that were so harsh people spat to cleanse their mouths after, she would grab him back and say, "Leave it. Just leave it. Will be over soon."

Those last days were long ones. Joey had wondered would he make it through without hitting back, doing some serious harm. There was always some cruel act, some senseless jibe, but Shauna contended with them all. He still admired the way she held her head up, floated above them all. Only one thing – the sight of young children pulled to their mothers – got to her, and later it brought her to tears when they were alone together. The older ones calling out names she could handle, even let Joey deliver a fong to the arse of any cur that was old enough to know better. But when they were both staying with her brother Barry and someone scrawled the word DAMNED on his doorstep, it sent her over.

"Tis too much, Joey. Tis all too much," she said when she saw the word.

Joey knew it was only chalked there by some child who had heard the grown-ups talking. "It's only kids messing," he said.

"No, it's what they think of us now. We're nothing . . . we don't exist." She was on her knees in the street for all to see. It was what they had wanted. She rubbed and rubbed at the step with her coat sleeve.

"Stop, Shauna. Come away in." There was a crowd formed to watch. Her tears were falling on the step and being smeared into the jagged letters. "Tis a holy show you're making of us," said Joey.

"Is that what ye think I am now?" she said.

"No, Shauna." She was better than them all; she had borne the taunts with dignity until now. It was all a heartscald to see her brought to her knees before them. What had they done to her? She was once so full of life, more full of it than anyone. It struck Joey deep to see her this way. He could never think less of her for it though, only more. Wasn't she worth more than he deserved entirely?

"You are ashamed of me as well, are ye?" she said.

"No. No . . . now stop. This is what they want, to see you broken."

"Well let them look." Shauna kept at the rubbing. Her coat was wearing to a hole, her palm was bleeding on the step as she forced it back and forth, back and forth. "Let them see me, it's broken I am now, are they happy? Are they happy now?"

Joey put his arms under her and lifted her back indoors. She screamed out, "No. No."

"Yes, Shauna, will be over soon like ye say."

"No. Joey, no . . . It will never be over," she said. There were tears rolling over her face, and then she buried her head in her bloodied and blackened hands. Her sobbing was silent, like all the noise was inside her, wrapped up inside the pain, unable to get out. When she removed her hands and tipped back her head, Joey looked at her face, smeared in blood and dirt, and wondered what to do. Her mouth was open. She was trying to wail but was unable, her screams stayed trapped in her. She was hollow, there was nothing left but the deepest misery inside her, and he knew it.

A hand was planted on Joey's shoulder. "Jaysus, tis a face like a constipated greyhound ye have," said a voice, and when he turned around Paddy Tiernan was standing there with a smile for all the world to see.

"What do you want?" said Joey.

"That's a fine welcomer is it not. I was about to buy ye a drink."

"Tis a free bar."

"Ah true, but the thought was there."

Joey fought an urge to tell Paddy a brain was needed for any manner of thought, and then he was glad when the urge passed and he kept it to himself.

"I hear ye were whisked away by the pretty little nurse, you low dog ye."

"It's not what you think, Paddy."

"Oh sure no, sure no . . . but keep in, Joey, keep in." Paddy laughed loudly and people turned round to see the source of the noise. It quietened Paddy down and then he started sticking his tongue out at the staring faces. Joey saw his chance and disappeared into a gap at the bar.

"Ah, Joey man," shouted Paddy. "I haven't forgotten and I won't forget sure . . . I still owe ye."

Joey nodded, pressed on to the bar. There were people starting to swallow up the gap between himself and Paddy, who got up on his toes and shouted, "And my offer is still there. Two heads are better than one, remember!"

"No thanks," said Joey. He was delighted to see Paddy cut adrift in the crowd. He collected his glass and slid away from the bar and Paddy. There was serious drinking to be done, alone.

20

"It's a fine pair ye make indeed. Well, we'll see how fine ye are when it's a cane ye feel flying across yeer bony arses, will we not," said Brother Aloysius. "I'll have the Devil lashed out of ye this day, so I will, for this behaviour is becoming a habit to ye both."

Brother Aloysius led Marti and Pat into Brother Michael's office where they would see the cane fly this day for sure and for certain. When they arrived there was no sign of Brother Michael, only Brother Declan, who sat in his chair with the gym shoes like the tennis players wear up on the big old desk.

"Where's Brother Michael?" said Brother Aloysius. "I have two here ready for the caning of their lives."

"Ah, tis a hospital visit – the old legs – won't he be back later on," he said. "I'm minding the place in his absence. What's the story with this pair, now?"

"This pair of curs, Brother Declan, are only after whipping up the entire school into a state of insurrection, beating young Gillon to a pulp and sending him fleeing for dear life, the arse hanging out the back of him, and a power of boys laughing like it was an episode of the Benny Hill Show."

Brother Declan swung his feet down from the big old desk and stood up. "Driscol, is it a report ye are after this day?" he said. A report was very bad; Marti knew only the worst boys went on a report. There were always brothers saying when a boy goes on a report tis the

140

end of them in this school entirely, because won't their names forever be on the lips of the brothers in the tea room. Marti didn't want to go on a report because he didn't want to be one of the very worst boys, and he told Brother Declan he was sorry and he felt the water in his eye for the trouble he was in.

"Shouldn't ye have thought about that before ye ran amok with this one." Brother Declan looked at Pat, and then he let fly with his hand across Pat's face and there was a wail from the pain of it. When Marti looked over, Pat had blood coming from his nose and Brother Declan was shaking his head. "Tis the Devil ye Kellys have in you. I beat it out of your brothers and I'll beat it out of you, so I will."

Brother Aloysius looked at Pat, who had the blood coming out his nose, and the brother's mouth was open very wide but there were no words said at all for a long time until his thin little lips started to quiver. "I-I-I think I can leave this pair in your capable hands now," he said.

"Grand so," said Brother Declan, and then he said these maggots would be returned later, in a better state than he found them.

The brother took out the longest cane in the rack and bent it between both his hands to show the give in it. The cane was very thick, thought Marti, and when the brother told the boys to bend over he felt like a big gap had appeared in his chest and his heart had been removed entirely. Marti's head felt very light, like it was filled with feathers, but there was room enough for one thought inside it: what would Brother Declan do with the big cane in his hands? When the cane cracked down on their arses, it sounded like a fire roaring, and then there were screams and tears from the pain of it. Pat's nose dripped blood onto the carpet whilst the cane came down and when the brother stopped the thrashing there was a dark stain left where the blood was.

"Right the pair of ye, move," said Brother Declan. "Tis just the start of it for yees. You will learn proper behaviour this day sure as eggs is eggs." Marti could hardly walk with the soreness which felt as hot as any hearth. He wondered if the pain would ever stop, and when he looked at Pat he saw him walking very slowly, with his legs sticking out to the sides like some manner of crab. Brother Declan led them to the main hall where his own boys were waiting to go in for the games. The boys looked at Marti and Pat like they were wondering why they were there and then Brother Declan said, "God bless us and save us, is it mocking me yees are – *get in*!"

The boys ran inside to change for the games and Brother Declan blew his whistle hard and said the timer was on them. Marti and Pat stood staring at the brother and Marti wanted to know what would happen next. Pat's nose had stopped the bleeding but he still looked very sore and Marti wondered if there might be a sore nose for him to come. Marti had to know why they were at the main hall when it wasn't their day for the games and when they had no games kit either and he decided he should tell the brother. "Tuesday is our day for the games, Brother," he said. "We have no kit."

"Are ye being facetious?" said Brother Declan. Marti didn't know what being facetious meant, but he thought it must have been something bad because the brother looked mad angry when he said it. Marti thought there would be a sore nose coming for sure if he said another word. Marti and Pat looked at each other and said nothing and then the brother spoke again. "You are a pair of dopes, do you know that? The clothes, boys, the clothes will come off."

Brother Declan said they would do the games in their underwear and bare feet and they could undress where they were. When they took off their clothes and folded them in piles on the floor, they stood and shivered in the cold of the main hall. Brother Declan blew his whistle again for the other boys to come in and when they passed Marti and Pat they all looked up and down and had a laugh to themselves. Marti felt very unhappy because of the shame, then Brother Declan blew his whistle very close to his ear and said, "Move," and he ran with Pat and the class of boys with the whistle ringing inside his head.

When the running was stopped none of the class of boys wanted to sit near Marti or Pat and there was laughing and jeering, even from the knackers, who had bare feet just like them. There would be a short game of hurling, but only a short game, so there would be no messing with the picking of the teams if you wanted any sort of a game at all, said Brother Declan, and then he said Finneran and O'Leary were to pick the teams.

Finneran and O'Leary ran to the front of the main hall and shouted out names very quickly one after the other, and the boys whose names were shouted out ran behind and started to point at other boys who they wanted to be picked for their team. The teams started to get big with rows of boys lined up and then the names started to be called out very slowly.

Marti and Pat still weren't picked and nobody wanted the knackers or the fat boy who was called Beany on their team either. Brother Declan said, "C'mon, c'mon," and started to clap his hands and then some of the knackers were picked and had big smiles on their faces when they ran to their teams and knew they weren't going to be the last one left. Pat was picked next and then there was only Marti and the fat boy who was called Beany. The two teams behind Finneran and O'Leary looked at them with scrunched up faces and didn't want either of them.

"Whose go is it?" said Brother Declan.

"Tis mine, Brother," said O'Leary.

"Well take yeer pick or I'll take it for ye," said Brother Declan, and there was some pointing at Marti from the team behind O'Leary and then there was some pointing at Beany and it looked like no one could decide until O'Leary said, "Beany."

When Marti walked over to Finneran's team none of the boys looked at him, and when he tried to get into the big group of boys he was pushed and told, "Feck off, knacker." Marti had never been called a knacker before and he wanted to say I'm not a knacker. He had never been picked last either and he hated being the one who was picked last, because it meant he was the worst boy in the whole class to have on your team, even worse than the fat boy who was called Beany.

There was lots of jostling and shouting about who would get the best hurling sticks and then Brother Declan said, "Stop that, ye shower of savages, or there will be no games played this day at all." There were too few helmets to go around and Brother Declan said if you have a soft head put up your hand now and there were no hands put up. Then he said he would use *the method*, which was hitting boys on the head with his knuckles to see if they had a soft head.

The first few boys in the line had good hard heads, said Brother Declan, and Marti heard the brother's knuckles on their good hard heads and then the boys started the rubbing where Brother Declan had hit them. When another boy was hit on the head he said, "Ahh, it hurts," and the brother said, "Ah, tis very soft indeed. Here, have a bonnet," and there was laughter from the class of boys.

"Can I give ye one?" said Brother Declan to one of the knackers with bare feet. "I won't risk touching yeer scabby head, though I'm sure it's very soft, I have no doubt about that."

A very tall boy with powdery blue eyes and big long lashes shouted out, "But it will get the fleas on it, Brother."

"It will, it will," said Brother Declan. "I thank you for your foresight, Collins. It must be a mighty brain ye have tucked away in that skull of yours. Here, have a bonnet to protect it." There was laughter when Brother Declan handed over the helmet, and then the method was started again and the laughter stopped.

"Get in yeer teams," said the brother. "We have half an hour before the Mass." Marti had wondered why he had said about the Mass. There would be no Mass for him surely because Mam had said he wasn't to go to the Mass. "And remember the rules of the game: play fair," said Brother Declan. "The rabble ye are will have enough to confess after the Mass as it is."

Marti knew there would be no Mass or confession for him, because Brother Michael had said tis an agnostic ye are, Driscol, and the Church is no place for the likes of ye. Mam had said the Church wasn't for them. It was for the likes of Aunt Catrin, who would gladly spend a day wearing her knees out for a sideways glance from some queer hawk in the next pew or, hope upon hopes, a gunner-eyed approval from the priest. Mam would have the women's look for making the milk sour whenever she spoke about the Church and Marti knew she would get mad angry if he ever even said a single word to her about the Church.

When Brother Declan spoke about the Mass again, Marti got very confused. "The Mass will have two special little sinners attending this day already sure. Kelly and Driscol will have plenty to confess after it, isn't that so?"

Pat nodded and said, "Yes, Brother Declan."

Marti looked at Pat and didn't know what to say and then the brother said, "Is it mocking me ye are, Driscol?" Brother Declan had

144

the whistle to his mouth before Marti could speak, and when he blew it in his ear the ringing started again and the entire class of boys stopped where they were and froze like a lot of statues. "I'll have a response from ye, boy, or is it a wrap in the snot locker like yeer friend you are after?"

"No," said Marti.

"No, what?"

"No, *Brother*," said Marti and when he looked away, Pat was shaking his head, with the wide eyes. "I mean yes, Brother. I have plenty to confess, after the Mass."

21

It was an awful morning, cold and damp, wet and windy. Joey looked out at Dublin's grey streets and thought there would be people all over Ireland staring at the sky, saying it's a terrible, terrible morning – sure it looks like it's been up all night. It was just like the Irish to make a joke of their weather. The seasons ranged from bad to worse – if you could call them seasons; didn't it just get wetter and wetter only. The same could be said of the place Joey had come from just five weeks ago, though half a world away it was the other way round. A gale took the breath from his lungs and the coldness of the day reached a part of him that hadn't felt a chill like it in a very long time.

The second his feet touched Irish soil, Joey knew he was in a very different place. The peculiar Irish lilt was everywhere and sounded familiar enough, but it was somehow strange to his ears after all this time. A drunk did a jig in the street whilst an old tug's horn sounded on its way round the dock. Joey was one of the first off the ship. He knew why he was there, in the one place he had said he would never be back, but even the thought of seeing Marti again for the first time in weeks wasn't enough to stop his mind nipping with the task ahead of him.

He shuffled his way along the wet streets, tipping his bag from shoulder to shoulder, making sure he had always a tight grip of the Superman picture. It would be a long trek to Kilmora, down on the coast. He had no money for the train, no job to go to, and no digs to go to either. He dug his hand in his pocket and looked at the few crumpled notes he had left after changing currencies. There was enough for a few days in a guesthouse at the most. Maybe a week or so in some cheap hostel or other. He would have to hitch in the rain. He would have to be bloody lucky too, to catch a ride the whole way. Nobody in their right mind would go to Kilmora if they didn't have to, he thought.

He slumped through the streets, the rain making his bag heavier as he lugged it from side to side, shoulder to shoulder. He tried to keep moving through it but then he felt himself taken off balance for a second and his feet slid beneath him. His arms were thrown out to break his fall and the bag was hurled onto the wet road; there was a loud clatter in front of him and Joey saw the Superman picture skiffing along the road.

"Bugger it," he said. A little rain and mud was spattered on the picture's glass, which had cracked clean down the middle. "Ah no way. I take ye all the way from Australia and the first day in Ireland ye smash." His heart sank when he thought of Marti's broken picture – wasn't it just a terrible thing to do to the boy, bring him it broken. He couldn't bear to look at the damaged picture and shoved it beneath his arm.

When he picked himself up and went to the wet streets again there was no attention paid to the thumb he held out. He felt sure he would have a better chance of a lift once he made it out a bit further. One of the busier roads or some well-used lay-by was needed for the ride, he thought as he lifted his feet, heavy as boulders, one after the other.

The further he got from the city the more the landscape changed on him. The greenness of the fields was as he remembered it, so bright it burned into your eyes if you stared at it, but the mist-swathed hills were more alive than he could ever recall. There were hares seen running in the bracken browns and soft violets, and Joey felt the tingling of a homecoming inside him. The dry, dusty reds of Australia seemed a million miles away.

Ireland was home and he knew it, but sure wasn't the place he was raised no place for Marti. The deeper he got into the country, the saturations of rain, the fields of potatoes and the rusted heaps of farm machinery all reminded him of his own godridden childhood. He felt the pain of Marti being so close to his own miserable memories. The boy would have no notion of the things he had seen, how could he cope with the likes?

Joey remembered the nightmares he'd had after starting school and finding out there really was a place called Hell. His mam had said it often enough but wasn't it only a word, the way she said it. The brothers had used more words to describe the place and by the time he got to bed at night he would hear the words over and over. *"Hell's tongues of blooded flame lashing spinning balls of fire into your belly; the filth of a thousand putrefying souls filling your nostrils; the disease-ridden flesh and entrails of sinners flooding your very own lungs and the Devil himself, poking and stabbing your eyes with the tips of his burning hot trident again and again and again for the sheer pleasure he found in it."*

The first time the nightmares came he woke frozen to the bed, drenched in his own sweat. He was too scared to scream even, for fear that the very ground beneath would open up and swallow him whole to Hell. He lay in panic for minutes and then he ran as fast as he could for his mother and father's room. He had glimpsed the very depths of Hell, had he not; surely they would understand.

A young Joey poured out the details of his nightmare, and his mother watched his distress with a look of worry, glancing sideways to her husband and back to her tearful son. The room fell silent and suddenly Joey's father shot out of bed like a cannon had fired him towards the boy. His face was red and his eyes were two dark holes ringed in white rage.

"Before God himself, ye better pray the Devil has a place in Hell for ye," he said. His father lifted him by the hair and dragged him back to bed; his mother followed, begging him to let the boy go, but he had the fury of all the ages in him.

"Come crying to me in the night, would ye," he said, and Joey was thrown onto his bed, his father's great hand lifted high above him. "I'll beat the fear out of ye . . . the Devil himself will look a fine prospect before ye come crying to me again."

Joey saw his father's hand fly down on him and when he felt it on him his whole body was shaken. The hand came down sharp and fast. Even when his mother tried to come between the hand and her son, it didn't stop. Joey could still remember his father's huge hand striking him, his mother's cries when she got in the way and was struck herself, and the red print of the hand on him as he lay in bed crying softly, too sore and too scared to sleep, more terrified than ever he was of Hell or the Devil himself.

An old cattle mover skidded to a halt on the road in front of Joey and the horn was sounded. The truck was empty, but had obviously been full of beasts recently, the smell of their confinement lingering above the diesel fumes spilling from the back. A bogman with mud caked on his face and a dirty tweed cap pushed back on his head roared out, "Where ye going?"

"South."

"Get in . . . get in," called out the bogman.

"One second. Let me get my things."

He got into the truck's cab and tried to appear friendly. He was grateful for the lift and to be out of the rain. "Howya, the name's Driscol. Joey Driscol."

"Hello so," said the bogman. He made no attempt to reveal his name, but Joey didn't mind. When it came to pleasantries, bogmen were known to be as tight as a cod's arse at forty fathoms. "Jaysus, yeer as wet as a field. Have ye no coat?"

"Ah, no," said Joey.

The bogman crunched the gears of the cattle truck and pulled into the road. He was still looking at Joey, shaking his head and giving no thought to his driving or others who might be on the road. "Jaysus, without the coat ye must be froze," he said.

"I'm too soon arrived from Australia. I think it's the Vitamin D I have in me or something. I don't feel it cold at all."

The bogman looked like he hadn't understood a single word. "I couldn't stand going about with no coat. I'd be froze. I would. Ye need a coat. Ye do."

"Ah well, sure maybe I'll get one when my luck changes . . . Are ye going far?"

"Yeer not going to put chat on me, are ye?" Two crossed lines appeared on the bogman's forehead.

"Ah, no," said Joey. "I can see yeer a man of few words. Will ye go through Kilmora, though?"

"I will."

"Grand so, that'll do me."

The bogman squinted at Joey from beneath his dirty tweed cap and Joey smiled back. You could grow potatoes on this fella, he thought, in fact roses probably – wasn't he covered in manure. He opened the window and tried to get a bit of air into the cab.

"Ah now . . . I don't like the windows played with. Close it up," said the bogman. "Close it up."

"Oh, sorry." The stench was powerful stuff. Joey wondered would he be seeing a repeat of breakfast, and then he remembered he hadn't eaten. On the ship he had thought missing breakfast was a mistake when he had little money in his pocket but now it seemed like a blessing entirely. He tried to breathe through his mouth and covered his nose with his finger, and the bogman looked far from offended – in fact, he looked none the wiser at all. They travelled in silence, only the occasional rustle of the newspaper Joey had taken from the dashboard with the bogman's say so.

The paper was an eye opener, he thought. It was full of stories about the Irish economy, which was flagging entirely, but sure hadn't that always been the way. Even when the papers said jobs and riches were coming round the corner he never saw any sign of them. Politicians were great at spinning a yarn but sure wasn't the globe awash with Irish youngsters looking for work; it made him wonder what he had come back to. The whole world had let in people like him for the last five hundred years, and just what would they have done back when they had the famine if great starving boatloads were turned back? None of it filled Joey with high hopes, and when he arrived in Kilmora he realised he must have been reading the paper, cover to cover, for close on two hours.

"Jaysus, are we here already?" said Joey.

"Tis Kilmora."

"Well, thanks for the lift. I would like to give ye something but, well . . ."

"Go way outta that," said the bogman, and Joey was happy his gratitude was enough for him.

When he hoisted his bag back onto his back he tried to take as wide a look as he could at the village. There were changes in the place for sure – it looked the same size, but somehow seemed to have turned into something else entirely. Everything was where he remembered it. There were houses and buildings had changed colour with fresh paint, but they were all where he knew them. Most of the bigger houses had been turned into shops selling Aran jumpers and green rugby shirts and silly tricolour hats with IRELAND embroidered across the front.

There were houses he remembered from years back that had taken boarders, now with signs saying GUESTHOUSE swinging above their doors. Old cray pots and tattered fishing nets had been tied up outside the houses to make them look quaint, but Joey thought it was all far from natural. Sure, any fisherman would be embarrassed beyond the life of him at the state of those nets.

When he walked the streets he saw faces he didn't recognise, and some of the faces were definitely foreign tourists. He felt like a tourist himself, like he was just visiting, and then he started to panic. There would be faces he remembered soon enough; this was Kilmora, sure, didn't his own father and mother live here. He felt the heart galloping in him. He knew Marti could be here and he wanted to find him, and then all his nerves were clattered together and he saw a face he did recognise, right in the middle of the village, over by the water fountain and the cross.

22

Marti had never been to the Mass before and he wanted to ask Pat what would happen but he didn't want Brother Declan to say it's a report ye are on now for sure, so he kept very quiet and walked in line with Brother Declan's class of boys all the way there. The church was a very old building with lots of very old glass windows with the pictures from the Bible like they had at Saint Joseph's School. The church looked scary on the outside, thought Marti, but when everyone went inside it felt very calm entirely and the big old ceiling with the wooden beams looked nice so far away that he felt he could float up there like a bubble.

The light came through in lovely rays and made patterns like the shapes of the windows on the floor. Nobody spoke and everyone was very quiet and sat with their hands together and looked at the front to the man who had the collar on like the brothers but was dressed all in white and not all in black. Marti liked the church inside. He wondered if Mam would let him go to the Mass all the time now, because he liked the church so much. But then he thought Mam would say no and he wondered if he would be in trouble and maybe even get the hot arse for going to the church when he wasn't even supposed to be listening to Aunt Catrin when she talked about the church.

All the boys from Brother Declan's class had to go on their knees in front of the man who was dressed all in white and opened their mouths while he dipped a little biscuit in a big gold cup. The biscuit was put in their mouths and Marti wondered what it would taste like until he was told to open up his mouth and he found it had no taste at all. He made the signs that were the cross like everybody else and then he went to sit in the pews with all the other boys. Everybody seemed to know what to do and what to say, except for him. They all looked very peaceful and quiet, even the boys who made the most noise usually, and they all looked like the angels in the pictures that were on the walls.

The church was like nowhere Marti had ever been before and even though he didn't know what to do or what to say, he didn't think it was at all like Mam had said it was. He had expected bad things to happen in the church when Mam had said he was never to go there, but it didn't seem like a bad place at all. He wondered why Mam got so mad angry whenever anyone said a single thing about the church. She got so angry sometimes she would shout, even at Aunt Catrin, and he could see the look on Mam's face when she was mad angry and he knew it was big trouble he was in for sure.

The boys from Brother Declan's class started to shuffle along the pew and over to a little box that looked like a shed with a pointy roof. Marti wondered why there would be a little shed in the church. He asked one of the boys was it the toilets and the boy started to laugh very quietly and said to another boy, "He thinks the confession is the jacks," and there was more of the very quiet laughing.

The boys queued outside the little wooden box and there was none of the usual chatter and fooling from them, and Marti wondered was it because God was watching. When the first of the boys went into the little box, Marti saw there was a small seat and there was someone to talk to on the other side. He wondered who it was on the other side and what was said. Some of the boys spent a long time inside and when they came out, they looked very white, like they had been given a fright. Marti wanted to know what it was they had heard or saw and then he started to get scared every time the queue of boys shuffled forward a few more steps. All those with the white faces had to kneel and pray in the church when they came out, but some of the boys would be very quick inside the little wooden box and when they came out they had the wide smiles. Marti watched them walk straight to the back of the church and sit, looking happy with the wide smiles for all to see, and he wondered would he have the smile or the white face when he came out.

When it was his turn to go in Marti's hands were trembling and his heart was beating fast. He sat down on a bench and his heart started to beat so fast that he could almost hear it echo off the walls. It was very dark inside with not a speck of light to be seen, and Marti felt like he did when he had the bad dreams about monsters and would wake up scared in the night and wondered was the monster in the room with him. His voice was very low when he said, "Hello, hello is somebody there?" A tiny door appeared in front of him. It was slid across very fast and then there was the sound of a throat being cleared, and a man spoke.

"How long has it been since your last confession?"

It was a loud, very old man's voice from the other side of the little wooden box. The voice sounded angry like the brothers sometimes did when a question was asked and they were in no mood for a wrong answer or to wait for the right answer. Marti wondered who the very old man was and what he should say. It was all dark and strange. He could see only a little bit of light from the side where the man was talking from and he thought it was odd entirely for a grown-up to be sitting about in some manner of dark little box.

"How long is it since your last confession, child?" he said again. Marti thought he would be in terrible trouble if he was caught going to the church and eating the little biscuit when he wasn't supposed to even go inside, so he told the very old man a lie, "It was a long time ago."

"All right so," said the man, "and have ye done any bold things since then?"

"I have." He heard his voice starting to crack when he spoke and he knew it was the sadness inside him. He knew he had done bold things because Aunt Catrin had said he was forever acting the giddy goat. Bringing the guards to the door was bold beyond belief and shouldn't he be ashamed of the life of him when it was a sick mother he had in need of the love and comfort of her only son.

"What have ye done?" Marti didn't know what to say and it was a very long time before the old man spoke again. "Have ye cursed?"

"I have," said Marti.

154

"Uh-uh, and have ye been a bold boy for yeer mammy and daddy?"

Marti dropped his head so low that his chin rested on his chest and made it hard for him to speak properly. "I have."

"What have ye done, child?"

Marti knew he had done lots of bold things lately but he didn't care about the fire or the bike or the fighting or even bringing guards to the door. He only cared about the worst thing of all, the thing that made him fill with tears whenever he thought of it. "I have stolen money and made Mam come to Ireland and leave Dad behind in Australia."

"Now, now . . . how did ye manage that, child?" The man's voice had changed and he didn't sound like the brothers at all now, thought Marti.

"I just did it. I am very bold . . . I took the money from Mam's purse when she had the Black Dog and now I've no dad and I'm sad too."

Marti started sobbing into his chest and he knew he was going to be the very worst of all the boys. He would look whiter than any of them and he would be kneeling at the prayers for longer than any other boy. He felt sad and he felt unhappy but he didn't care about the white face or the prayers; he only cared about what he had done to his mam, and his dad, who he hadn't seen for a very long time and who was all alone now.

The very old man on the other side of the little wooden box leaned forward and spoke in a whisper, "I'm sure your father, even though ye are separated by distance, still loves you a great deal."

Marti felt the wetness in his eyes start to overflow and run down his cheeks. "I love him too," he said. "C-can you give God a message, to tell Dad I love him, so he can come to Ireland and make Mam laugh and chase away the Black Dog, so she doesn't need to go in the Cabbage Farm and leave me with Aunt Catrin?"

The man went very quiet and Marti wondered had he said something that you shouldn't say in the church. There was no noise for a long time and then the very old man moved. There was a rustle noise like a curtain makes when it's pulled and then he let out a long breath and said, "I shall pray for ye, my child. Go away and say three

Hail Marys and two Our Fathers. God is great. God forgives ye." Marti saw the very old man make the signs that were the cross before the little door and then he told Marti to go back and join the class of boys.

When Marti went out the light in the church hurt his eyes and then another boy went inside and Brother Declan moved his hand at a row of boys where Marti was to go and sit down. All the boys in the row were saying the Hail Marys and the Our Fathers. Some said the prayers in the Irish and some said them in English and Marti had to listen to the ones who said them in English and try to copy them.

When Marti was halfway through there was a hand placed on his shoulder and a voice said, "Driscol?" It was Brother Michael, and he looked very confused and maybe a bit angry too, thought Marti. "What are ye doing in here, Driscol?" he said.

"I was told by Brother Declan, *Brother*."

"Ye were told, have ye taken the Mass?"

"I have, Brother," said Marti.

"Ye have. Oh Lord." Brother Michael's big old grey eyebrows were forced so far to the top of his head that they looked like they might disappear entirely. Then he made the signs that were the cross himself and called over to Brother Declan, who was still at the little wooden box and pointing to boys to go and sit down.

"Yes, Brother," said Brother Declan.

"Was it ye who told this boy to take the Mass today?" said Brother Michael.

"This boy, yes it was. I hope ye have confessed to the trying time you gave us all this morning, Driscol."

"*The confession too!*" said Brother Michael, and then there was a great sigh and a look upwards and he made the signs that were the cross again, very quickly. "Brother Declan, this boy is from an *agnostic* family. Ye are only after making a heathen take the Holy Sacrament."

"Oh," said Brother Declan.

"Oh. Yes, *oh*," said Brother Michael. "I will have a fine time explaining this to his mother, will I not. It's wasted at Saint Joseph's ye are, Brother Declan, shouldn't ye be on the missions in Africa!"

23

In the middle of Kilmora the water fountain and the cross stood where they had always been. All of the village's roads and streets ran into or around the two granite landmarks and if there was a manoeuvre or an errand to be performed it would be done in full view of them or not at all. Joey remembered the dread and fear he had felt passing by them in his final days in Kilmora. There was always a group of crones in shawls and headscarves, clucking away like proud hens, at their vantage point. The group of them would gather to pass judgement on the village's affairs and Joey knew himself and Shauna were never far from their lips.

As he approached Joey saw the water fountain and the cross had only one slender figure to keep them company. He recognised the man with his head turned close to his shoulder in an unnatural pose, trying to focus on him. When Joey put down his bag and stood before the man he thought it was as if the old raw order of the place had been defeated by this one slight figure alone.

"Joey Driscol, ye old dog," said the man. "Sure I thought it was yourself." It was Old Nelson with the one eye from Gleesons Bakery.

"God above, tis yourself," said Joey.

"The very same. How are ye?"

"Ah well, I could complain, but sure who would listen?"

"You look well enough." Old Nelson ran his one eye over the length of Joey, his teeth like tiny fossils stuck out from his wide grin. "Back from Australia, are ye?"

"I am so."

Old Nelson's look suddenly changed. "Ah sure, will be the sad business of yeer father brings ye back, is it?"

"My father . . . God no. What sad business is this?"

Old Nelson's one eye widened and the black patch on his other twitched upwards. "Ah . . . well, eh . . . I only hear he isn't keeping so well these days."

"Oh," said Joey. Talk of his father's health, sick or otherwise, held no interest for him. Old Nelson seemed to sense Joey's unease and quickly changed subject. "Are ye still with the books?"

"The books . . . God no."

"I don't believe it. Always with the books ye were, a terror for the books ye were. There goes Joey Driscol with another book, tis some library he must have in that head of his, I used to say at Gleesons."

"Ah, tis a long time since I picked up a book." Joey could still remember the power of books Old Nelson had handed him in his days at Gleesons Bakery, the heavy linen covers and the yellowed pages that he had thought smelled of knowledge. He had loved the books. There were no books in his father's home and the ones Old Nelson shared with him made him feel special. Joey didn't think he had even said goodbye to Old Nelson before he left for Australia with Shauna, it all happened so fast. To see the old man now made Joey wish he had said goodbye and thanked him for the books but it also made him feel like he had let him down badly.

"Tis a shame . . . and the studies will be by with as well, I suppose," said Old Nelson.

"Before they got started, they were over." Joey realised Old Nelson knew nothing about Trinity. ". . . Didn't the Bishop say it would only give me notions. I don't think they wanted the likes of me cluttering up the place."

Old Nelson shook his head. "Tis a terrible shame – doesn't life have a way of wringing the passions out of a man . . . and others yet simply walk away from theirs."

Joey tried to look at Old Nelson but his gaze dropped. He had no response for him. "And you? Still with Gleesons, I suppose," he said.

"Ah no, I'm long passed my working days, but sure wasn't it a changed place entirely since it was sold to the Yanks. Tis process this and process that. They make them wash their hands a dozen times a day in there now . . . and wear a hairnet, would ye believe it? I bet ye never would."

"So it's sold," said Joey. He knew he would need to find work soon and if there were new owners about the place his long walk away in shame might be forgotten entirely. "Do they need men?"

"Ah tis desperate for more they are, sure they run the place on teenagers and old women since the likes of ye took off for foreign shores." Old Nelson pushed back his hat.

"Sounds like there's been some mighty changes about the place," said Joey. "I like the sound of my chances."

"Ah tis changed days indeed, Joey . . . way better than when Gleeson himself run it to impress the Bishop, the gicker-licker that he was. There's none of that now. The bakery is very egalitarian in its desperation for good workers."

Old Nelson tipped his hat again and got into a stride. "I'll leave ye to it, Joey," he said, "sure, I bet ye have a power of things to do about the place. Good luck and God bless ye."

Old Nelson doddered as he went. He was an old man but a happy one, thought Joey, happier now than the days when he stoked the ovens at Gleesons Bakery. It was quite a turnaround – wasn't Kilmora shaping up to be full of surprises, he thought.

He crossed the road to a building with a guesthouse sign swinging out front. The owner, Mrs O'Shea, was eighty if she was a day and walked with a stick about the place. Her hair was a white cloud that floated above her head and she spoke with a soft voice, giggling like a schoolgirl when Joey made attempts at humour. She had moved from Mayo to be near her sister, who had packed up and retired to Kilmora after just one weekend's visit. Joey knew neither of them but thought Mrs O'Shea was a real improvement on the folk he remembered from when he was last in the place.

"So, do ye have any room at the inn?" he said.

"Ah, sure there is room but no inn," said Mrs O'Shea, and there was a giggle from her.

"Ah that's fine . . . sure, I have no plans to drink on this visit."

"Is it the one room, or a double?"

Joey fidgeted and looked at his shoes. "Ah, just the one." Jaysus, wouldn't the tongues wag at that, he thought. He was glad Mrs O'Shea was a stranger with no call to ask where his wife was.

When he dropped off his bags in the tidy little room Joey knew he had no time to spend admiring the comforts of the place. He quickly walked back downstairs, where Mrs O'Shea was padding about with her walking stick by the front door. "Back out so soon? I think there's a spit of rain coming," she said. "Will ye take an umbrella?"

"Thanks," said Joey. He gave her the best yard-wide smile he could muster. "You're too kind, really ye are."

The rain started as soon as he stepped out of the door and he raised the umbrella and huddled beneath, pulling it down to hide his face whenever anyone approached. Wasn't it a terrible reddener to be back in Kilmora, he thought. Memories jumped out at him with every step. They weren't all bad memories, some were good ones. In happier times he could have seen himself walking the streets with Marti, pointing out where he learned to go a bike, where he got his first comic, the trees he climbed as a boy and still had his name carved in them.

There were trees he had carved Shauna's name in too, alongside his own, and Joey remembered them yet, where they were and when he had hacked away at their bark with a penknife. He could remember the places he and Shauna had gone to be alone as youngsters, the parks and the benches, where they had laughed and joked and kissed into the night. He could hear Shauna's voice calling him across the street, could see her waving to him, full of smiles for him, her long black hair flowing behind her.

The first time he asked her to come out with him Joey had ran up the main street of Kilmora looking for people to tell. He was full of handshakes and hearty smiles for everyone he met and told them all his news: he would be stepping out with the girl of his dreams. He couldn't have been happier if it was a movie star. A young child with golden pigtails in her hair had pointed at Joey and he looked to hear her ask her mother who that man was, the one who loves everyone, she had said. She looked lovely when she said it, all smiles herself. She had got it right as well. Wasn't the world a grand place, he thought.

On the night of their first date, Shauna had done most of the talking. He was so nervous he didn't know what to say. They had walked around Kilmora, sitting under bus shelters when the rain came down, and after a while she took his hand. It was the greatest feeling, thought Joey. Her hand felt so soft next to his that had been toughened by carrying the coarse and heavy sacks of flower around Gleesons. He felt like a giant with her, and walking through the village he hoped there would be lifter boys galore spotting him just striding about with Shauna, the pair of them hand in hand.

He felt so proud that he didn't want the night to end, even though he knew it had to. They went to get chips for the road home and giggled at a drunk old woman who filled the chipper with songs from Ireland's sad history. She carried a rose she had plucked from a garden and when she saw Shauna with Joey she stopped singing and approached them. The old woman handed the rose over to Shauna and touched the side of her face, then she said, "You can tell when they're in love, really in love, so ye can."

Joey had felt embarrassed and looked away, but Shauna thought it was all so sad.

"She looked close to tears, didn't ye think?" said Shauna when the old woman went.

"She looked fluthered."

"Ah go way, Joey, she was sweet . . . when she spoke it was like she was thinking of a lost love." Shauna brought the rose up to her nose and smiled behind it at Joey. "Or maybe she was thinking her time for love was by."

Shauna had laughed and Joey wondered why she never thought the old woman was being a silly drunk or having a cod with them. She carried the rose all the way home, laughing and smiling, and said she would put it away, pressed in a book and keep it forever. Joey had wondered why she would want to bother with it but later he tried to imagine it was all really true and that Shauna believed it. Later yet, years even, when Shauna had shown him the rose again

161

and asked did he remember, it had only made him sad to look that far back and think about the way they once were.

They'd had some happy times together, sure they had, but hadn't there been bitter times as well. The image he had of Shauna smiling behind the rose suddenly went. This was Kilmora, the place they had gone to the other side of the world to be away from. The place that had broken her. No matter how many good memories they had together there would always be the bad ones to blacken them all. Joey still had a picture in his mind from the time they were the talk of the place and Shauna couldn't go out without crying in the street. He remembered when they were right outside the butcher's shop, people lined up inside for the weekly cuts, old women in shawls and headscarves pointing and shaking heads at the pair of them. Emmet Driscol's boy brought down a peg or two, they were saying, and his wild lass too; hadn't they got what they deserved. It was lovely hurdling the job they had done on the pair of them, was it not, thought Joey.

How on God's green earth could Shauna ever come back to this place? Were things so bad in Australia? Joey couldn't focus his mind, his thoughts were everywhere. The time had come to confront his wife, to get to the bottom of this, find the truth and ask what he had ever done to deserve her taking his boy from him and making him come back to this place.

Joey lowered the umbrella, bared his face to the rain, and stared ahead at a house made of stone.

24

When Brother Michael took Marti home and banged on the door of the house made of stones all piled up on top of each other right to the roof nobody answered for a very long time and Marti wondered where was Mam, or Aunt Catrin even. Brother Michael said this was no use entirely and it was a journey for nothing through sheets of rain they had had, and then there was the sound of the key going in the door. When Mam opened up she was still wearing the baggy jamas and when they went inside there was no fire going and it was so cold Marti could see Brother Michael's breath whenever he said a word.

"Tis like an icebox in here, Mrs Driscol. Have ye no housecoat?" he said. Mam shook her head and took one of the brother's cigarettes. "Okay so," he said, "we will have to get this fire lit I think. Marti, ye can pull out the grate there, save me old legs, which are a terrible affliction I have these later years."

They got the fire started while Mam watched the rain out the window. She stared and stared like she was expecting a visitor and smoked her cigarette down to a tiny stump that looked like it might burn her fingers. When the fire was high enough Brother Michael told Marti to put on a clod of peat and then another, and soon the whole room was filled with the lovely smell of burning peat that would nip the eyes and make them water.

They sat in silence and stared at the fire for a while and Brother Michael said it was a rare and roaring fire which was a blessing indeed.

Marti wondered when the brother would tell Mam about the Mass and the confession, but he didn't look like he was going to tell her at all when all he would talk about was the fire and the grand heat it had brought to the place. Mam said nothing either and Marti knew it was the Black Dog keeping her quiet. Mam could spend days and days saying very little, but wasn't it worse when she said nothing at all.

Marti heard the back door clanging open and there was a gust of wind brought through the house which made the flames of the fire dance and little cinders fly up. Marti knew it must be Aunt Catrin, and when she appeared in her long grey coat with the scarf on her head she looked straight at Brother Michael with big staring eyes. The brother smiled but said he wouldn't get up because of the terrible bad legs, and Aunt Catrin took off her scarf very quickly. "Oh wasn't there no need, Brother," she said, and when she looked at Marti the big staring eyes became very narrow.

"I had come to have a little chat with Mrs Driscol . . . about young Marti," said Brother Michael, "but I think I have caught her a little under the weather."

"Ah now, Shauna hasn't been herself lately. Tis a trying time for her, what with the move and the boy settling in school and so on."

"Ah sure it must be."

"But, Brother, ye can talk to me – amn't I family and taking every interest in the boy's raising these days."

"Grand so," said Brother Michael, and he rubbed his lips together like he was after tasting something very sour. "But first could I trouble ye for a glass of water. The fire is rare and the heat blessed, but sure it dries the throat something terrible."

"Indeed it does, Brother," said Aunt Catrin. "I don't know what you must think of me making ye sit there without so much as the offer of a cup of tea . . . I'm so sorry, will ye ever excuse me?"

"Ah go way now . . . but tea would be grand, with maybe a biscuit. Haven't I a terrible sweet tooth these later years."

Aunt Catrin smiled at Brother Michael and called Marti to help her wet some tea but when they got into the kitchen she grabbed at his shoulders and started on at him.

"Marti Driscol, this will never do," she said, "bringing the brother home from the school is a reddener for yeer poor mother – wasn't

164

the guards bad enough. Is it a broken heart ye want to add to your mother's troubles?" When Marti said no Aunt Catrin said well it's the proper way yeer going about it. "If you was a boy of mine ye'd feel the back of my hand bringing home a brother like this. The kip of ye, standing there as if butter wouldn't melt."

He was getting tired of Aunt Catrin going on and on. She was always saying the same things over and over. Aunt Catrin said it's a silly boy ye are to Marti and she wasn't put on this earth to be minding silly boys who should know better, especially those with sick mothers in need of the love and comfort of their only son. Marti didn't think he was a silly boy because he knew the names of all the counties in Ireland and he knew how long the longest river was in Ireland, which was the Shannon. And he knew how to ask for the toilet pass in the Irish and he even knew for sure now that the little green flower thing on Dad's arm was called a shamrock. Sometimes in bed at night Marti would lie awake and remember Dad making the shamrock dance on his arm and it made him sad because now he knew what it was called, but Dad wasn't there to tell.

Acting the like and bringing the brother home was no joke and it was no laughing matter at all, said Aunt Catrin, when Mam might have to go up the hill to the Cabbage Farm. Marti would have to be doing some growing up in a hurry, she said, or it's some serious form of hurt that he would be doing to Mam. He would have to keep an eye on her and mind she didn't start with the long puss, said Aunt Catrin, because wasn't the long puss just the tip of the iceberg entirely and wasn't the road to recovery a lengthy one.

When Aunt Catrin was finished giving out, she told him to butter some bread for sandwiches whilst she wet some tea. A big slab of cheese and a jar of pickle sauce was put out on the table, and Marti thought Brother Michael must be very important because there was nothing like this ever seen in the house before.

"That's a fine mess ye have there, is it not?" said Aunt Catrin when Marti was after cutting the bread.

"I don't know."

"Well, let me tell you it is, Marti Driscol. A fine state of affairs is what it is. Sure, wasn't there more butter on that knife than on the bread."

"I hadn't finished."

"It's a disgrace, that's what it is, a living disgrace. Can ye do nothing right? And ye have the kitchen table left like some manner of tip – don't ye know that's how ye attract rats? It is, it is, it's rats is the next thing ye will be adding to our troubles . . . and what in the name of the Lord is that?"

"What?" he said.

"That, what is it?"

"It's a sandwich."

"I can see that, sure I'm not an entire fool, Marti. Haven't ye only gone and cut it into triangles . . . what is wrong with the squares as a cut?"

"I like the triangles."

"Cutting sandwiches into triangles is getting above yeerself and haven't ye no call to be getting above yeerself and adopting all manner of airs and graces." Aunt Catrin shook her head and took the plate of sandwiches onto the tray beside the teapot and left Marti standing behind in the kitchen. When he went through to sit beside the fire Aunt Catrin was pouring tea for Brother Michael and apologising for the sandwiches, which she said weren't of her making.

"Ah they will be fine," said Brother Michael.

"I have no biscuits but the pickle is very sweet," said Aunt Catrin, "and I think the boy has spread enough of it about for ye to get the taste of it, Brother. He has been a constant source of worry to his mother and myself of late, Brother, so whatever ye have to tell us this day will be no surprise."

"Ah now, it was more of an inadvertent error, ye might say."

"An error, Brother?" said Aunt Catrin.

"Like I say. Sure there is no way of soft-soaping this for ye; hasn't Mrs Driscol explained the family's agnosticism very clearly . . ."

"Ah no. No. I have the Faith, Father," said Aunt Catrin, "sure tis her alone is turning her back on Our Good Lord." Aunt Catrin made the signs that were the cross when she spoke and Brother Michael's eyebrows were lifted up on his head.

"I see . . . ah sure, that puts a different complexion on things entirely. The family has Faith, ye say?"

"No, *we* don't," said Mam. She turned from the window and threw her cigarette butt in the fire and there were little sparks shot up above the flames. "What is this all about? I want to know now."

"Ah, Mrs Driscol, tis a minor mistake, an inadvertent error like I say," said Brother Michael.

"What has happened?"

"Well, ye see there was a mix-up and young Marti was taken, quite innocently, to the Mass."

"Mass . . . ye went to Mass?" said Mam, and Marti looked at her and nodded.

"And, eh . . . the confession as well," said Brother Michael.

"*What?* How did this happen?" Mam had the fury on her when she spoke and Marti wondered why she was so angry when the church wasn't bad at all. The church had been quite a nice place, really, and Marti thought it was all a holy show over nothing. He didn't understand why Mam was so mad angry and why Brother Michael would even bother to tell her about the Mass and the confession. The only person who looked happy in the whole room was Aunt Catrin, who had the wide smile on her when she stood up and touched Mam on the arm.

"Now, now, Shauna," said Aunt Catrin, "sure tis not the end of the world."

"Get off me," said Mam. She pulled her arm away and pointed a finger at Brother Michael. "I told ye, I gave ye specific instructions, did I not?"

"Ye did. Ye did," said Brother Michael, "and I can only apologise that I failed to follow them."

"Tis easy to say after the event, is it not?" said Mam, and Aunt Catrin tried to get her to sit down but she was for none of it. Her face had red patches all over and her eyes never stopped moving about the place, like they couldn't settle on one thing.

"I can say the brother who made the mistake has been repri-manded if it is of any consolation."

"It is not," said Mam. "It's of no consolation at all." She called Marti over and grabbed him tight. There were little kisses placed on his head and then the brother said perhaps it was time to leave.

"I am very sorry for the distress I have caused ye," said Brother Michael. "I can promise ye there will be no repeat of this incident in the future."

"Oh is that what ye say, is it?"

"Tis, Mrs Driscol, sure don't we all make mistakes in this world – real and genuine mistakes – but amends can be made with honest contrition . . . I can tell ye are a good woman, ye love yeer boy and that is good. I hope ye can see I'm sorry."

"Is this the Church now, is it?" said Mam. "Still making the mistakes, but saying sorry for them now?"

"I'm sure there's been many changes in the Church since ye last had the Faith, Mrs Driscol. I will pray ye can find some peace."

Aunt Catrin made the signs that were the cross when Brother Michael made his way to the door, and then Mam stopped stroking Marti's head and ran into the hall after him. "Don't bother praying for us, we don't need your prayers!" shouted Mam, and then the door was opened and she threw her hands up to her face.

Marti stared at Mam, who had the shocked look on her that grown-ups sometimes say is like when a ghost is seen, then he heard a man's voice he knew say, "Shauna," and when he turned, he saw his dad standing on the doorstep like some manner of dream had just come true.

25

Joey had come all this way for Marti, but wasn't it the sight of Shauna stood before him in her nightclothes, her hands over her face, unable even to look at him, that jabbed at his heart the hardest. She was worse than ever he remembered her in Australia, the sadness not just in her eyes now but all over. Didn't she look a wreck entirely. It was a shock to see her so beat-looking, stood there like some manner of wet rag. He felt like picking her up in his arms and running to the hospital. He didn't know what to expect from her, whether it would be shouts or tears, he didn't know how he would take seeing her again, but this feeling was surely the strangest so far.

Her sister, Old Kiss the Statues, pushed past him, leading some old priest onto the street, and Joey saw Shauna drop her hands and reach for Marti. The boy was grabbed tight but he struggled free and ran straight into his father's arms. "Son, son, son . . . my beautiful boy. God, it's good to see you," said Joey. Marti tightened himself like a limpet, squeezing and hugging and saying the word, "Dad, Dad," over and over. Joey held the boy tight and when he looked beyond his shoulder he saw Shauna was trembling as she watched the pair of them together.

He didn't know what to say or do. He had so many things stored up that he had to say to Shauna but none of them seemed right now. He had started off hating her for taking the boy away from him and then he had tried to fathom why she would ever do such a thing, and then somehow, somewhere along the way, he had got snared in confusion. All he knew as he stood holding his son was that he must do whatever it would take never to lose him again.

The front door slammed, raising cinders from the fire and dust from the grate, and then Catrin walked back into the room. Her face was pinched, her mouth closed as tight as a vice, and her eyes like two black old pennies burned right into Joey like he was the Devil himself stood in her own godridden home. "How can ye dare?" she said. "How can ye dare to show your face here?" She reached out for Marti and tried to loosen his hands that were gripped on tight.

"Can ye leave the boy, please?" said Joey. Marti thrashed out at her with his arms and started to whine; he was close to tears. "For his sake if not for mine," said Joey, and stepped back, out of her clutches.

"It's ashamed ye should be . . . ashamed to come back here," she said.

"Oh, that I am. I can assure ye I feel very ashamed to be back here." He felt his own jaw tighten when he listened to Catrin. He could only speak through gritted teeth. "But what was I supposed to do when my wife is after running off, taking my son?"

Catrin let out a shriek and tried to grab for Marti again. "Leave, leave this house. Ye have done enough damage—"

"Catrin, no," said Shauna. It was the first words she had said and her frail voice was a shock for Joey. "Leave him be."

"Leave him be . . . tis him should be leaving yees both. Hasn't he brought you to death's door." Catrin's eyes burned deeper into Joey. "She is a flitter away from going up the hill, don't ye know. A broken woman she is, thanks to you. Is it another member of my family buried outside the Church ye want?"

What on God's Green Earth was she going on about, thought Joey. He had done nothing wrong. He had worked his fingers to the bone in a miserable job to keep a house and home for his wife and son, that was all. Was it his fault she had saw fit to throw it all back in his face and come to this, the one place surely she should have been glad to leave behind her forever more?

Shauna screamed out, "Catrin, stop. Stop it, now." The outburst looked like the breath had been taken from her entirely, and Shauna slumped down in the chair by the fire. "Joey, give the boy to her. She can take him whilst we talk."

"Talk, what's to talk about?" said Catrin. She was so mad angry that she couldn't stop herself spitting out the words.

"Please, would ye just leave us," said Shauna. Marti started to cry and hang on to Joey, and his mother tried to pacify him. "Be a good boy, Marti, ye can maybe see your dad later, once we have had a little talk."

Marti was still crying when he was led away by Catrin into the next room. He clung on to the jamb of the door and when his fingers were pried free he held his arms out to his dad as though he thought it was the last time he would ever see him. The sight put the heart crossways in Joey. Had he come so far to see nothing but pain? Catrin pulled the door until it was almost closed and said she would be no more than a footstep away and wouldn't her ears be open for any manner of carry-on by himself. Joey said nothing but glowered darkly at her, and then he was left alone in the room with Shauna.

"Ye might as well sit down," she said.

"I'm fine where I am."

"Why did you come here?"

Joey tutted. He couldn't believe she was asking him this – wasn't it his question to ask, surely. "Are you serious? I would think it was feckin obvious why I came here – because my wife left me and took my boy, perhaps!" He felt more confused than ever. He knew Shauna was ill, but did she really expect him to have done nothing? Did she really expect him to just write her and the boy off after what had happened? "It must be a mighty shock to ye, I suppose, to see me standing here like this. Was it too afraid ye thought I would be? Were ye hoping this was the last place on earth I would turn up? Was that your plan, eh?"

"No," said Shauna. She had a look on her face that Joey couldn't read. She was neither found-out nor guilty. There was a hint of shame in her but for what it was he couldn't figure. Did she see what she had done to him? What she had done to Marti? Or was it the same sense of shame Joey felt just being in Kilmora, where everyone knew them and their secret that he'd tried all these years to forget? That he had tried all these years to get away from.

"You just wanted to hurt me, didn't you? You wanted to bring me back here to shame me, didn't you? Well, you've done that. I feel shame for what happened here. I feel the eyes on me in the street, feel them pointing – whether they are or not, I feel them, pointing and saying, 'There goes Joey Driscol. Get a good look at a man whose eternal soul is damned straight to Hell.' I feel it, Shauna, does that make ye happy now? Do you think I'm suffering as much as you now?"

"No. No. No. Joey, that wasn't it." Her eyes were a mass of tiny red veins, tears spilling down her face. "Why does it have to be me? Always me. It was you . . . you made me come here."

"I never did. I didn't. How could you think I would ever do that?" Joey pushed the suggestion back at her. He was having no part in her plan to put blame on him. It was like when he had read her diary all over again – the hurt, the shame and the anger, all rolled into one. She wasn't right. He had tried so hard to be a good man, to fix things after what they had done, to mend the mistake they made in Kilmora all those years ago.

"I killed the child inside of me, Joey . . . It was our child and I carried all the shame." Shauna had never spoken of her abortion. Never in more than a decade. It was ancient history, and there was no point dredging up ancient history, thought Joey. They had made the decision together but it was Shauna crossed the water to England herself. It was Shauna bore the most pain and Joey knew it. Nothing could erase the pain she had felt. He had his pain too – hadn't she done it for him, to save the dream he had for their life together – but how could his pain compare to hers?

Joey remembered the night Shauna told him she was to cross the water. "Will be best," she said. They were on the pier end, huddled together from a storm out at sea, rain lashing the tin roof over their heads. They held each other tight and cried for what she was about to do.

"I won't let ye go," said Joey.

"No, I must," said Shauna. She had taken the notion and there was no stopping her, no turning her back. The thought of what they were about to do frightened Joey but she seemed so sure. She seemed the strong one.

"You cannot."

"Joey, I must. Wasn't it for the best only . . . You will have the Trinity soon and we will be together after. Now is no time for the likes of this."

"But, Shauna, it's our child."

"Joey, we have our whole life to face. A child now would destroy everything, your only dream. What would you be then if you gave it up? What would you think of me then?" She was so firm, so sure. She knew Joey would waver and she took to the boat alone.

When the boat pulled out to sea with Shauna and the child she was carrying, Joey watched with tears streaming. The boat's lights were fading into the distance, the course was set, but he wanted it to be different. If they stayed there would be no Trinity and no future other than Gleesons and the pair of them forever under Emmet's roof. What life would it be, for them and for any child born of sin raised under his father's roof? Shauna knew it; she saw Joey's hopes for them wasted and she would have none of it. She put herself through it for them.

Whilst she was gone, Joey prayed to God for forgiveness, begged absolution for the grand sin committed by them both, but nothing would cleanse his guilt. How could he imagine how Shauna must have felt, especially later on? The way people reacted when they knew she had committed a sin worse than any other sealed their fate. And when the Bishop said no to Trinity, everything had been for nothing.

"I did it all for nothing. I killed our child for nothing, Joey," she said. "By God, Joey, what have we done?" Shauna was so young, too young to carry a burden like it, and it broke her. She was never the same girl again; nobody in Kilmora let her be.

Joey felt the rage fly into him when he remembered the people who spat in front of them in the street, the foolish old women who blessed themselves and kissed the beads and crosses round their necks at the sight of them. They were like lepers, pariahs they were.

Australia was supposed to mend it all – wasn't it supposed to be a fresh start, a chance to put it all behind them, forget about it. Wasn't that the plan, thought Joey. It had worked for a while, then the Black Dog appeared and Shauna became like a crazy woman, picking up babies in the street and bringing them home, breaking down worse than their own mothers when the children were returned. It all changed again when Marti was born. They were happy then, sure they were . . . until she started with the babies again, bringing them home again. But there could be no more babies after Marti, wasn't that what the doctors told her. Why couldn't she see Marti was special? He was her child as well. They could do nothing about the child lost, but, God above, didn't Marti need a mother.

"Marti is your child, Shauna. How could you do this to him?"

He looked at Shauna. She had dried her eyes. She was lucid like she hadn't been in ages, like she was unburdening herself. "I did this for him, Joey. Don't you see that? I did it *for* Marti."

None of it made any sense to Joey. "What are you saying?" he said.

"Open your eyes for once, please. Try and see, for once. I took Marti away from you so he would be happy."

"He was happy."

"No, Joey. He wasn't, none of us were. Raising the boy in an unhappy home with a father who had given up on himself wasn't what I wanted for him."

The words lunged into Joey. He had only ever done his best for Marti. He loved the boy, loved him in more ways than he could count, loved him a million times more than his own father had ever loved him. "How can you say these things to me, Shauna, how can you? I am a better father than I ever knew."

"That's it, Joey, suffocating Marti with affection doesn't make up for the love ye never got from Emmet. Shutting out our past and abandoning your dreams, somehow hoping your son will fill the gap is wrong . . . The boy learns from example and you're not the example I want for him."

It was wrong; it couldn't be right, thought Joey. Even though she meant it, it was all wrong. How could she say these things to him? Had they been stored up? Had she blamed him for it all – for everything – all this time and said nothing, hoping somehow that he would stumble on the answers by himself? None of it made any sense. Joey didn't recognise the person she was talking about. It wasn't him, it just couldn't be him, because if it was then he was the problem surely.

"Shauna, do ye think I am to blame for everything?"

"No, Joey, I don't think that."

"But you've just said so."

"Joey, I haven't. If you don't understand what I have said to you, then you've had a wasted journey."

"What do you mean by that?"

"I don't want you to see Marti."

"You can't mean it."

"Can't I? I think you should leave now, Joey."

26

All morning Mam was at the bubbling with the tears. Marti had said he wanted his dad, that he wanted to see him and didn't want to go to school, but Aunt Catrin said there would be school this day as sure as there's a hole in yeer arse. Aunt Catrin had to make the signs that were the cross when she said arse, and Marti thought she must be very angry to be saying a bad word when she was the very image of piety like everybody said. Marti knew the image of piety meant believing in God and he thought God was great like Aunt Catrin said, because now Dad was back and hadn't the Mass and the confession and the visit to the little wooden box just done the trick.

When he set off with Pat for school there was a cold chill in the air that sometimes turned to mist and sometimes turned to little bursts of rain that were like icy needles. It was Miss Glynn, the music teacher, who was taking Marti and Pat's first class and Marti knew there would be the singing. Nobody liked the singing, apart from Colm Casey who was soft in the head and would clap and dribble along with the others' singing and would tap his foot to the tune when Miss Glynn played the piano. All the boys in the class would laugh and nudge each other and say, "Lookit, Casey's foot tapping away."

Pat said Miss Glynn had a mighty backside on her and wasn't it like looking at two eggs in a handkerchief when she bent over in the corduroy trousers, but Marti had never really noticed Miss Glynn's lovely backside before. He thought it was the diddies you were supposed to be looking out for and he thought it must have been Pat's brothers, Brendan and Kenny, who had spotted it and told Pat it was mighty and worth the looking at.

Miss Glynn's class was always very noisy before she got there in the morning, with the boys clanging on the cymbals and making the chopsticks on the piano keys. Colm Casey sat with his feet up on the rim of the chair and his hands up over his ears and dribbled and then a boy went over and said, "Casey, Casey, there's the firebell!" He went mad and ran around, screaming and wailing like a wild thing. There was laughter at him running around, and when Miss Glynn came in the door with her long red coat all wet and an umbrella dripping with rain she had a look of meanness in her eye.

Miss Glynn threw the umbrella down on her desk and there was water flown everywhere and the boys nearest said, "*Ah, Miss. Ah, Miss,*" and lifted their arms over their heads like it was a downpour.

"I will have no more of this," said Miss Glynn. "Do ye hear me? No more of this." The class was silent when Miss Glynn spoke and when her rust-coloured hair fell down over her face she threw back her head for all to see this was not a day to be trying her patience.

"You, the books," she said, and Ciaran O'Dwyer jumped out of his seat and ran to the press to fetch the books with the songs printed in them. There was to be no talking and no acting the maggot, said Miss Glynn, and the first one to step out of line would feel the sharp end of her tongue. Pat looked at Marti when she spoke, and when Marti looked back at Pat he thought he would run out of the class-room or climb down the drainpipe at any second to get away from Miss Glynn and the singing.

"Now, tis the 'Bunch of Thyme' we're singing, so after me," said Miss Glynn, and she started, "*Come all ye maidens young and fair.*" She played the notes out on the piano and the class joined in. "*All ye that are blooming in your prime.*"

Marti heard Pat singing, and when he turned to look at him he saw him making the words of the "Bunch of Thyme".

Always beware, and keep your garden fair,
Let no man steal away your thyme.
For time it is a precious thing,
And time brings all things to my mind.

Marti watched Pat at the singing and he felt himself start to giggle at the sight of it.

Time with all its flavours, along with all its joys,
Time brings all things to my mind.

It was really hard to watch Pat at the singing, he thought, and then Pat started to poke him in the ribs with his elbow and make the rolling movement with his eyes that he knew meant *go away*. The poking only made Marti worse, though, and then it was too late to stop the laughter coming out and Miss Glynn stopped playing the piano and shouted, "You boys, get out here this instant." The look of meanness in Miss Glynn's eye was all for Marti and Pat when she spoke, and Marti wondered what would be said or done when they walked out to the front of the class.

"Is it a joke ye have, Driscol?" she said.

"No," said Marti.

"Oh, there's no joke, so it is disrupting the class and depriving these boys of an education the pair of ye are at, is it?"

"It wasn't," said Pat, and then he was quiet and bowed down his head.

"No, I didn't think that was it – sure isn't it always the empty vessels make the most noise," said Miss Glynn, and she wrapped on their heads with a ruler to try and make the noise of an empty vessel. Miss Glynn said it was casting pearls before swine she was and there was not one boy who could afford to act the maggot in the music class. Wasn't the Driscol boy and Pat Kelly a fine pair to be coming in looking for a laugh and a joke when it's on their knees praying for the miracle of enough voice to hold a tune they should be.

"Is it rivals to Christy Moore yees think ye are?" said Miss Glynn, and there was more laughing in the class.

"No," said Marti.

Christy Moore was a true artist and a lovely and blessed man into the bargain, said Miss Glynn, and if she found another voice like Christy Moore's for Ireland she would gladly meet her redeemer a happy woman. She said there were no Christy Moores to be found in this class, but as sure as God made the birds sing in the trees she would hear the "Bunch of Thyme" sang properly this day and Marti and Pat would be doing the singing.

She made them sing the song all the way through by themselves and it was so bad that not even Colm Casey was after tapping his foot. There was laughter in the class by some of the boys and others sat with their mouths open when Marti and Pat were at the singing. Miss Glynn said if she had heard a worse pair carry a tune in her lifetime then she must have blocked it out of her memory, because that was truly woeful and worse entirely than hearing any heathen curse or malediction make its way to your ear. If this was the level of singing these two boys had attained after all these years of schooling then she was ashamed of her profession and ashamed for them. They would face life unable to utter a note in tune and spend their days confined to humming and whistling their way through parties and weddings and many other social occasions. Wasn't it just the limit and more than she could bear entirely to think of these two boys giving praise in Our Lord's house when it was like two wounded cats they were.

"I can see this problem is further gone than I thought, boys," she said.

"How do you mean?" said Pat.

"There is severe remedial attention required here, boys, and I will see to it that you get it." There was laughter when she said remedial, which was where Colm Casey who was soft in the head went for extra lessons, and when Pat looked at Marti there was a worried look on his face and Marti wondered what was coming. "Yes, ye will both report to me for detention tonight . . . I will start ye on the tin whistle and when ye can hold a tune ye can go."

"But, Miss," said Pat.

"No buts. Ye can thank me later tonight . . . when I have ye whistling away like a pair of sweet larks."

At lunchtime Pat said it was sick to the back teeth he was with school and music especially, for didn't Miss Glynn have it in for the pair of them because of the old sexual frustration. It was two fine figures of men they were, said Pat, and wasn't the detention for that reason only, sure wasn't she just getting her own back entirely. She could take her tin whistle and she knew what she could do with it, and if she could make a tune whilst she was at it, then it's a stage she should be on and not minding the likes of them at Saint Joseph's. Pat said he was for mitching. He didn't care about the detention, and it didn't matter anyway, because he was going to Italy one day where he would get the scooter like they have on the films and ride around Rome giving the two fingers to the Pope.

"Are ye coming, Marti?" said Pat.

"To Italy?"

"No, Jaysus, on the mitch with me."

Marti knew he had been in a lot of trouble lately. He'd already had the guards at the door and the brothers, and hadn't Aunt Catrin said it was time to stop acting the giddy goat when it was a sick mother he had in need of the love and comfort of her only son. Marti knew if he went on the mitch with Pat and missed the detention then there would be more trouble, from Miss Glynn this time, but he didn't care anymore. He hated living with Aunt Catrin, who was always making him and Mam cry, and he didn't care if he made her angry anymore.

"Okay, I'll mitch . . . but can I say where we go?" said Marti.

"Sure ye can," said Pat, and there was a *yee-ha* noise from him when the two boys ran off to squeeze through the gap in the railings where they could get out of the school without the pass.

Marti didn't really know where he wanted to go but he knew he wanted to find his dad. He told Pat about his dad coming all the way from Australia and about Aunt Catrin dragging him away. Pat said Aunt Catrin was a bockety-arsed old witch, sure she was, and shouldn't she be minding her own business. Pat said Aunt Catrin wasn't Marti's mam and he didn't need to do what she said anyway. Marti thought it would be terrible to have a mam like Aunt Catrin because it was bad enough the way things were. He hoped Mam would get better soon, because if she needed to go to the Cabbage Farm then he would be left all alone with Aunt Catrin and that would be like she was his mam, and then he would have to do everything she said.

"So where is your old fella, Marti?" Pat wanted to meet Marti's dad because Marti had said he always had lots of funny stories and wasn't the type to be giving out like other grown-ups. Pat wondered if Marti's dad might even have brought some presents from Australia, because weren't people always bringing presents when they came from far away places.

"I don't know where he is . . . We would have to look for him," said Marti.

"No bother at all. Sure isn't Kilmora only small and he would have to be in one of the places people stay."

"Like a hotel?"

"Or a guesthouse." Marti had never heard of a guesthouse, but Pat said he had stayed in one in Cork with his mam and dad when he went to kiss the Blarney Stone. He said it was like a hotel, but smaller, and there was more of them in Kilmora than anywhere else in the whole world.

"Really?" said Marti.

"Well, I think so, sure my dad's forever saying the place is turned into the world capital for guesthouses now."

Marti didn't like the look of their chances if there were so many guesthouses about the place, but when they got to the water fountain and Pat pointed to the little signs on the houses he could only count twelve of them. There didn't seem to be too many places that Dad could be staying, and then Marti followed Pat when he started running in and saying, "Howya. Have ye an Aussie staying here?"

Marti told Pat his dad wasn't an Aussie and didn't speak like him, and Pat looked very confused when Marti told him Dad was Irish and had to change what he said to the people in the guesthouses.

"Howya. Have ye an Irish fella from Australia staying with ye?" said Pat. They went down the whole street with Pat asking the question and then they crossed over to the other side and started to walk back the way they had come. In the next place they tried, a very old lady with hair the colour of snowflakes started laughing at Pat when he asked the question, and Marti wondered what was so funny.

"Oh ye will be talking about my new fancy man, Joey," said the lady. "'Tis a lovely man, a gentleman entirely." She smiled when she spoke and sometimes let out a little giggle, and Marti thought she must be a very nice old lady and he liked her more because she liked his dad.

"Can we see him?" said Marti.

"Ah, well ye could, son, surely, but isn't he away out. He's looking for work, ye know. Not one to sit about waiting for it to come to him, my Joey."

Marti and Pat walked away from the old lady and when they said thanks she said it was no problem at all, at all and gave them both a butterscotch for showing such lovely manners. Marti and Pat decided they would wait by the water fountain until Marti's dad came back, but when the hours started to pass Pat said he would have to go home. Mitching school was one thing but missing his tea was another entirely, and he didn't want his arse blemmed by his own old fella, who was as fat as a bishop and put his weight into every lash.

"Are ye coming, Marti?" said Pat.

It was starting to rain again and it was very cold, but Marti didn't want to leave without seeing his dad. "No, I think I'll wait for him."

"What about Old Kiss the Statues? Won't she be sour at ye?"

"She always is anyway," said Marti. "I'm staying for my dad."

Marti stared down into the water fountain and remembered when he had dropped in the coin and made a wish for his dad to come to Ireland for him. He wanted another coin to make another wish and ask for his dad to make Mam happy and chase away the Black Dog so she wouldn't have to go to the Cabbage Farm, but Marti had no coin and he knew there could be no more wishes made.

27

So there it was, he was back at Gleesons Bakery, after leaving the place a disgrace entirely. The little man in the brown suit shook Joey's hand and said he could start Monday week on the early shift. Joey remembered the morning starts at Gleesons were a mighty awakener. Frankie Fogarty, who used to mind the ovens, had told him once, "Sure, ye get used to them, and don't the early starts mean the early finishes." But he knew the early finishes were no good to anyone because didn't the entire working day spent yawning only make you ready for bed at the end of it.

' He walked through Gleesons and there was the smell of bread baking and the sound of the tin trays being tapped into the ovens with long wooden poles. The place seemed familiar enough but hadn't it changed entirely. There were no windows being opened for the men to spit out the white flour below and there was no swearing and cursing heard like there was in the old days when the men burnt themselves on the ovens and started calling for a spanner to take them apart.

When he got outside Joey loosened his tie and lit a cigarette. It felt good taking a smoke and being away from the place, but wasn't Monday week very close altogether. He stared at the big building and remembered the faces that would flood out covered in flour on a Friday night, blue mouldy for a pint, and screaming to get down the dancing for a chase of the old skirt. Joey never went down the dancing because he always had Shauna waiting for him on the Friday night and there would be whoops and whistles from the men when they saw her. When he remembered her waiting to meet him, his heart kicked inside his chest. There was no way she would be waiting to meet him now, wasn't that a certainty. Hadn't she taken it into her head to blame him for all the ills of the world.

It was a saddener to think about the things Shauna had said. He knew she wasn't happy – she hadn't been happy for a long time – but wasn't that the trouble? If Shauna could get over the abortion, stop blaming herself for what they had both done together, then surely she could be happy. She had been happy once since, when Marti was born. With a babe to mind she was steady, she knew she had to keep it together, for didn't a child need its mother there every second of the day. But Marti had grown now, he didn't need his mother as much as he once had and the space he left was soon taken by the Black Dog.

Joey didn't want to think about any of these things. He didn't want to think about Shauna and the Black Dog that had followed them around since they had got rid of a life, a life they had created together, but he couldn't stop. It was like the abortion had been locked away in a box and now Shauna had forced in the key and opened it all back up.

He had thought it would be best to run away from it all, to start again in Australia, where nobody knew either of them, or what they had done. They had started again and Joey had never mentioned a word to anyone about the abortion, not even Shauna, and now here she was saying he had been wrong to do it. She had carried all the shame, that's what she had said, but worst yet wasn't he a bad father. That's what she had said, more or less, that he was playing out his own father's mistakes on Marti.

Joey drew hard on his cigarette, took the smoke deep into his lungs. If there had been poison gas to hand he would have done the same. To say he had been a bad father was like a knife going in him. Hadn't he only ever tried to give Marti his best, always. The thought that he had been a bad father to the boy was harder to think about than any of the rest because he didn't know why.

He reached inside his pocket for Shauna's diary. He still felt a twinge of guilt for reading her private thoughts, but he had to know what she meant. If there was a chance he could find a clue to what he had done, he was going to read.

So, Dr Cohn, what do you know about children? As much as me? I bet you don't. I live with three children. One is a spirit that I take with me everywhere, she is a little girl, she looks like me sometimes, but other times she shows up in the faces of all little girls. She's forever smiling, forever happy, forever my little girl. I call her Alannah, my darling angel. I know I will never see her properly, never touch her, or hold her, put her hair into bunches, or even talk with her about dolls and dresses or other little girls' things. But she doesn't seem to mind. She seems to know I love her and that's enough for me.

Joey put down the diary. His throat was dry and stiff. He had to suck on his bottom lip to stop it quivering. He had sometimes thought about the child, but he had always forced himself to stop. Shauna hadn't. She had thought about the child every day of her life and she had never told him once. No wonder she was hurting, he thought. Why did he never see it? Why did he never open his eyes? He picked up the diary again.

The other two are not so easy for me to write about. My son, Marti, is only eight, but he knows something is wrong at home. He can be such a happy boy, playing like all boys do, but he can turn to sadness, so quickly. He doesn't know why things aren't right between Joey and me, and sometimes he blames himself, thinks he's the problem. He can't feel like this, I can't have him growing up feeling like this. I know he cries in bed at night when Joey and me fight and it breaks my heart. Joey tries so hard to show his love for Marti, but I think he might be better without it. We're tearing the boy apart.

What did she mean? How could Marti be better without his father's love, thought Joey. There had been fights, for sure there had, but never around Marti. He knew Marti sensed his parents' troubles, but he was only a lad and Joey loved him. He never tired of showing him – surely that was enough. When he read the next entry, he froze.

My third child, Dr Cohn, is Joey. Joey is hurting, I know it, but he won't admit it to anyone, not even himself. I have tried to reach him but he pushes me away. For more than ten years I have tried and failed. I don't think anyone but Joey can help himself now. Somewhere inside him

185

he is still a child, running scared from his father, from the lashings and the harsh words, from the shame of never measuring up to the high and mighty Emmet Driscol and the shame of the sin that hurt us all. But he cannot see any of it, he is blinded with a kind of rage. A rage at his father, a rage at the world and a rage at himself. Joey may have failed in his father's eyes, but never in mine. He gave up on himself but I never did, I just can't do anything for him, my love for him isn't enough and Marti is hurting as well.

The writing in Shauna's diary was suddenly changed, fat spots of rain were falling on the pages, making the words blur and ink smears run down the page. Joey tucked the diary back in his shirt and looked down at his shoes. Black dots were welling on the leather. He started to walk into the downpour. There was only one place left to go now, one place which might hold some answers.

The road to his father's home was winding and potholed. Branches of trees hung over the way, creating a dark arbour, and the wind picked up, whistling shards of rain into him like tiny darts. When he saw the house in the distance, it had changed entirely. Where every other house in Kilmora had been spruced up, painted and turned into a tourist attraction, Emmet Driscol's home had gone to ruin. Slates were missing on the roof and long grass and weeds sprouted around the timber staves of the fence. There was grey paint peeling from the door, showing the black beneath, and the lion's head door knock was covered with a slimy-looking verdigris.

"Jaysus, they've let the place go a bit," he said to himself.

Joey scraped the gate along the ground and it caught on an uneven flagstone, forcing him to squeeze into the gap. At the door he knocked three times, his heart speeding up with every rap of his knuckles. He wondered what he would say to his father and mother. Would they even recognise him after all these years? If they did, would they let him in?

He remembered his father's words the night he told them Shauna had had an abortion. He raged at him and called him a murdering bastard, who would be damned straight to Hell. He had said he never wanted Joey to darken his door again and it made him smirk because he thought that it was something only people said in the films. When his father saw the smirk he raised his hand, but Joey grabbed it. He stepped up to him and looked in his eyes – he felt his father reading his thoughts – then Joey spoke in a whisper, told his father the days of laying into him were long by.

Joey grabbed for the door knock and the noise was like thunder in the heavens, then the door started to creak, and was slowly opened.

"Hello, Mam," said Joey. His voice was soft.

Peggy Driscol stared out wide-eyed, with a look that said she had seen death wakened, and then she made the sign of the cross and motioned her son in. The house smelt stale and damp like something was rotting away beneath the floor, thought Joey, and when he looked down he saw the carpet was worn away and the boards were exposed beneath. It was the same carpet he remembered from when he was a boy, and his eyes jumped to see it still in place. When they went through to the front room Peggy sat down and sighed out, then said she didn't know what to say. She looked older than Joey remembered her. Her hair was iron grey now and there were hollows in her cheeks, but her eyes still danced with a look of intelligence.

"Well, it has been a long time, has it not," said Joey.

"It has," said his mother, touching her quivering lips, "that it has."

He thought she seemed more gentle than he remembered, but then wasn't she very frail. "Are ye well, Mam?"

"I have no complaints . . . yeer father is not a well man," she said.

"I heard."

"Oh, ye would have. He is not a well man but still a *known* man in Kilmora." The words seemed to give her strength and the old composure was back with her once more. She straightened her back where she sat, and Joey saw there was still a power of pride left in her.

"Where is he?" said Joey.

"He's through in bed," said Peggy, "tis a terrible strain for him to move about now . . . It's his heart, ye know. He is very weak."

"Mam . . ." said Joey, then broke off.

"Ye will want to see him, I suppose."

"Is he fit for visitors?"

"Go on through – haven't I just brung him his soup. Ye know where the room is."

Joey stood up. His knees were weak when he tried to walk. Why would he ever want to be there? There was nothing his father could

187

say that would change how he felt, surely. Didn't Shauna, who knew him better than anyone, better than even he knew himself, see the damage this man had done? He didn't want to feel like this. He knew his bitterness had hurt more than himself. It was that thought alone which made him turn the handle and face his father.

"*Joey* . . . Is it yeerself?" said Emmet. He was pale and old, his skin grey from the weeks spent indoors. There was none of the terror left in his eyes at all. Joey stared at him and found the image hard to take in. Had this pathetic man blighted his childhood, and still blighted his life yet? How could he feel so much hatred for him? Any hatred he had felt was for another man, surely.

"Joey, come away in." Emmet held out a hand to his son and motioned to his bedside. The hand looked feeble, bony and arthritic, the fingertips purple where his weak heart had failed to pump enough blood to keep the circulation going. Joey stared at his father's hand and wondered could it really be the same hand that had gripped a hurley in the All-Ireland and made grown men tremble? He stared and stared at his father. He wanted to find the words to say how he felt. How he felt when he was whipped as a boy and how he felt as a man when his own father turned his back on him in his hour of greatest need. But he couldn't find any words. All he could find was a mix of hurts and anger rolled into an almighty bolus of hatred.

"I'm glad ye came," said Emmet. His voice trembled over his dry lips. "I had hoped ye would."

Joey nodded but there were still no words found in him. His voice was somewhere else, hidden in the depths of him. To sound a breath even was beyond him. It felt as though he had not yet learned to make a noise, never mind learned the power of speech.

Emmet gripped his hand and seemed to speak for him. "I know why ye came, son. It wasn't for me, sure – I don't deserve any visitors. Yeer sisters and brothers have all stayed away. I don't fault them for that . . . they have their own lives now. But you were different, sure. I hoped ye would come."

Why was he different? Why was it him sat there and not Megan or Clancy or any of the others? Emmet had fathered six children. The idea that Joey had been singled out for his father's scorn hit him like a bolt in the belly.

188

"Why?" said Joey. The word scalded his heart, nearly choked him on the way out. It was only one word, one small word, sure, but didn't it mean the entire universe to Joey Driscol.

"Ye were the firstborn, son, and I was hard on ye." Emmet spluttered when he spoke. His dark eyes were blood red and circled in black. "I learnt to be a mite gentler on the others, but the habit with ye was hard to break."

"Why?" said Joey. Didn't it always come back to the same question for him.

"I had such high hopes for ye, my first boy. I wanted you to be *my* boy but weren't ye always yeer own man. I thought I could win ye round by being hard on ye . . . It was what I knew. I got what I wanted by being hard – a hard player I was. I thought ye needed the same."

"You were wrong."

"I know it. I know it now . . . son. I see it now, I do. I see what I did was wrong."

"Why didn't ye see it then?" Joey spoke through his teeth, his jaw clamped tight. "That was when I needed you to see it."

"I saw what was in ye and it wasn't the same as what was in me, Joey. I wanted to change it, I wanted to make ye more like me."

"I could never be like you." Joey spat out the words. He wanted to look at his father when he said them but he couldn't face him.

"You are better off being nothing like me," said Emmet. "Didn't my flower bloom only briefly."

"None of us missed it, and sure all of us would have been glad to."

"I know it. Now the Good Lord is close to his harvesting it feels like I finally understand. I know why you're here and the others are not." Emmet brought his hands up to his face, tried to cover the tears in his eyes. "You are a very different man to me, different entirely. I tried to shape ye the only way I knew how, but I was wrong. Ye cannot mould a child, tis wrong to try. The best ye can do is live yeer own life well and hope the child follows your example."

Joey looked at his father and thought he understood something of him. He saw he was sorry; he didn't need to hear the word even. In his own way Joey knew he had tried to do the same with Marti, that's what Shauna meant with the suffocating. He had suffocated the boy

189

with love in just the way Emmet had starved him of it. It couldn't work. It was as wrong to try and mould Marti into the man he never became as much as it was for Emmet to have tried to mould him.

"Joey, son, ye have a good head on them shoulders. I always knew that – didn't it only confuse me though. I never knew what to do with ye . . . me a muck savage, how could I?" Emmet began to sob, streaks of tears rolled down his cheeks and held like icicles to his face.

"Don't, Da," said Joey. "Just don't. Isn't it too late for that now."

"No, son, ye don't understand. I knew when ye left for Australia I had ruined ye . . . ruined ye I had. Sending you out to Gleesons when you could have been in pinstripes. When you left, it was too much, too much entirely for me to think of what could have been."

"Da, stop now . . ."

"I was a coward, Joey. Was my hurt pride only sent ye away, pushed ye away like I always did . . . and why? Because the tongues were at the wagging in Kilmora. I thought they were laughing at the mighty Emmet Driscol. Jaysus, son, I'm sorry. I was a fool then but aren't we always learning, right to the end, so we are. That's why it's never too late, son, it can't ever be too late to change, to say yeer sorry. Can it?"

Joey looked at his father in the bed before him. He was exhausted now, the effort shown in his face shocked Joey. His father was wasting away. And wasn't that what he had done with most of his life – just wasted it away. He could see that playing in the All-Ireland meant nothing to his father now that he was dying, alone, without his family.

"Dad, it's all right," said Joey.

"Don't make my mistakes son, *please*," said Emmet.

"No, Da . . . I won't do that."

Joey removed his father's hand from his and left the bedside. When he closed the door his mother stood up. "What is it?" she said.

"I've made some terrible mistakes, Ma," he said. "Some terrible mistakes."

28

The rain lashed down on Marti, soaking his hair so much that it stuck to his head. There were great drops of it hanging off his nose and his eyelashes even and sometimes the drops would run down his back and the shivers would start. It was freezing cold and dark out and Marti wondered where his dad could be. He would never go back to Australia, surely. Aunt Catrin said if Dad would only up and take himself away back to Australia, wouldn't that be a blessed release for everyone and wasn't that what was needed, especially for Mam, who was buckling under the strain of it all, so she was.

Marti started to cry when he thought about Dad going away back to Australia. He didn't want him to leave. He wanted him to stay and tell the funny stories that made Mam laugh and chased away the Black Dog like before. It wasn't fair that Mam was sick and in need of the love and comfort of her only son like Aunt Catrin said. He didn't want her to be sick and he didn't want Dad to go away again. He wanted to be just like all the other boys who had a mam and a dad and didn't need to worry about the Black Dog or one of them being taken away or told to leave.

Marti didn't think his dad was ever going to come back and he didn't know what to do or where to go. He knew Aunt Catrin would be mad angry at him for being so wet and staying out so late and he knew Mam would be making a holy show if he went home. He stared up at the night sky and watched the rain falling in the moonlight and he wished it would rain and rain until the whole place was one big river and he was swept away somewhere else. When Marti looked up at the rain falling he heard someone shouting at him and when he looked to see who it was, he saw the very old lady with hair the colour of snowflakes.

She called him over to the guesthouse and said was it grim death he was after, for standing in the downpour was a sure way to find it, was it not. The old lady took Marti inside and made him sit by the fire, where the peat was burning away and making little crackle noises. She said her name was Mrs O'Shea, and Marti thought she was a very nice old lady.

"There now, will ye dry yourself on that," she said, and handed him a fluffy white towel that was so big it could be wrapped around him more than twice. She gave Marti a warm drink that made him cough when he sipped at it and then she laughed and said, "Tis only a tot added, boy . . . drink up the toddy."

Marti liked sitting by the fire and drinking the toddy with Mrs O'Shea, and when Dad came back Marti asked could he stay there now, but Dad looked shocked and said he couldn't.

"Marti, yeer mam will be worried where you are."

"I don't want to go back there, Dad."

"Why not?"

"Because Aunt Catrin is always telling me I'm bold and Mam is always with the Black Dog . . . I want to stay with you, before Mam's taken to the Cabbage Farm and I'm left with Aunt Catrin forever." Marti started to cry, and Dad picked him up and sat him on his knee. He knew he was too big to be sitting on Dad's knee but wasn't it grand to be sat up on his knee getting the hugs again.

"Dad, did Mam take me here because I was a bold boy and took the blue ten dollar bill?"

Dad's eyes went really wide and then he spun Marti round and looked straight at him. "No, son . . . No way. It was nothing you did at all. Do you hear me? I don't want you thinking that now."

Marti nodded.

"I mean it," said Dad. "It was my fault entirely . . . not yours or Mam's either." Dad looked very sad when he said it was his fault Mam had taken him to Ireland and Marti didn't want Dad to be sad. It had been so long since he had seen Dad that all he wanted was for him to be happy and have a laugh and a joke like they always did before. Dad rubbed at Marti's hair with the fluffy white towel and then Mrs O'Shea said about the toddy and Dad said, "I think he'll live, sure." A soaking to the skin was no laughing matter though, said Dad, and hadn't Marti better be getting home for some dry clothes and the sooner the better.

"Okay, fella, up ye are," said Dad. "'Tis time we got you home to Mam. There could be guards out looking for you."

Dad carried Marti, wrapped inside the towel, all the way to the house made of stones all piled up on top of each other right to the roof.

When Aunt Catrin opened the door straight away she reached out for Marti with her hands and he was grabbed away from Dad. The fluffy white towel was pulled away too, and thrown into the street like it was some manner of dirty old rag. "'Tis soaked to the bone he is," said Aunt Catrin. "Why haven't ye got him out of these wet things?"

Dad's mouth was wide open when Aunt Catrin spoke and Marti thought he looked more shocked yet, but didn't Aunt Catrin only seem to care about shouting and screaming at everyone. "Up them stairs now and get some dry clothes on," she said, "or is it a child with pneumonia ye want to add to your mother's troubles?"

"Leave the boy, will ye," said Dad. "You can save the giving out for me."

"Oh, I have plenty to say to you, Joey Driscol, don't worry about that," said Aunt Catrin, and then she made a long mean look at Dad.

"Where's Shauna? I want to see my wife."

"Oh, yeer wife, is it? Well in name only, sure. She is out pacing the streets, sick with worry, looking for her only son, the only child to survive your unholy union. 'Tis a disgrace the way ye have treated that woman."

Marti stood on the stairs and watched Dad and Aunt Catrin fighting. He saw them stood on the doorstep and the rain falling on them both with the *plink-plink* sound. "I didn't come here to discuss my affairs with you," said Dad.

"Oh, no, ye wouldn't, would ye? I have heard all about your reluctance to face responsibilities, sure." She was leaning forward and waging her finger at Dad. Marti wanted to tell her to stop or to grab the finger and snap it right off but he knew he had to be very quiet on the stairs. "That boy of yours is running wild, so he is. Tis had a terrible, terrible effect on the boy, yeer behaviour."

"Terrible effect?" said Dad. "I know Marti's upset and confused, but—"

"I'll have none of yeer buts – wasn't he traumatised, sure, acting like a child possessed by the Devil himself. If it's not the guards at the door, it's the brothers, and tonight it was the music teacher. The music teacher, would ye believe it? I bet ye never would. What class of cur acts up in a music class?"

Dad said nothing back to Aunt Catrin, only stood staring and staring in the rain, and then the door was slammed hard in his face and Marti ran upstairs to get changed into the dry clothes like Aunt Catrin had told him. He knew he was in big trouble for mitching with Pat and missing the detention, but he didn't care what Aunt Catrin would say to him and he didn't want to see her after the look she had put on Dad's face. Marti thought his dad looked very sad when Aunt Catrin was at him with the finger poking and he wondered would he maybe even cry. Dad had never cried before, but he looked very near to it, thought Marti, and then he started the crying himself.

Marti cried for a long time; he didn't want to go back downstairs because that's where Aunt Catrin was. Even when he started to shiver in the cold upstairs, and even when he heard Mam come back home, he still didn't want to go back downstairs where Aunt Catrin was. Marti was tired of all the fights with Aunt Catrin, which were worse entirely than any fights had ever been between Mam and Dad in Australia. He shut his eyes tight and shook his head. He wanted all the bad things he was thinking to go away, but he knew they would never go away as easily as that and he knew he would have to face Aunt Catrin again and again.

When Marti finally went downstairs he saw that Uncle Ardal was back hanging out the rabbit traps and he wondered if he was still the lousy feck like Aunt Catrin had said. There was very little talking in the house, even Mam said nothing when she saw Marti, only lifted her hands to her face and then sat and stared into the fire. The only time she spoke was when Aunt Catrin asked Uncle Ardal to help with the tea. She said the ignorant bogtrotter had put his feet back under the table now, and Marti knew Uncle Ardal must still be the lousy feck like Aunt Catrin had said. When everyone sat down to eat Aunt Catrin said there was hardly enough of the cabbage and potatoes and a bit of a stew to go around but wouldn't she do her best to make it stretch to the four of them.

Aunt Catrin had very little on her plate at all and when she spooned out the great load of potatoes onto Uncle Ardal's plate, Mam made the *huh* sound very loudly and Aunt Catrin said, "Sure amn't I hardly famished and doesn't the man need a good feed after working the entire day."

Uncle Ardal started eating before Aunt Catrin had finished with the spooning out and Mam looked away with the folded arms and made the *huh* sound again. Uncle Ardal ate very fast with his fork and didn't even touch his knife at all, and Marti thought he was as fast an eater as the knackers at the chipper. Uncle Ardal would smash the potatoes and cut the stew to bits with his fork and scoop it all up into his mouth and then he would poke at the cabbage and cram that in behind it very fast until his cheeks bulged out like he had two great big red apples on the sides of his face. Mam shook her head when Uncle Ardal ate very fast and when she did it Aunt Catrin said, "We had yeer lousy feck round when ye were out."

"Joey?" said Mam.

"Don't get excited. I put him straight . . . had Ardal been here then he would have put him straight in the street."

Mam had no words at all for Aunt Catrin.

"Wouldn't ye know it – brazen he was! But I put him straight, all right. We won't be seeing any more of him I shouldn't think."

"What?" said Mam. She had the shocked look on her face and the wide eyes were staring out at everyone, darting back and forth with the wondering. "Marti, where is he now?"

Marti didn't know what to say to Mam. He might say the wrong thing and get Dad into trouble or he might say the wrong thing and get the hot arse for himself. "He's gone," said Marti. "Aunt Catrin told him to go."

Mam went straight into the hard bubbling with the tears and Aunt Catrin said stop it now, for she had no call to that type of behaviour. "I will have no tears shed at my table for that lousy feck, Shauna—"

"Stop it. Stop it," said Mam.

"I will not. Hasn't he done ye enough damage? Lookit the state of ye now; tis Barry all over again."

"Stop it. Stop it. Stop it." Mam was screaming, really loudly, and everyone stared at her, even Uncle Ardal stopped smashing at the potatoes and poking at the cabbage with his fork to look at Mam. She was red all over her face and even her hands were red where she was banging at the table so hard the plates were made to jump.

"Shauna, will ye control yeerself," said Aunt Catrin, and she was out of her seat and grabbing Mam by the arms and shaking her. "Shauna, Shauna," she said, but Mam just kept at the screaming and the wailing, and then Aunt Catrin slapped her across the face. There was another loud slapping sound and then Mam looked away, but her eyes seemed like they couldn't see a thing and the screaming was started all over but this time sounded even more desperate.

"Oh, Sweet Jesus," said Aunt Catrin. "Oh, Dear Lord." There was another slap and Aunt Catrin grabbed Mam by the shoulders and started to shake her so much Marti thought she was going to fall off the chair and land on the floor. There were more slaps from Aunt Catrin and then Mam looked so tired that she slumped back in the chair like she was almost sleeping, but with her eyes wide open. Marti wondered what was wrong with her and why she had the strange look, then Aunt Catrin started shouting to Uncle Ardal. "Tis Barry all over, Ardal. I told ye it would be," she said. "Come on, move yeerself, quick."

Uncle Ardal had a mouthful of potatoes and started to chew very fast when he was told to move himself. He stood up and grabbed Mam around the waist. She looked very light and easy to lift when Uncle Ardal picked her up and put her over his shoulder, and Marti wondered what he was going to do with her.

"Where are you going?" said Marti. He ran after Uncle Ardal and watched him open up the back door and go to the car, where he put Mam on the back seat. "Where are you going?" said Marti. He felt the panic going through him because he didn't know what was wrong with Mam or where she was to be taken, and then Aunt

Catrin came out in her long grey coat, a scarf tied on her head and a little brown suitcase in her hand. "What's happening?" said Marti, and the panic was all through him again.

"Get back inside, Marti. Yeer Mam is not a well woman," said Aunt Catrin.

Marti looked at the little suitcase and wondered how Aunt Catrin could have packed up Mam's things so quickly. "Where are you going?" he said.

"Back inside. Yeer Mam is sick. We're taking her away."

"I want to come. I want to come." Marti dropped to his knees and grabbed onto Aunt Catrin's long grey coat. "*Please, please, please . . .*"

Aunt Catrin pulled her coat out of Marti's hands and he fell face down onto the wet road. "Marti, up the hill is no place for a child," she said. He watched her get into Uncle Ardal's car and drive away and then he started to chase after it but it was too fast.

Marti shouted for them to stop as he watched the car take his mam away from him, but the car didn't stop, only kept on going, taking his mam away from him, away along the street, then away up the hill, and then away to the Cabbage Farm.

29

Joey never expected to feel anything but it was a terrible fright to hear Emmet had died in the night. Sure, he went quickly in the end, said Peggy, which was a blessed relief to everyone, especially those who had watched him hanging to life for months, and please God he's happy where he is now. There would be no great occasion made of the funeral, she said, because only Joey's sister Megan would be making the journey, but weren't the notices posted and ye never could say.

Joey didn't know how to feel about his father's death – didn't it all happen so suddenly. He knew Emmet felt he had done wrong by him and it had hurt him. But hadn't he been hurt too? When he felt like he was sorry for his father he wondered was it really himself he was feeling sorry for, because hadn't he done the same to Marti. He knew now that the person he was wasn't the person he wanted to be.

Catrin had laid it down to him. The boy was running wild, with guards and the like at the door. Say what you would about Emmet's ways, hadn't he at least taught his children right from wrong. When Joey was a boy he knew he would have been scared witless at the thought of bringing a guard to the door. Jaysus, he thought, it was a failure he was to Marti entirely.

He had tried to shape the boy in his own way, had he not? Sure, there were no lashings and no harsh words, he used the very opposite, but only made different problems for him. It was a heartscald to think of how he had tried to raise Marti with all the love he never had. He showered him with it and Shauna knew it was wrong – wasn't he only setting the child up for disappointment. Shauna knew Marti would be forever looking for the same kind of love in the wider world, and he would never find the like of it.

Joey understood Emmet's ways now. He had taught him to be tough, to keep the feelings he had locked away, and hadn't that only made things worse for Marti, and for Shauna. They were both hurting, and he knew it was all his fault. Hadn't she the measure of him. And Marti himself carried the blame for his father's mistakes, thinking he caused it all by taking a few lousy dollars from his mother's purse. It was too much; wasn't Shauna right, the boy was better off without him.

Joey straightened his black tie in the mirror. He found it hard to even look at himself, but he knew what he had to do. He would tell Shauna she was right. He was no good for either of them; he could see that now.

He walked to the decrepit house where he had said his farewells to his father. A black crepe scarf dangled from the lion's head door knock, a handwritten card told when Emmet's remains would be removed. Joey pulled down the card and crushed it in his hand.

Inside, his father's coffin was balanced on the kitchen table, his mother sat beside it, dabbing her eyes with a handkerchief. Joey's sister Megan stood up and smiled at him. She came over and kissed him on the cheek, then seemed to remember the occasion and pulled herself away, straightening the sides of her skirt.

"Are we it?" said Joey.

"We are," said Megan, and then she looked at Peggy. "Dermot's wife is expecting again and Clancy, well ye know Clancy, busy, busy, busy."

"The others?"

Peggy interrupted and put down her handkerchief. "Ye have all lives to lead. Come on, will ye?" Three men in black armbands helped Joey raise his father's coffin; he recognised none of them. They could have been old hurling players or old drinking partners, it didn't seem to matter either way. Without the rest of the family wasn't the occasion a farce entirely.

The slow cortège made its way to the churchyard, with Peggy out front wearing a brave face for all to see. People on the street greeted them with nods of the head and said they were sorry for the family's pain. Old women stood outside their doors and blessed themselves as the coffin went by and there were some said they would pray for Emmet's eternal soul.

Joey didn't know any of the people who spoke. He may have once – a word here and there as a child, a pint taken together when a man – but sure hadn't times changed in Kilmora. He hardly recognised the place. It seemed to have been scrubbed clean. Its past was being rubbed away.

In the churchyard the sun was blinding. A yellow oblong led the way to where the earth had been broken and the priest stood with a small crowd. They were just more strange faces to Joey, people he may once have known but not now. Even the priest was a stranger, a young fella with pale blond hair and paler cheeks. He stood sweltering, sweat dripping down his flat forehead. It all looked very difficult for him, thought Joey as he watched the priest start to stammer.

"Emmet Driscol was known the length of the country," he said. "In his day he knew faith. Not only faith in the Lord, for faith comes in many forms, but faith in himself. When he took to the hurling field Emmet Driscol showed his faith in a strong arm and a winning determination. He showed skill and he showed heart and he was an idol to many." Joey tried to block out the priest's voice. Every word was a reminder of what he would sooner forget. "In these times of change, we see the worship of many false idols but it is in men with faith, in the Lord and in themselves, we can look forever to for guidance."

Joey had heard enough. He loosened himself from his mother's arm and walked away from the gathering. Shading under the church-yard's mighty Irish oak, he lit a cigarette and watched whilst his father was lowered into his final resting place, and then as his mother scattered earth over his coffin. When the little crowd dispersed Peggy came and stood by him and said, "Tis over."

"Yeah, tis," he said. "All over."

"Ye know, he talked about you at the end."

"Did he?"

"Every night. He was forever wondering about ye over in Australia. You were his son, ye cannot change that."

Joey looked at his mother. She took his arm again. "We all have feet of clay, son . . . If ye don't follow your own parent's mistakes, ye make fresh ones of your own."

Joey smiled at her, and she smiled back. "All ye can hope for, son, all ye can hope is that they survive." Peggy patted him on the arm and turned back to the mourners. "I think that fella wants a word with ye . . ."

"Who?"

Joey looked to a plump figure in a dark suit. There was a brightly coloured shirt, open at the collar, flapping in the breeze beneath. "Howya, Joey," he said.

It was Paddy Tiernan, the sight of him made Joey fumble his words. "What the hell are ye doing here?"

"That's blasphemy. Tis sacred ground yeer on."

"Is it? How did ye get here?"

"I drove my car . . ." Paddy pointed to a silver saloon parked beyond the churchyard gates. "D'ye mean, how did I find out? It was in the paper. Your old fella was a bit of a star."

"Was he now?"

"Look, I can tell yeer still with the grief. I only wanted to see ye, have a word . . . Will ye take a drink?" People were filing into Molloy's pub across the way, but Joey knew it wasn't a day for him to be drinking. "I'll have the one."

"Grand so."

"I mean it, mind. Just one . . . tis my new limit."

People from the funeral had spread themselves out inside Molloy's pub. Little groups huddled round tables, staring gloomily into their dark pints. When Paddy came back with the drinks, Joey thanked him. The mood was tense. "Sure ye won't go far wrong with just the one," said Paddy.

"Tis just an idea," said Joey. "Better than swearing off it, I reckon." Swearing off the drink hadn't worked, sure, but only one drink taken a day might remove the wonder, stop the build-up that always ended in a skite, and more trouble, thought Joey.

Paddy wrinkled his forehead, then raised his glass. "Well, good luck to ye."

"Paddy . . . but why are ye here?"

Paddy sat up straight, rummaged in his pockets, then held a hand out to Joey. "To give ye this." He handed over a bundle of notes, rolled together in a rubber band. "I put some interest in there."

Joey looked at the bundle. Paddy had added more than a bit of interest. There was a time when Joey knew he would have raised the roof with his excitement at this, had the lot of it buried away for Marti's education, but not now. "Paddy, I don't know what to say."

"Say nothing, sure tis all yours. I couldn't cheat a decent Irishman who was only after doing the best for his boy."

Joey knew he had got Paddy wrong; he wasn't the first he had got wrong either, and the thought grabbed at him. "I never thought, well, ye know."

"Ah well, I had a bit of a win on the horses, an accumulator . . . Sure doesn't bad luck run out just like the good."

"Thanks," said Joey. "Look, would you mind me dashing out on ye? It's just . . . I have somewhere I need to be."

"Jaysus, man, I'll be fine here m'self. Run yeer errand," said Paddy.

Joey tipped his one whiskey down his throat and left the pub alone.

The sun was high outside as he headed to Catrin's home, clamping the bundle of notes in his hand. Wasn't it the least he could do now, give the money to Shauna. She could do what she liked with it – she would know what was best for Marti, and for her. She deserved the chance of a fresh start, so she did. A chance to get herself and the boy right again.

He stood at the door of Catrin's house. There was still a power of heat in the day's sun and he was sweating as he loosened his tie and knocked on the door. Catrin took her time answering and let out a shriek when she saw him standing on her doorstep. He saw Marti run into the hall behind her, but when he called out to the boy Catrin spun herself round and held him back from his father.

"Get inside. Get inside now." Marti reached out for Joey, but Ardal appeared at the back of him, raising him up and carrying him away. The boy kicked and wailed, and Joey remembered Catrin's words about him running wild, bringing guards and the like to the door. Sure wasn't it a terrible effect Joey had had on him. It was the Devil Marti had in him now like Catrin said, and hadn't his own father put it there.

"I'm not here to cause any trouble," said Joey.

"Well I can tell ye I won't be having any of it now – not at my door. I have Ardal there will sort the likes of ye with no messing." Ardal appeared behind Catrin again, swinging the door wide open and pushing out his great stomach. Joey heard Marti calling out from upstairs, banging on the door, but he knew he was best kept from the boy.

"I only came to see, Shauna. I have something to say to her, something for her," said Joey.

Catrin leaned into his face and there was little more than a nose between them when she spoke. "My sister is in the insane asylum, thanks to you."

He didn't know what to say to her. He had thought he couldn't feel any worse, but hadn't he been wrong entirely. Catrin stepped forward and her finger wagged in front of him. "Ye come here stinking of drink, upsetting the boy and by what right. Have ye no shame coming to me? Me with a brother already buried outside the Church. Tis you I will be blaming if it's a sister I have next."

Joey felt numb. He muttered, "Sorry, I didn't mean—"

"No, your sort never do," said Catrin. "Leave this place. I don't want ye coming round here anymore." Catrin pushed him back and followed into the street, prodding him in the chest, pushing at him. "The child is staying with us now. Aren't we the only family he has capable of minding him . . ."

Joey stumbled and fell in the street, throwing his head up to the sky where the sun hurt his eyes. As Catrin towered over him he caught a brief glimpse of Marti crying in the upstairs window, watching his father being shamed beneath. "Shauna's to have him signed over – sure tis all legal. Now there ye have it. Go. Go. There is no place in the boy's life now for a drunken father that's driven his own wife into the asylum."

Joey raised himself on his feet and Ardal stepped forward, standing in front of his wife like some manner of minder. There was no need for it, no need entirely, thought Joey. Wasn't the woman right. Marti was better off without him. He stared up at his son, crying in the window above, and waved to him. He knew both their hearts were breaking, but what could be done, wasn't it the best thing for everyone. He had messed everything up for so long. It was beyond repair now.

As he walked back to Molloy's pub he felt like the world had ended, not instantly like in an explosion, but slowly, like it always had been dying on him, only he never knew it. Nothing was ever going to be the same now – wasn't life as good as over. Not even Marti would be in his life now and Joey wished he could just be dead and buried, like his own father.

He went back to Molloy's pub where Paddy had a row of creamy pints of Guinness lined up on the bar for everyone. He placed a hand on Joey's shoulder and said, "What can I get ye?"

Paddy's eyes were weary, the slow blink of the drunkard settling on him. Joey wanted no more than to take one of the creamy pints and pour it down him, join Paddy in oblivion, but he'd been there often enough to know there were no answers to be found. "I'll have a lemonade, please," he said. "Just a small one."

"One small lemonade it is," said Paddy. He took the glasses back to the table and sat with Joey, talking and talking. There was no talker like Paddy Tiernan, thought Joey. Couldn't he talk the leg off an iron pot. He'd been on his travels again and had some grand tales to tell but wasn't he more interested in Joey's story. He was like a priest wheedling a confession out of him and didn't it all come out in between the dark pints Paddy swallowed.

"It's easy enough solved, sure it is," he said.

"Solved . . . There's no solving it. None," said Joey.

"I think you love Shauna yet . . . and can't you see she loves you."

"Bollix, man."

"It's as simple as that, Joey. She's brought you here because she loves you, nearly killed herself with the love she has for you."

What was he saying? Joey heard every one of Paddy's words, sure hadn't they chimed in his ears. He knew he'd got this fella wrong in the past, but none of this was right, surely. Had he really been so lost in his world as not to notice the obvious? Paddy had had too much to drink, a few more scoops and he'd be falling over.

Joey said goodbye to Paddy and took himself back to the guest-house where Mrs O'Shea greeted him with a smile and was kind enough not to be offended when she never received one in return. In the room he collapsed on the bed and felt his body shaking. His whole self shook, inside and out. Wasn't this the limit? There was nowhere to go from here, surely. Paddy might be right about how he had felt for Shauna all along, but wouldn't he have to be dead wrong about how Shauna felt for him. Even if she had led him back to face up to things, hadn't he failed her entirely, and led her the way of her brother Barry.

Joey felt sick in his stomach. The bed started to spin slowly and he took himself up from it. It was time to run. Anywhere would do, just away. Far, far away. He started to throw clothes in a bag and then, under a shirt pile, he uncovered Marti's Superman picture, propped against the wall.

Joey looked at the picture he had carried all the way from Australia. It was cracked clean down the middle. He pushed together the pieces of broken glass and wondered could it be mended yet? Couldn't most things be mended with a bit of effort, he thought.

30

Marti prayed to God. He prayed as hard as he could because he knew it was a miracle he was asking for. But if God had brought Dad back to him once already, then couldn't he do it again? And if he could bring Dad back to him then couldn't he bring Mam back too and maybe then it could be like it was before? Marti wanted it to be just like it was for all the other boys and he wanted to have a mam and a dad again. He didn't want to live with Aunt Catrin, who was a bockety-arsed old witch, and he didn't want to live with Uncle Ardal, who was the real lousy feck.

Marti told God there would be no more acting the giddy goat and there would be no more mitching if he could just be like all the other boys again. He promised to behave entirely and he told God if he would only fix things one more time, then wouldn't he be the best boy in the whole world and he would even tell Pat Kelly to be a good boy too. Marti made the signs that were the cross like he had seen everyone do a million times over and then he went downstairs to watch out the front window to see if God would answer his prayers.

Aunt Catrin was making a big old pot of porridge in the kitchen and she was shouting at Uncle Ardal, who wasn't holding the drawer properly. Marti hated the porridge that went in the drawer to set and would be cut up every morning for him to eat before he went to school. He wanted Uncle Ardal to be shouted at because then mightn't he panic and spill some like he was always doing. Aunt

Catrin said Uncle Ardal was a clumsy article who was always making a mess of everything, and when there was finally porridge spilt on the floor she shouted at him some more and said, "That spill will go for yeer pigeons now, I suppose."

Marti went through to the kitchen to see Aunt Catrin at the shouting and to see how much of the porridge had been spilt. There wasn't that much on the shiny kitchen floor, but Uncle Ardal had got it on his boots and had started to walk all through it, making the porridge footprints everywhere. "Off. Off with them boots," said Aunt Catrin, "or is it through the whole house ye want to traipse it?" Uncle Ardal took off his boots and carried them out the back door, and Aunt Catrin told him he was a fool entirely. "Ye can get cleaning them up yeerself," she said, "and ye can close the door behind ye. I'm not burning peat to heat the yard."

When Aunt Catrin saw Marti staring at her she was mad angry and started the roaring shouting again. "And what call have ye to be stood there idle . . . tis indolent ye are. Honestly, the head on ye, boy, and the price of turnips." Marti was handed a wet rag and told to clean up the holy mess that had been made on the shiny floor by Uncle Ardal, and when he got on his knees there was a loud knock on the front door.

Aunt Catrin told Marti not to concern himself with the loud knock because didn't he have more than enough to be getting on with where he was. The big old drawer full of porridge was left on the kitchen table and Marti was told to mind he didn't go tipping it over because hadn't Aunt Catrin had enough of clumsy men this day already. The loud knock on the door came again and Aunt Catrin started to rush for it, saying, "Where's the fire, where's the fire?" She tried to take her apron off as she went for the door but then the loud knock came again and she left the apron half on and half off.

When Aunt Catrin opened the door there was a mighty shriek from her giving out at somebody and then there was more shrieking and calling for Uncle Ardal to get in from the yard. When Marti turned to see what the shrieking was all about he saw Dad standing in the doorway, holding out his hand to him. Dad's face was all red like he was just after running and when he tried to speak there was only a little splutter noise made. Marti went to grab his hand but then there was the sound of the back door swinging open and Uncle Ardal ran in, sliding about on the shiny floor in his stocking soles. He grabbed Marti by the collar and pulled him back with a hard yank, and when Marti started to wriggle Uncle Ardal was nearly falling all over the place.

"Let him be, Ardal," said Dad. His voice was very firm suddenly and there was a look on him that said he was in no mood to be waiting, but Uncle Ardal didn't let Marti go. He only looked at Aunt Catrin with his mouth open wide.

"The boy stays," said Aunt Catrin, and she was pointing at Dad with her finger again. "Tis what his mother wants, his mother ye put in the asylum."

Dad shook his head and there was a big breath taken but nobody said a word at all, and then Dad very gently lowered Aunt Catrin's finger. "Shauna will be staying in no asylum if I can help it."

"What . . . ye are full of it, are ye not, Joey Driscol. What have you in mind for her this time? Where will ye run to this time? That's yeer game all over, is it not. Sure it was fine for ye both to swan off leaving the tongues wagging after the grand sin ye committed, was it not. But hadn't some of us to stay behind and face the music for ye, picking up the pieces whilst the pair of you sunned yourselves. And it was no picnic for me when I had a sick brother in need of the love and comfort of his family."

"A sick brother ye packed off to the Cabbage Farm," said Dad. "A sick brother who ye left there to rot till he took the only road out . . . I tell ye, I'm not letting the same happen to Shauna."

"No, it's not true," said Aunt Catrin. Her voice was a quiet tremble now, her eyes all misted over. "Tis your mistakes was the cause of it . . ."

"God woman, would ye ever wake up to yourself? Do ye think I don't know I made mistakes? I mightn't have known at the time, but God do I ever know now." Dad was shouting, but then Aunt Catrin started to raise her hands to her ears and he started to speak softly. "I'm going to try and put my mistakes right, Catrin . . . I hope to God it's not too late for you to do the same."

Aunt Catrin's face was as white as the porridge setting in the big old drawer. Her mouth was wide open like when Uncle Ardal fell asleep at the fire and Mam said it was the flies he was catching. Marti wondered if Aunt Catrin was going to scream or attack Dad with punches and scratches, but then she very slowly went to sit down by the table and said, "Let the boy be, Ardal."

Uncle Ardal made a noise like a grunt and Marti started to wriggle again but his collar was still held tight and he couldn't get away. "But he's staying, sure. Ye said he was to clean the floor. I heard ye say it, so I did."

"Clean yeer own mess!" screamed Aunt Catrin, and when she stood up the table was shook and the big old drawer landed on the floor, splashing porridge over the whole place. "Out. Get out all of ye," said Aunt Catrin. She was screaming again, with porridge in her hair this time and hitting out at Uncle Ardal, who let go of Marti and ran into the yard in a hurry.

Marti watched Uncle Ardal run into the yard with Aunt Catrin at the screaming and hitting behind him. He thought they looked mad entirely and wasn't it this pair that should be taken to the Cabbage Farm. There were neighbours started to look over the fence and they were in flitters with the laughing when Uncle Ardal and Aunt Catrin fell over into the rabbit traps set to keep the cats from the pigeons. There were traps snapping all over them, catching at arms and legs and even one at Aunt Catrin's apron strings.

Marti thought it was all a gas, sure it was, and hadn't he never seen a thing like it, but then Dad said they had more important things to do and they could leave the likes of them behind.

Dad grabbed hold of Marti's hand and started to run through the streets. Dad was a faster runner and he had bigger steps taken, but Marti tried to keep up with him because it was all very exciting. Marti wondered where he was being taken, but sure didn't none of it matter, really. Wherever Dad was taking him would be better than the house made of stones all piled up on top of each other right to the roof. They ran past the water fountain and Marti wondered had all his wishes came true and everything would be just like it was when he had a mam and a dad and he was just like all the other boys.

"Dad, where are we going?" said Marti.

"We're going to get your mam."

"Where will we take her?"

"Wherever she wants to go, son . . . Sure that will be up to your mam entirely."

Marti and Dad ran for a long time through the streets and then there was a big hill ahead of them and Dad stopped the running and said wasn't the hill too much for him. Dad said the Cabbage Farm was at the top of the hill and when Marti looked up there was an old building made of dirty bricks and there were hundreds of high dark windows with little glass panes in them. Marti thought it looked like a very bad place entirely and he didn't want Mam to be in there. When they got closer to the building Marti saw there were little white bars on all the windows and it looked like somewhere people who have done bad things go.

"Dad, I don't like this place." He felt scared to be going inside, but then Dad lifted him up and carried him in and he wasn't afraid anymore. There were ladies dressed in black with big white pointy hats on their heads inside the Cabbage Farm and when Marti said were they nurses Dad said, "No, son, they're nuns, which ye call sister."

Dad spoke to a sister behind a big old desk and she said there were proper visiting hours to be observed, but Dad said hadn't he only heard his wife had been taken in and he needed to see her desperately. The sister said it was irregular but what was her name, and then she pointed down a long corridor and said a number on a door for Dad to look out for.

Mam's room was very big and there were lots of beds in it and lots of people wandered around and looked like Colm Casey who was soft in the head. There were people walking around and making little waves to Marti with their hands and there were people who dribbled all over themselves and just stared. There were sisters sat with some of the people and Marti wondered what the sisters could ever say or do to make the people better when they looked so sick entirely.

Mam didn't look like any of the others at all, thought Marti when he saw her sitting on top of a big white bed, looking out the window, staring and staring like she was expecting a visitor to come along at any moment. Mam was one of the only ones in the room wearing proper clothes, not nightclothes. Marti wondered did she like the Cabbage Farm better than Aunt Catrin's house where she would always be sitting about in the baggy jamas with the very long sleeves over her hands. Marti heard Dad gulp when he saw Mam sitting on the bed and then he put Marti down on the ground and said, "On ye go, son. Go to your mam." Marti ran over to Mam and stood by her bed and when she turned round she didn't look like she had seen him at all, only stared and stared and stared, and then she jumped off the bed in a hurry and hugged Marti tight, so tight he could hardly breathe.

"Marti, Marti, you're here. How, how did ye get here, son?" she said.

"Dad took me," he said, and when he turned to point to Dad he was already there beside him.

"Hello, Shauna," said Dad.

"Joey . . . why?" said Mam. She let Marti go and then she sat back on the bed.

Mam looked like she didn't recognise Dad at all, thought Marti. He wanted to say something and try to explain about the fight with Aunt Catrin, but then Dad started talking and Mam started to look like she recognised him again. They talked and talked for a long time and Dad said he had lost his father but found himself, and Marti wondered how anybody could find their own self or how it could be lost even.

"Shauna, I want you to come away with me . . . with us," said Dad, and he lifted Marti onto his knee.

"Why?" said Mam. "Why would you want that?"

"Shauna, I know why you brought me here. I know what you wanted me to see . . . I see it now. I've faced it, Shauna. Things would be different for us now."

"Joey, you know I had to do it. I had to. You were in hiding in Australia. I couldn't live like that anymore, I thought . . ."

Dad reached forward and touched Mam's lips very gently with one finger. "It's okay, Shauna. I know now, I see it, you don't need to explain."

"No, Joey, I do. I needed to make you see this is what you were running from. I wanted to make you see you had nothing to fear from the past. I thought if you could face it, get over it and just move on . . . I thought we might have a chance."

211

"We do, Shauna. We have another chance, now we do. It can't ever be too late to change, to say you're sorry."

"Are you sure, Joey?" Mam leaned forward and tried to look in Dad's eyes. It was the truth she was looking for, Marti knew it because wasn't Mam always checking himself for the truth.

"I am sure," said Dad.

"Are you really, though? I mean, you need to live too, Joey, and not just through Marti."

"Shauna, I think we can all be happy, we can move on, can't we? We can put the past behind us, tis the future that's important, I see that now."

Mam leaned forward and hugged Dad and Marti together and there was clapping heard from around the room. Mam started to cry, but they weren't sad tears, thought Marti, sure didn't everyone look happier than ever. He felt the happiness inside him and it was a lovely warm feeling.

"Dad," said Marti, "can you show us the green flower, the shamrock dancing?" There was laughter from Dad and there was more of the little happy tears rolled down the side of Mam's face.

"Are ye serious?" said Dad.

"I am. I want to see it."

Dad smiled at Mam and then he started to roll up his sleeve, over the shoulder. "Once there was a lucky little shamrock that stood in a field."

Marti started to smile too when he saw the shamrock and he felt like he was a very special boy again.

"A lucky little shamrock, in a lucky little field," said Dad, "and all through the day he'd stand in his field, thinking what a lucky little shamrock am I, am I, what a lucky little shamrock am I." Dad's voice started to creak and break and there were more tears rolled down the side of Mam's face, and then a big breath was taken by Dad. "To stand in a field and grow strong, said he, to stand in a field and grow strong." Dad turned up his arm and the shamrock's stem straightened.

"He's starting," said Marti.

"And when the night turns to day, I go wild, he said. When the night turns to day I go wild, wild for song and the dance of a song and I dance in a field all night long." Dad turned his arm back and forth making the shamrock dance. It rolled and reeled on his shoulder and Marti watched, smiling, as Dad kept the shamrock rolling and reeling.

"I love the shamrock," said Marti when Dad was finished.

"And the shamrock loves you, son."

Epilogue

Writing people wasn't something Joey was very used to, but sure wouldn't he have to start. There had been no letters sent home to Ireland when he was in Australia, but wasn't that when he had no one to write to. Now they had decided to settle in Kilmora there was Macca to write to – hadn't he to be told to stop holding the job open, for starters; they would be making a go of it where they were. And there was his own mam to write to since she had moved in with Megan over in England. Wasn't it for the best when the old house was too much for her, sure she was right to sell it, and the new owners were right to pull it down and put up a guesthouse. But wasn't Peggy asking too much expecting a letter every month from Kilmora. There had been a power of news from the Driscols just lately, but it couldn't keep up, surely.

They were all having a grand laugh at Marti's new brogue. He was becoming a proper little Irishman, so he was. Playing the hurling even, a power better than his old man ever did, and speaking the Irish better than him too. The boy had had a tough time of it, but wasn't he brighter than ever now. Joey knew Marti would find his way in the end, just like he had. And wouldn't he be there to support him, whatever his way was. The boy had learnt some harsh lessons at an early age, but it would show him life was no grand stroll. Things would be better for him in the future. Marti had no call to run away from anything.

Joey knew he would be a better father now too. He was happier than he ever had been, for a start. He was still only carting the flour in and the bread out at Gleesons, but there was bags of time after the early finishes to read the books. And wasn't there more time yet and more energy entirely with only one drink a day taken. Mightn't he even give the studies another go some day – nobody ever said learning was just for youngsters.

Shauna was happier too. There were some real tough times when they would talk into the night about the child they had never given a chance to. There were some tears shed when they thought about what she might have been like, how she might have turned out, who she would have taken after. But weren't they lucky to be talking at all after everything that had happened, thought Joey. They would always talk about things now, he knew it. Shauna's new doctor had said Joey could talk for Ireland, sure she had never met anyone so full of stories, weren't most people quiet as mice when they started the joint therapy sessions. But no one had surprised the doctors more than Shauna.

The letters back from Peggy were more accomplished than Joey's ever were. Her writing was full of a wisdom he had missed, but he would have plenty of time to catch up on it now. He knew things had changed for everyone; it was hard sometimes to keep up with it all. Peggy had said it was down to Joey himself, for sure didn't the Bible say, *"For whosoever hath, to him shall be given, and he shall have more abundance; but whoever hath not from him shall be taken away even that he hath."*

His mother was full of lines like that from the Bible, but Joey wasn't too sure about any of them. One thing he did know was that the Lord definitely moved in mysterious ways, for wasn't Shauna carrying again. The doctors in Australia had said it could never happen, but there it was. Joey knew now that no one could be certain of anything in this world, except perhaps that he was definitely one of the luckiest in the whole of it.

Marti was so excited to have a new member of the family on the way – wasn't he just bursting out of himself with the idea of it. And Shauna, she had never looked more beautiful in all her days, there was a composure about her since the news came. Blooming, she was, didn't everyone say it. The baby inside her was beautiful as well, just a beautiful thing entirely. It was a beautiful baby girl; they knew it. This one was special, sure. She was all their hopes for a new start, for their future together, and they were going to treasure all the many blessed days they had ahead.